WINDSWEPT

SUSAN HAYES

ABOUT THE BOOK

When Vivian Waverly arrives in the small coastal town of Tofino for her best friend's wedding, romance is the last thing on her mind – until she meets two men who might just be able to tame her restless heart.

Tucker Pine and Byron Triggs are selkies, shapeshifters living in secret. Bound by blood and magic, they're destined to share a mate – and they want it to be Vivian.

Finding each other took an act of fate, but to stay together this trio will have to break the rules, defy tradition, and forge a new path for themselves and the colony of Kismet Cove.

Windswept

Copyright © 2019 Susan Hayes

Windswept

E-book Publication: July 2019

Published by: Black Scroll Publications Ltd.

ISBN: 978-1-988446-50-9

For my parents, who always encouraged me no matter what dream I was chasing. And to Karen, who listens to me rant and ramble about the worlds that exist only in my head, and has never questioned my sanity. (Even when she probably should.)

CHAPTER ONE

"TANYA, you already said I could have the time off!" Vivian pulled the phone away from her ear and gritted her teeth as she resisted the urge to hurl it across the terminal. Her boss's shrill voice blared through the speaker, grating on her already frazzled nerves.

She took a deep breath and interrupted the diatribe coming at her. "My ticket's non-refundable and I'm out of here. For fuck's sake, I'm at the airport right now, about to check my luggage. There is no way I'm going to cancel my first vacation in two years and drive back into town to babysit the shop while you fly to Hawaii! This is not me being difficult, this is me telling you, no. In fact, this is me telling you good-bye. I quit!" She hit the disconnect button on her phone and turned it off before her former employer could call her back.

When she looked up, she found herself the focus of several curious looks, and she smiled blandly as she swept her tousled, red- and black-dyed hair back behind her ear. "It looks like my vacation just got extended," she

1

explained with a shrug. With that she dropped her phone into her carry-on bag and decided to postpone panic until after she'd gotten her boarding pass and could find a lounge to hide in, preferably one with a well-stocked bar.

By the goddess, she needed a drink right now.

It took her another twenty minutes, but she finally sank down into an overstuffed chair and took a slow sip of her Irish coffee. If quitting her job a few, short weeks before Christmas wasn't a reason to indulge in a boozy pick-me-up with double whipped cream, she didn't know what was. She leaned back in her chair with a sigh, letting her eyes flutter closed as she did a mental inventory.

Job? No. Money for rent? January was covered, but after that, another no. Best friend? Now living on the other side of the country and getting married in three days to not one, but two men Vivian had never met. It was official. The winds of change had come storming into her life again.

Well, at least my life never gets boring.

She took another drink of her whiskey-laced coffee and tried to think things through. When she got to Tofino, she'd have to get her Tarot deck out and do a reading for herself. She'd brought them with the intention of reading Jess's cards, but it couldn't hurt to read the signs so she could prepare herself for whatever change was coming.

Her best friend, Jess, had left Toronto a few months ago to spend some time at her family's cabin out on the west coast, and Vivian had missed her more than she cared to admit. They'd been best friends since childhood. With Jess gone, life hadn't been the same.

Now she was flying out to stand up for Jessica as she committed herself to two men who had swept her off her feet. As happy as she was that things were working out for Jess, Vivian had felt a hint of selfish panic at the idea of losing her best friend to love and long distance. It wasn't something she was proud of, and she had hoped that once she'd seen for herself that Jess was truly happy, she'd be more ready to accept that her friend was never coming home.

And now I'm getting maudlin.

She sat up a little straighter and closed her eyes, imagining a quick, cleansing flare of white light all around her, burning away the negative energy she was gathering around herself like tiny storm clouds. There was no point in wallowing in self-pity or panic. The holidays were here, she was only a few hours away from seeing Jess again, and apparently she had no pressing reason to rush back from her long overdue vacation. The rest of the fallout she could deal with eventually, given enough time and possibly another Irish coffee.

Many hours and two time zones later, Vivian walked into the Tofino terminal and was hit by a short, platinum-blonde tornado. "You're here! I've missed you so much!" Jess squealed and let her go only to hug her again twice as hard. "Rory and Evan can't wait to meet you and I can't wait for you to meet them! Did your flight go okay? Is this all your luggage? The guys wanted to come along but I told them I wanted you all to myself for a bit."

"Whoa! Slow down!" Vivian grinned down at Jess. "Is this what love has done to you? You're actually glowing! And laughing!" She couldn't believe the difference in her friend. The sad, quiet woman who had left with her mother's ashes and a heart full of grief was radiantly happy and almost bursting with cheer. "I've got to say, this is a good look for you, girl."

Jess grabbed one of Vivian's suitcases and nodded. "I'm happy, Viv. So happy it's almost scary. I have so much to tell you, and show you. The cabin is gorgeous. You're going to love it. I'm so glad you're here!"

"I'm glad to be here. I've missed you!" Vivian followed Jess out into the parking lot, shivering as the damp chill in the air sucked the warmth from her body three steps beyond the doors. The sky was a deep gray and the shadows were already deepening, despite the fact it was only three in the afternoon. There weren't a lot of vehicles in the parking lot, and Vivian headed for the sensible, gray, four-door sedan nearest the door.

"Uh, Viv? Not that one." Jess called and pointed to a bright red Jeep. "That one."

"You bought a Jeep? Good gods, you've only been here a little while and already you've gone native! If you tell me you've given up lattes for herbal teas, I swear I'm going to call for an intervention."

"Not to worry, I will always be a caffeine junkie. I've got the nicest espresso machine set up, I'll make you something as soon as we're home, I promise. You look a little wiped out, rough flight?"

"The flight was okay, more turbulence than I would have liked, but that's on par for the the kind of day I've had." Viv tossed her bag into the back of the Jeep and climbed in. "How do you get in here with those short little legs of yours?"

"Very funny." Jess climbed into the passenger seat and stuck her tongue out before admitting, "The guys had a step installed."

"I think I like them already," Viv said, unsuccessfully trying to repress a snicker. "That was very thoughtful."

"Laugh it up, Miss Long-Legs! Not all of us got bonked on the head with the tall, svelte, and sexy wand!" Jess was laughing as she pulled out of their parking spot.

"Well now, I bet I can name two men who would say you're more than a little sexy. Two very hot men, I might add," Viv pointed out, and grinned as Jess blushed and nodded in silent agreement. It was worth the trip just to see the changes in Jess since she'd left Toronto. She was her old self again, with a double dose of confidence.

"There's plenty of time to talk about me, I want to know what's up with you. You said you'd had a bad day, so tell me what happened."

Viv groaned and rolled her eyes. "What happens every time I try to get away from the shop?"

"Tanya suddenly needs to go out of town and you're left—You're kidding me. She did it again?"

"Yep. This time she actually waited until I was standing in line at the airport counter waiting to get my boarding pass. I shouldn't have answered the phone."

"No, you shouldn't have, but you wouldn't be you if you'd ignored a possible emergency at the shop." Jess glanced over at her with a frown. "So, do you have to cut your vacation short? You're going to be here for the commitment ceremony, right?"

"Cut my stay short? Uh, not exactly. I may have let my temper get the better of me and told her I quit."

Jess squealed with joy and bounced in the driver's seat, which was not exactly the reaction Viv was expecting. "You quit? Finally! You were the best hairdresser they had and they treated you like crap. I am so glad you're done."

"Well there's the whole matter of my being unemployed now, but I have to admit, I'm pretty happy I'm done too. She actually wanted me to miss my vacation with you so *she* could go to Hawaii."

"You see? She's been taking advantage of you so long she actually thought that would work!"

"As if I'd miss my best friend's big day! Not even a horde of fire-breathing dragons would keep me away," Viv said and meant it. Jess was the one person Vivian would always be there for, because Jess had always been there for her. They'd been best friends since they were kids, and nothing would ever change that.

"You know, when Dad gave the place over to me you said it was kismet, so now I'm going to say the same thing to you. This is fate! I'm moving out of the cabin in a few days, so you can have the whole place to yourself for as long as you want. Stay for the holidays. Hell, stay forever if you want. You're the only thing I miss from my old life. If you moved out here, I wouldn't have to miss my best friend anymore."

"I think that is the sweetest thing anyone has ever said to me, *and* the most insane. I can't just stay out here in the wilds! I have a roommate back in Toronto, and my bike, and rent, and…well, stuff!"

Now Jess was openly laughing at her. "I cannot believe what I'm hearing. You're the one who helped me pack up my stuff and told me to go have fun and not worry about things too much. Now it's your turn and you're telling me you're worried about rent?" She made a clucking noise at the back of her throat.

"Hey, I'm not a chicken!" Viv protested the good-natured teasing. "I quit, didn't I? But I have a personal rule never to make life-altering decisions while jetlagged, so you're not getting any kind of an answer tonight."

"Fair enough, but I promise when you see the men here you are going to be phoning your roomie and giving notice for the end of January. My guys aren't the only hotties out here and it's the off-season. You'll get a sample at the ceremony in a few days. Rory and Evan's entire community are coming to this thing. It's going to be fun."

Viv saw an opening to ask one of the questions she hadn't been able to voice in their Skype sessions. "So, what exactly is this community they're part of? I know they all live together on the land next door to your cabin, and judging by their pictures they're not tree-hugging hippies, so what exactly *are* they?"

"I dare you to tell Rory you thought he might be a tree-hugging hippy," Jess snorted with laughter at the idea. "They definitely aren't like that. It's a bit hard to explain. They're all originally from Scotland, their ancestors came here a long time ago and bought up a large tract of land, and they all live on it together."

"And they're all poly?" Viv asked, cutting to the point she really wanted to understand.

"Most of them are, yes." Jess glanced her way, her gentle features suddenly knotted with worry. "You aren't freaked about the fact I'm going to be with two guys, are you?"

"Freaked? No." Viv decided to come clean about her doubts. "But you have to admit, it's pretty unusual. If you hadn't looked like you were glowing with happiness I'd be a lot more concerned, though."

"Good." Jess grinned. "Because as I recall, *you're* the one who told me to go for it."

Viv faked a horrified shudder. "I said sleep with them. I never said anything about a lifelong commitment! I can't commit to the same hair color for more than a couple of months. I have no idea how to commit to the same guy forever. You're sure this is what you want?"

"Absolutely, completely, utterly sure, and once you meet them you'll see why. They really do make me happy."

"They better, or I'll be having very unladylike words with them! I promised your mom I'd take care of you, and I will."

Jess snorted with laughter. "You call telling me to sleep with two guys taking care of me?"

"Yep. You needed to cut loose and have some fun. And clearly I was right about that, look how it all turned out! Speaking of fun..." She glanced out the window at the forest around them. "What exactly is there to do for fun around here? I'm seeing an alarming number of trees and not a whole lot of anything else."

"Oh, we're not going through town. I'll show you Tofino tomorrow. There are shops and even a Starbucks, not to worry. And there's Breakers, which is one of the local bars. It's run by Rory's cousin and it's totally your sort of place."

"Rough, cheap, and full of hot guys?"

"Exactly! And we're going there tomorrow night for a sort of a co-ed bachelor party. I thought you'd want a chance to meet everyone before the big day."

"Perfect. I am dying to meet your guys, *and* all these hot men you keep promising me live out here."

"Oh believe, me, you'll meet at least a few of them

tomorrow night. And I've told them all about you already."

Vivian chortled. "Well, that wasn't very sporting of you! Now they've been warned!"

"I STILL DON'T UNDERSTAND why they couldn't have the reception here. It's a Sunday night, we could have closed it down for a private party, no problem," Tucker grumbled as he finished one last walk-through before they opened the doors for the evening.

"Dude, look around you. I own half this place and there is no way I'd want to celebrate a new chapter of my life here. It's a dive bar. Stress on the word *dive*." Byron popped his blond head up over the aged wooden bar and flashed his best devil-may-care smile. "You need to get out more. This will be good for you."

"I own a fucking bar. That means I don't need to get out to socialize. I just open the damned doors and the people come in, saving me from having to go out. It's a good system, I don't see the point in messing with it."

"Going to see Rory and Evan bond with Jess isn't messing with your precious system, it's celebrating a major milestone while getting drunk on someone else's dime for once. Now lighten up and go see if we have any customers." Byron tossed a bar rag at him. "Besides, we both know why you really don't want to set foot in Kismet Cove, and it's got nothing to do with your antisocial streak."

"What are you, my shrink now? Keep your opinions to yourself and get the music on." Tucker flipped his middle finger up at his best friend and business partner before heading over to open the main doors. There were a few of the regulars already loitering outside, and as he greeted them he was nearly deafened by AC/DC's *Highway to Hell* booming through the sound system.

"Welcome to Breakers. Come on in out of the cold and the wet. The bar's open!" He greeted the customers and led them back inside, taking a second to tap one of the strobe lights back into place as he passed the dance floor. At six foot four, he was tall enough to reach the lighting without needing a ladder.

As he joined Byron behind the bar and started filling orders, he kept a careful eye on the floor, making sure the waitresses were attentive and no one was getting too friendly. His staff could all handle themselves, but lately there'd been a few incidents with patrons getting unruly and harassing the serving staff or picking fights with the bouncers.

The tattoo parlor that leased space on the south side of the property had been a nice source of income, but since it had changed hands a few months back it had been attracting a crowd that was rough even by his dubious standards. He'd talked to the new owner, but so far Steve Trask hadn't done much to impress him, and neither did the shop's new name, The T-Spot.

Breakers did well because it catered to everyone, and it wasn't uncommon to see some of the local businessmen having a brew or playing a game of pool with a biker or a surfer or a gaggle of sunburned tourists. All that would come to an end if his bar got a reputation as a hangout for troublemakers and criminals.

As if on cue, three of the guys who liked to hang out at

the tattoo shop walked through the door and grabbed a corner booth. They were already leering at Patricia, his head waitress, leaving him with no doubt they were going to be a problem at some point in the evening. He was going to have to talk to Trask again and make the man understand that if he wanted his lease renewed at the end of the year, he was going to have to do something about his buddies.

"You okay?" he asked as Patricia dropped her tray on the bar.

"All good, boss. Just make sure the other girls leave that table to me. I can handle them."

Tucker poured the beers and set them down on her tray. "If they get out of line, you throw up a flare."

"You know it." Patricia winked at him and waltzed away, tray balanced in one hand as she ducked and darted through the gathering crowd. Not bad for a Thursday night. Tomorrow night was going to be packed, because on top of the regular crowd, Rory and Evan had reserved an entire section for what they were calling their bachelor party. It wasn't really one, considering it was all co-ed, but if it meant getting his friends in his bar for a night of drinking and fun, Tucker was all for it, whatever the excuse. He may not have much to do with the colony of selkies he was born into, but he still had friends there, and he missed them. Not that he'd ever admit it.

"Tucker? Dude, snap out of it." Byron hip-checked him as he went past, hoisting an armload of clean glasses. "You're the cheapskate who won't hire another bartender for the midweek shift, so quit daydreaming and fill those orders!"

"And this is why I don't need a wife, I have you to nag

me," Tucker muttered good-naturedly. Byron was his best friend and blood-brother. While they didn't see eye-to-eye when it came to women and living by the rules of the shapeshifting clan of seals they belonged to, he was the only person Tucker trusted completely. When everything in Tucker's world had fallen apart, Byron had been there with a joke and an outstretched hand, committed to getting him back on his feet again. That meant he was also the only person in the world allowed to bitch at him. All in all, it was a fair trade.

CHAPTER TWO

"Now this place has potential!" Viv declared as they pulled into the parking lot and she got her first look at Breakers. Jacked up trucks, SUVs, and a handful of motorbikes were parked out front, despite the fact it was December. The place was busy too, as there were only a few parking spots left in the large lot. The music was loud enough she could hear it the moment she hopped out of Jess's Jeep, while the entire parking lot was lit up an eerie blue and white by the large sign that proclaimed the bar's name.

"So why Breakers? They break out of jail? Break plates? Noses?"

"Sorry to disappoint you, but it's just another name for a big wave," Jess answered as she pointed to the stylized curl of water crashing over the letters. "Byron's a surfer. I'm betting the name was his idea."

Viv took a second to adjust the turned-down cuff of one of her soft leather boots, shook her bangs down over one eye, straightened the sleeve of her cropped black leather jacket and mentally declared herself good to go. "I still can't believe people surf this far north. I dipped my toe in the ocean this morning and it damned near froze off!"

"I know." Jess snickered and linked their arms. "I heard you shrieking and swearing all the way up at the cabin. It *is* winter, you know."

They opened one of the main doors and were greeted by a blast of warm air and raucous music, along with the mingling scent of bar food and booze. Viv whooped softly, "Oh yeah, this is my kind of place!"

Jess rolled her eyes and led her deeper into the bar, completely oblivious to the appreciative looks she was getting from around the bar. Viv grinned to herself, knowing that was one thing about her friend that wouldn't change. Jess had never noticed a tenth of the male attention she got, because she didn't think she was worthy.

They rounded the back side of the bar into an area where the music was much quieter and suddenly Jess's face lit up until she was damned near glowing. She let go of Viv's arm to run straight toward two men, one blond, and one dark. She threw herself into their arms as they stood up to greet her.

As the guys pinned Jess between them and kissed her hello, Viv felt an unfamiliar ache in her chest. She tried to puzzle out what it was. Not jealousy, because she was nothing but happy for her best friend. This was something else, this was…envy? Oh hell no. She put a stop to that line of thinking right away.

She wasn't looking for Mr. Right. She wasn't even really in the market for Mr. Right Now. So whatever part of her heart had suddenly decided that Jess's life was looking good needed to take a seat and get a grip. Vivian Waverly was a lot of things—hairdresser, techno-pagan, and occasional lunatic—but she had never imagined herself as the happily-ever-after type. Not with her baggage.

"Viv, this is Rory and this is Evan. Guys, this is my best friend, Vivian." Jess made the introductions, bouncing in place with nerves as she did so.

"Nice to meet you two at long last," Viv greeted them and then squawked as Evan leaned past Jessica to hug her.

"Nice to meet you too. We've heard a lot about you." He grinned and then let her go. "Don't panic, I'm the one who hugs. Rory will just nod and shake your hand."

"We're still housebreaking him, sorry." Rory offered her his hand. "I'm really glad you made it out. Jess has been pacing around for days waiting for your flight to arrive."

"And she's staying!" Jess announced happily. "At least for a little while. She quit her job and so she's got no reason to go back to the snows of Toronto for a while."

"I'm not sure whether to offer condolences or congratulations, so how about we buy the first round?" Evan said and then asked, "What are you two drinking?"

Rory immediately turned and frowned playfully at Jess. "You're going to say tequila shooters, aren't you?"

Viv laughed. "Of course she is. Two shots, please. With lime and salt."

"I thought we agreed no more tequila after the last time?" Rory grumbled in protest even as he raised a hand to flag down one of the serving staff.

"You said it, but I never agreed to it." Jess stuck out her

tongue at her very large boyfriend and Viv nearly cheered. *This* was the Jess she remembered.

They ordered the drinks and got settled, with Vivian sitting beside Rory and Jess wedged between her two men. "So where's everyone else?" she asked, curious.

"We wanted to have a few minutes to hang with you before the rest of the gang arrived," Evan said. "Tucker and Byron are already here. They own the bar. They'll be out later to say hello."

"Right. One of them is Rory's cousin, right?"

"Tucker." Rory nodded. "But Kismet Cove is a small community, so a lot of us are cousins of some kind, many times removed."

Viv grinned. "I'm from Toronto. By comparison this whole town is small. It's cute though, and the scenery is nice." She made no attempt to hide her appreciative stare as a well-built blond guy with sun-streaked curls and green eyes headed their way with a tray full of drinks.

Evan chuckled and shook his head. "Damn it, I'm going to owe you money soon, aren't I?" he asked Jess, who was laughing too.

"Did I miss something?" Viv asked, still watching the man make his way through the crowd. He moved with a dancer's grace, but he wasn't built like any dancer she'd ever seen. Even from a distance she could make out the cut of his biceps and the heavy curve of his shoulders beneath his dark blue shirt.

He was smoking hot, and Viv found herself wondering if he was as graceful in bed as he was out of it. She had to tear her eyes away from him as Jess began talking again.

"Oh, Evan didn't believe me when I told him I already

knew which of their friends you'd think were hot." Jess nodded to the blond. "*That* would be Byron."

"You know me well." Viv grinned at her friend. "So why is he going to owe you money soon? Did you actually bet on this?"

"Twenty bucks," Jess crowed. "But not yet. It's a two-part bet."

"Bit of advice for the soon-to-be-almost-weds, never bet against my girl. She won't bet real money unless she's already sure of the outcome."

"Oh sure, now you tell me," Evan joked, and then glanced up to greet Byron.

"Hey, Byron, the place is hopping as usual."

Viv noticed both men laid a possessive hand on Jessica and she barely managed to hide her amusement. Jess had clearly found herself a pair of possessive guys. For the hundredth time since Jess had told her she was forming a permanent relationship with two men, Viv wondered how they dealt with the finer points of sharing one woman. Maybe if she got enough tequila into Jess tonight, she'd find out.

AFTER YEARS WORKING THE BAR, Byron had developed something of a sixth sense when it came to detecting the presence of pretty women and trouble, likely because they were often the same thing. It wasn't anything definite, just a shift in the energy when something drew the attention of a bunch of his customers at once. He felt that shift and glanced up, looking for the source. When he found it he forgot what he was doing and stared. There was a goddess in his bar.

Long legs, black leather jacket and a tumble of short, cherry-red hair with streaks of what looked like either black or purple, it was impossible to tell in the dimmer light. Just looking at her made his cock stir and his heart beat a little faster.

She walked with confidence through the crowd and Byron marked her progress, trying to figure out who she was and what group she was joining. He'd need to know so he could find her later. There was no way a woman that beautiful was leaving his bar until he had her name. That was when the crowd moved a little and he realized she was arm in arm with a very familiar blonde.

Jessica.

Byron inwardly cheered. That meant the sexy redhead must be her best friend, and *that* meant he was going to get a chance to chat up the bombshell in black leather.

When the order from their table came in, he told Patricia he had it covered before signaling to Tucker he was taking a break. He glanced down at the order and laughed. Tequila, he should have known. The first time he had met Jessica she'd ordered two shots of the stuff and then nearly gotten into a fight with another woman over her men.

Byron had learned later that had been the day Rory and Evan had planned to tell her the truth about their selkie heritage, but miscommunications and bad timing had resulted in their mate sitting at Breakers, learning the truth about seal shapeshifters from Rory's second father, Torin. Byron was confident that when his mate finally appeared in his life, he'd be better at communicating with her than his friends had been.

He set the tray down on the table and passed out the drinks before glancing at the redhead, and his cock twitched behind the fly of his jeans as he got his first good look at her. Big hazel eyes, creamy skin and a full mouth that was currently quirked up into a grin. Before he could say anything, she stuck out her hand, and as he took it he noticed she was wearing a collection of silver rings on nearly every finger.

"Hi, I'm Vivian."

He was a sucker for a woman with confidence, and this one had it in spades. "Hello, Vivian." He shook her hand gently. "I'm Byron, welcome to Breakers. If there is anything you need, just whistle."

She grinned up at him. "Oh, don't worry, I know how to whistle. I just put my lips together and…blow."

Well damn, she actually knew the line!

He realized he was still holding her hand and belatedly released her.

"You watch Lauren Bacall and Bogart movies?" she asked.

"I love old movies. *To Have and Have Not* is a great one. Not many people are into the classics."

"I love them. It was a side effect of a misspent youth. Nothing else on in the middle of the night, so I watched those and developed a taste for them."

"I think you were using insider information when you made our bet," Evan muttered, and shot Jessica a dirty look.

"Bet?" Byron asked. "What bet?"

Jessica laughed, Evan winced and Rory rolled his eyes, but none of them said anything until Vivian chimed in.

"Oh, Jessica bet Evan that she could figure out which guys I'd find attractive before I even got here. She's just collected on the first half of that bet."

"I see. Do I get to find out who the other half of the bet is?" Byron's dick twitched again and he was thankful the high table was hiding his very apparent reaction from the others.

"Nope." Evan shook his head. "I've still got a chance to break even here."

"So I was the first half?"

Jess nodded and Vivian gave him a playful wink before letting her eyes drift over his body with obvious approval. "Oh yeah. She knows me pretty well."

"Apparently she does." He winked back at her. "And, slim, the feeling is mutual."

Her already lovely face lit up as she realized he'd called her the name of the character in the movie they'd just been discussing, and Byron knew right then he wanted to get to know Vivian better. Human or not, she was the first woman to actually spark his interest instead of just his dick in a very long time.

"I need to head back before Tucker gets overrun at the bar, but I'll be back later to join the party." Byron decided to go for broke and reached out to tuck a strand of Viv's hair back behind her ear, caressing her cheek as he did so. "I'll see you soon, slim."

She just grinned as he moved back, grabbing the tray and the bills Rory had left on it to cover their drinks. "Next round is on me, I'll tell Tucker the party's starting."

As he headed back to the bar he spotted a few more of

the Kismet Cove colony arriving. He gestured for them to head to the back, pointing them toward the right tables. The crowd had gotten thicker in the brief time he'd been away, and by the time he got back behind the bar Tucker was going full out to keep up with the orders.

"Where the hell did you go?" Tuckered demanded as he pulled drafts.

"Jessica arrived, I went to say hi." Byron called back over the noise. "She brought her friend, Vivian. I'm starting to think we need to go visit Toronto. The women back east are hotter than I thought!"

"You'd be miserable there, no surfing."

"Damn fine point, but that's okay, since Vivian happens to be single."

Tucker shot him a dubious look. "She's that hot?"

"Next chance you get, go say hi." Byron slid two more drinks across the bar to waiting customers. "Try to avoid scowling at her…or talking for that matter. Just smile and nod and maybe she'll like you."

Tucker loaded another tray and then cocked his pierced eyebrow at Byron. "How much to make you shut up so I can finish up these orders?"

"You can't afford it."

The two of them worked in relative silence after that, leaving Byron free to consider his reaction to Vivian as he kept pace with the steady demand for fresh drinks. She'd definitely piqued his interest. Enough that he intended to get to know her better once the other bartenders arrived to take over later on in the evening. Just thinking about her had his jeans feeling two sizes too small. He wanted to get to know her a *lot* better.

He'd hand over the night's profits to find out who the

second half of the bet had been about. If Jessica thought there was even a chance Vivian would be interested in Tucker too, then the moment he'd been waiting for might finally have arrived. Tucker's rift with the colony had made it almost impossible for them to find a selkie woman of their own. The blood-bond they shared would compel them to live together and protect their mate, but none of the local selkies wanted to live away from Kismet Cove, and Tucker refused to go near the colony land unless there was a damned good reason.

Instead, he had converted the space over Breakers into an artist's studio and apartment, while Byron lived alone in Kismet Cove, in the house that he should have shared with Tucker. It wasn't the way they were intended to be, and Byron kept hoping for more. He wanted what his three parents had, and what Rory and Evan were building with Jess. He wanted a family.

He caught a strain of sultry laughter coming from the far end of the bar, and he somehow knew it was Vivian. He had only shared a few words with her, but her voice was already imprinted on his brain.

JESSICA'S MEN and their friends were all good people, that much was already clear to Vivian as she watched them all interact. They were laughing and joking with each other, and they'd all gone out of their way to make her feel included. They'd all done another round of shots, but after that Jess had switched to cola, reminding everyone that she was the designated driver for the night. Vivian was under no such restriction, so during a lull in the conversation she headed over to the bar to order something a bit more subtle than another shot.

She was standing on tiptoes, trying to look over the crowd to see if Byron was at the bar when someone jostled her from the side and she lost her balance. She staggered back a step and bumped up against a solid mass of what was either a man or a tree, and she was still trying to decide when a hand wrapped around her waist, helping to steady her.

"I got you." A deep voice rumbled by her ear.

"Thanks." She turned around and found herself nose-to-chest with her savior. She had to tip her head way back to see his face, but it was worth nearly putting her neck out to get a good look. He was one good-looking man. He had short, black hair, and sitting above one slate-gray eye was a gold eyebrow ring which added an edge to his already intimidating presence. Her gaze slid down his neck to the elaborate, tribal-style tattoo that began below one ear and flowed underneath his dark blue shirt.

"There has got to be something in the water around here," she muttered, giving voice to the thoughts running through her head.

"I beg your pardon?" He quirked that pierced eyebrow up a notch at Viv's comment and her stomach did a little flutter.

Damn, he is hot.

"Sorry, that should have been my inside voice. You just caught me by surprise." She splayed her hands wide, indicating the width of his shoulders. "When I first ran into you I thought I'd bumped into a tree. Now I think you're a lumberjack. Paul Bunyan, maybe."

He smiled at that and a dimple appeared in his right

cheek, softening his expression. "Name's Tucker, not Paul. I do know an ox though, or at least someone as stubborn as one."

"Nice to meet you." She realized this had to be the other owner of Breakers and grinned at having the advantage. "You must be Rory's cousin. I'm Vivian. I believe we're both going to the same non-wedding in a couple of days." The crowd surged around them both and Viv found herself pushed up against Tucker's hard body. He was solid muscle and completely unaffected by the surge of humanity around them. He kept one arm around her waist, acting as her anchor until the crush eased up again.

"So you're Jess's best friend? The one she told me was a trouble magnet?" he asked as he released her.

"That's me! Though my reputation as a chaos attractor is completely undeserved," she said as she took a step back, putting some space between them so she could get her brain firing on all cylinders again.

"It's nice to meet you, trouble. I was actually just heading over to join the fun. Why aren't you with the others?"

"I was on my way to find Byron and see what you guys had stashed in the back for someone who was tired of tequila." Viv cocked her head and smiled. "So what do you say? Want to show me the good stuff?"

Curiosity gleamed in his eyes as he looked down at her and then finally nodded. "I could do that. What exactly were you hoping for? If you're yearning for a light Chardonnay with a hint of summer berry, you're in the wrong bar."

Viv choked back a laugh. "Not even close. I was

wondering if you have something in a ten or fifteen-year-old scotch. And if you try to tell me ladies don't drink scotch, I'll happily confess I'm not much of a lady."

"Scotch? Now for that, I think you're in exactly the right place." He took her hand without another word and started making his way through the crowd. People seemed to instinctively give way to the big man, and before she knew it they were passing by the bar. Tucker grabbed two glasses and kept going, leading her to a door clearly marked "employees only." He pushed it open and led her to a well-lit and carefully organized stock room, which was a complete contrast to the rustic décor of the main bar. In here everything was itemized and labeled, and the stillness was welcome after the crush and thrum of the crowd.

She breathed a sigh of relief and caught him doing the same.

"I never realize how loud and crazy it's gotten until I step away from it for a bit," he explained, and handed her the glasses before reaching to an upper shelf to snag a distinctive, green glass bottle. "Glenlivet." He held it up for her approval. "Other options include an eighteen-year-old Macallan, or I've got a fifteen-year-old Dalwhinnie here as well."

"I vote for the Macallan. That's one of my favorites."

"Good choice." He set the Glenlivet back and grabbed another bottle from the same shelf. "Do you want to head back out, or are you good to hang here for a minute? I wouldn't mind taking a moment to enjoy the quiet, but I don't want you to feel like you have to stay."

"I'm good here." She was more than good, actually. Meeting new people was never easy, and as inclusive as they had been, it was something of a relief to get a break from the group, not to mention getting to spend a few minutes alone with Tucker was no hardship. Between Byron's early flirtations and now Tucker's attention, Vivian was feeling hotter than she had in a very long time.

In the brighter light he only got better looking, and as she estimated the height of the shelves she realized he had to be around six foot four, which was why he dwarfed her though she was almost five foot ten, if you included the small heel on her boots.

"Well, since we're calling a time out, why don't we enjoy a drink while we're here?" He cracked the seal on the scotch bottle and she held out the glasses as he poured a measure into each and then set the bottle aside. "What should we drink to?"

"New friends?" she suggested.

"To new friends." He touched his glass to hers. "And to women who like good scotch."

"Here, here." She raised her glass and drank, enjoying the rich flavor and the warming sensation as it travelled down her throat. "Now *that* is the good stuff."

CHAPTER THREE

HE'D NEVER BROUGHT a woman back into the storeroom before, and he wasn't quite sure how he'd ended up back here with one now. Not that he hadn't picked up women from his bar a time or two, but he'd never let anyone he'd been attracted to cross the line between business and pleasure. Pleasure meant going upstairs for an evening's fun and then sending them on their way.

A relationship with a human woman was damned near impossible given the number of secrets he had to keep, while selkie women all wanted more than he was able to give. So why was he having a drink with Vivian in his stockroom? He didn't have an answer to that one. She'd asked, he'd taken her hand and led her back here without a second thought.

As she took another sip of scotch, he leaned back against the wall across from her, letting his gaze wander over her. She was tall and leggy, her soft leather boots clinging to the subtle curve of her calves. She was wearing a pair of jeans with none of the sequins or bling that some of the women wore, and her green top was a flowing, simple affair that wasn't tight or low cut, but somehow looked as if it were. What intrigued him the most was the fact she was wearing a motorcycle jacket, a real one and not a fashionable copy.

"You ride?" he asked. If she did, he suspected he was going to be looking for an excuse to get her on the back of his bike. The idea of those long legs snugged up behind him was a very tempting one.

"Every day until the first snowfall. My baby's off the road for the winter, though. I saw a few bikes out front, is one of them yours?"

"Mine's in the back. I actually live upstairs." He pointed to the ceiling and silently willed his cock to stop rising in response to her answer. She didn't look like any biker he'd ever laid eyes on before.

"That's a very short commute," she observed with a grin. "What do you have?"

"Harley," he said. "You?"

"Kawasaki. "

"Ouch. No wonder you retire it for the winter. I cannot imagine trying to navigate one of those things during a Toronto winter."

She grinned. "It's not the bike that's the problem, it's the other drivers. If they would just get out of my way I'd be able to ride all winter. I take it you can go year-round here?"

He didn't miss the gleam in her eye as she asked her question and he knew without a doubt he'd be looking for an opportunity to give her a ride while she was here. Hell, He'd ride her any way she wanted. He banished the graphic images of her body under his and tried to answer her question. "You can, for the most part. The times I can't I use the work truck or I call Byron and get him to give me a ride."

"He's the other owner here, right? And you're both part of that Kismet Cove place?"

Tucker tensed and took another sip of whiskey. He really didn't like talking about the colony. "Byron is. I'm sort of the black sheep. I live here and don't have much to do with them, really. Rory, Evan and Jessica's ceremony will be the first time I've set foot in the place in a long time."

"Oops, sorry. I didn't mean to hit a nerve. I've only been here a day and I'm still jetlagged and trying to figure everything out. Jess means the world to me, and I want to be sure she's going to be happy here, you know?"

He relaxed a bit as she explained. "Yeah, I get that. I can tell you that Rory and Evan are completely nuts over her, and she's settled in like she was a long-lost member of the family." Because she is, he added mentally, but of course there was no way he could tell Vivian that. Vivian was human, and clearly she had no idea that her best friend and her mates were all seal shapeshifters, modern-day descendants of creatures out of legend. The colony guarded their secrets tightly, and Tucker had to be sure he didn't inadvertently say too much.

"Her mom's last wish was for her to come out here. I'm glad she did, but her mom also asked me to look out for her. It's been hard knowing Jess is never coming home."

The confession seemed to startle her, and she took another drink and then another, clearly not sure what to say. The outburst made him like her even more. She had a loyal streak, and cared deeply for her friend. Those were traits he could admire. He had the luxury of a blood-bond with Byron, which meant they were linked for life. They were closer than brothers, able to sense each other's thoughts and feelings thanks to their bond, a telepathic advantage when they were in human form, and a necessity when they were seals and had no other way to communicate with each other.

They didn't leave the link open all the time, though. They'd figured out how to close it off long ago to allow them both their privacy. After all, they'd been bonded as boys, and they were both over thirty now. That would have been a lot of years of inadvertent eavesdropping.

"From the amount she's talked about you, I'd say she's missed you too. Every time she's been in she's talked about how happy she was you were coming out."

"Yeah, but she's got Rory and Evan now..." Viv trailed off and blushed. "Damn, that sounded needy, didn't it? I'm going to blame the tequila, drink this scotch and get over myself." She took another drink and grinned, her hazel eyes glowing with sudden mischief. "I don't suppose the owners are supposed to hit the dance floor, are they?"

"Only on special occasions, so you're going to need to give me a reason, trouble."

"You keep calling me that, you're going to give me a complex!" She drained her glass, throwing back her head and exposing the long lines of her throat. The sight made his cock stir and he wondered if her skin was as soft as it looked.

"I think it suits you."

"Fine, then. You can keep calling me that, but you have

to dance with me. You can claim we're celebrating my baptism."

He downed the rest of his scotch and grabbed the bottle. "Then you have yourself a special occasion. Let's put this behind the bar and you can show me how they dance back east."

They headed back into the bar, and as the crowd pressed in he found himself once again reaching for her hand. She twined her fingers with his as he led her through the crowd, using his size to advantage. As they passed the bar he handed the bottle of scotch to his assistant manager, Tim. He left Tim looking bemused as he made his way to the dance floor with Vivian still in tow.

The song that had been playing ended and instead of another upbeat tune, Foreigner's *I Want to Know What Love Is*, came over the speakers. He thought about stepping off the floor again, but decided to see how far he could push his luck and tugged her into his arms.

She came willingly, her eyes dancing as she slid her hands up his chest in a flirtatious caress that had his dick hardening and the blood pounding so loudly in his ears he could barely hear the music. He hadn't tried to slow dance with a woman while sporting a hard-on since high school, and he was disconcerted to discover it hadn't gotten any easier in the years between.

This close to her, the scent of her perfume struck his nose and he breathed her in, enjoying the subtle flavor of vanilla that rose from her skin and hair. They fit together well, her body brushing up against his as they moved to the music, neither of them trying anything fancy.

"I think we've been spotted." She murmured, stirring

in his arms and lifting one hand to wave at Jessica, who had appeared at the edge of the dance floor.

"She probably wondered where her best friend had disappeared to."

"Likely, but she knows I can take care of myself. I've been doing it most of my life."

He heard a wealth of meaning in those few words, and they struck a chord deep inside. Maybe that was why he'd been drawn to her so quickly. She had the same independent streak he did, and he had no doubt that if he got to know her, he'd find out that her upbringing had been as screwed up as his.

"We've got that in common then."

"That, and an appreciation for good scotch and two-wheeled transportation." She laughed up at him and rubbed her body along his, her hip brushing over his cock just hard enough to make his breath catch. The woman was trying to kill him in the middle of his own bar.

"I don't think that's all we have in common." He dropped his lips to her ear. "I'm pretty sure we have chemistry, too."

He felt her shiver and he knew he'd been right. She was feeling the attraction between them, too.

"Mhmm." He barely caught her soft hum of agreement. "That too."

The song ended, and all around them couples untangled themselves before heading off the floor. She'd felt good in his arms, so when the time came he let her go with more than a little reluctance. As she stepped out of his arms her cheeks were flushed and her eyes were sparkling. "We should get back to the party so you can say hi to everyone else." She glanced over toward the others.

"Yep, we should. But before we head over I want to know if you'd be game to go out on my bike sometime. I'll give you the nickel tour of the area."

She smiled and he felt his heart kick up another notch. Oh yeah, he had it bad.

"I'd love it. Any time after Jess and the guys leave on their honeymoon works for me. I'm going to be on my own for a few days."

"What a coincidence, me too. Byron's heading out of town for a couple of days next week."

"Great. I'll make sure you have my number before we head home tonight. And of course, I'll see you at the commitment ceremony."

"Yes, you will." He headed off the dance floor and noted that the knowledge that she'd be there made going to the ceremony far less of an issue than it had been. Vivian was something new and interesting, and those were things that didn't come into his life too often these days.

VIVIAN WAS FEELING ALMOST GIDDY, and she knew it had more to do with the man leading the way back to their table than with the alcohol she'd consumed. She got her fair share of male attention, but it had been a long time since she'd had two very hot and very different men flirt with her on the same night.

When they arrived back at their tables the party had grown, and she was greeted by several more new faces with names she knew would all be a blur very soon. There were simply too many people to be able to keep track of them all. Her seat had long since been claimed, so once the latest round of introductions was done she looked for a spot she could claim and maybe inveigle Tucker into a longer conversation.

At least she would have, if she could see where he'd gone. She felt a prickle of disappointment when she discovered he wasn't with the group any longer. He had said he was coming to join them, so where had he gone?

Putting Tucker's vanishing act out of her mind, she managed a brief wave to Jess and then slipped around the knots of people to the only empty seat she could find. She found herself sitting right beside a mural that stretched the entire length of the wall, depicting a beach scene she was certain was of the local area. It had been painted with breathtaking detail.

The closer she looked at it the more tiny elements caught her eye. The waves looked real enough that she could imagine them crashing down on the rocks at any moment, while birds and other wildlife were hidden among the trees and grasses that lined the shore. When she took a good look at the ocean, she spotted a number of seals frolicking in the waves. That was when she noticed that there were murals on almost every wall, depicting beaches and forests where most bars had sports posters and memorabilia.

Interesting.

Leaning back in her seat, she relaxed and then cursed as she realized she didn't have a drink.

"Miss me?" Tucker's deep voice sounded from behind her and a bottle of scotch with two fresh glasses appeared in her vision. "I went back for our drinks."

"My hero."

"She took the bottle and glasses from him and then

laughed as he walked around and placed another stool in front of her. Instead of sitting in it properly, he threw a leg over the seat and sat in it backward, so the back was against his chest and he could fold his arms over the top.

"I thought you were coming over to join the party?" She gestured behind him to the bulk of the people gathered.

They'll come say hi when they want to. I did mention I'm the black sheep, remember? So I thought I'd keep company with the other unknown element." He took back one of the glasses from her and then held it out for her to pour. "This time, you can serve me. Anyone asks, just say you work here."

"You offering me a job?" She poured him a measure and then herself one before setting the bottle down on the nearest flat surface.

"Why, you looking for one?" He cocked that pierced eyebrow at her again and she felt her nipples harden as a wave of lust rolled through her. What was it about him that had her hormones in a tizzy?

"My boss demanded I leave the airport and come back to cover the shop for a week so she could fly to Hawaii at the last minute," she explained with a shrug. "So I quit. I've worked in clubs before, but honestly, I am much better at cutting hair than making drinks or waiting tables."

"So, you're thinking about staying out here?" He seemed surprised at the idea.

"Maybe. I don't know. Hell, two days ago I was missing my best friend and booking clients for New Year's Eve styles and sets. Now I'm on the other side of the country and unemployed. I know Jess would be happy if I stayed, but I have no idea if that's what I want. Not to mention the fact my bike and stuff are still back in Toronto."

"If you decide to stay, you won't have any trouble finding work once the tourist season starts. This whole town fills to overflowing. It's a big change from the world you grew up in, though." He grinned and his dimple flashed. "You're more likely to get attacked by a bear than a mugger, for one thing."

"A *bear*! There are bears around here?" Jess hadn't mentioned anything about any damned bears. "Tell me you're kidding."

Tucker was laughing and shaking his head. "I'm not kidding. Bears, deer, cougars. Even the occasional wolf. You have landed in the wilds of the west coast. You still think you want to stay here?"

"Who's staying? And why are you telling her about the bears already, Tucker? Jeez, man, how many times do I have to tell you not to traumatize the visitors?" Byron appeared beside them, laughing. "Pay no attention to him. He's trying to mess with you. The bears are quite happy to stay out of town, and the deer are only a threat to people who are foolish enough to try and grow a garden. Those things eat *everything*!"

"Hello again. Are you both out from behind the bar for the night now?" Vivian's gaze bounced from one to the other, once again amazed that both men were clearly interested in her. Jess had said most of the folks in Kismet Cove were poly, did that mean these two were as well? Wicked thoughts filled her head for a moment and she had to mentally shake herself back to the present.

"I am free for the night. Barring catastrophes, bar

fights, or kitchen fires, that is." Byron eyed the glass in her hand. "That's not tequila."

"Nope, Tucker found me something better." She pointed to the bottle of scotch. "*Much* better."

"He did, huh?" Byron whistled low when he spotted the brand. "Eighteen-year-old scotch? How did you get him to part with that, slim?"

"I asked nicely." Viv fluttered her lashes at Byron. "It works wonders."

"Besides, I'm joining her." Tucker held up his own glass, still half full. "But you don't have enough appreciation for good scotch to lay a finger on that bottle, you heathen."

"Not a problem." Byron threw up his hands in mock surrender, revealing he already had a drink in his hand. I'm driving home later so I'm sticking to unleaded for the rest of the night. Kitchen is about to bring out some nachos and appetizer platters. I came to warn you that if you're hungry, you better be prepared to move fast. The locals are very friendly until you get between them and their food supply, then they get ornery."

As she hopped off her stool she found herself between them both, with Byron's hand on the small of her back and Tucker's resting between her shoulder blades. They escorted her back to the main table as several servers appeared, all laden down with food. She could feel her stomach rumbling even if she couldn't hear it over the music. She decided to throw discretion to the wind and enjoy all the indulgences the night had on offer. Good food, fine scotch, not to mention the attention of two men that she wouldn't see again once she went home. After all, she *was* on holiday.

CHAPTER FOUR

THEY WERE ABOUT DONE CLOSING down for the night when Bryon turned and grinned at Tucker. "So, are you as smitten as I am?"

"Subtle, dude. Very subtle." Tucker snickered. "If I am, then what?"

Byron chose his next words carefully. "Then I think we should see how she feels about seeing us. Both of us."

"There are a few flaws in this plan of yours. For one, she's human," Tucker pointed out.

"She is, but I think that's a plus. She's not a selkie, so she's not going to have expectations of how this is going to work. We could figure it out for ourselves. Jess was so sure Vivian would like us both she bet Evan twenty bucks over it, and Evan made sure I knew he'd lost the bet. I'd say that's a damn good sign we have a very attractive woman who is at least nominally interested in both of us."

"Do you think she's interested in both of us as a package deal, though? That's not exactly normal human dating."

"I think the fact she flirted with me, then danced with you and then paid us both equal attention for the rest of the night speaks for itself. Maybe she's more open-minded than you think. Maybe she's curious to see what Jess's life is like now. I'm not really worried about why. I just want to know if you're game to try."

"I might be. "I'm willing to grant that neither of us has had much luck dating separately. She is smoking hot, and smart too. I'm game. But if we are going to do this, we're going to need a plan."

Byron grinned at his best friend. "I'm working on one."

"There's one other minor problem. She's only visiting for a few weeks. Now, she mentioned she might be staying, but what if she doesn't?"

"You've got the cart so far before the horse that the horse hasn't even been born yet. Let's see if she's actually willing to go out with us first." Byron felt the first stirrings of real hope. He'd wanted this a long time, but it had never worked out for them. Maybe this time would be different. There was something different about Vivian. Something that was already tugging at the sleeve of his soul, demanding his attention.

"So how would this work?" Tucker asked, and Byron could see he was hopeful too.

"Well, we know she's going to be busy until the ceremony, so we'll see her there, get to know her a bit more and see if she's still interested in us both. I'm gone as of Monday morning, and that should give you a few days to hang out with her. When I get back, it's my turn to get to know her. Fair enough? Vivian's a grown woman, she can make up her own mind. If she says no, that's it. If she decides she only wants to see one of us while she's here,

I'll have to hope she prefers her men hot and blond instead of cranky and covered in ink."

Tucker snorted in derision. "You can hope all you want, but it's never going to happen. You're the Goose to my Maverick. I'm the pilot, you're the wingman."

"*Top Gun* references, really? Do you remember how that movie goes? Goose dies!" He clapped Tucker on the shoulder. "And on that cheery note, I'm going home. See you tomorrow."

"Have a good one." Tucker headed over to the light switches and glanced back at Byron. "You're going to call her tomorrow, aren't you." It wasn't a question.

"Of course I am." Byron said, hand on the door. "If you want to keep up, you might want to do the same."

"So it's going to be like that, is it? So be it. Game on, bro."

"Game on," Byron called back and headed out the main doors, stopping to make sure they were locked behind him. That had gone better than he could have hoped for. Now he just had to hope Vivian was willing to consider this half-assed plan of his.

She's going to have to be equal parts insane and brave to take us both on. Please gods, let her be the one.

Twelve hours later Byron was standing in a flower shop, signing his name to a card that would be sent along with a bouquet of coral and yellow roses. He hadn't sent flowers to anyone but his mother in years, but the thought had struck him on the way home the night before and had still been with him this morning. As he handed over his credit card and the address of Jess and Vivian's cabin, he couldn't wipe the grin off his face. If Tucker was going all out, then he was going to have to bring his *A* game too. Vivian deserved no less.

~

VIVIAN WASN'T QUITE finished tying the purple and silver ribbons around the guests' favors when there was a knock at the door. With her fingers tangled in the midst of yet another bow, she barely looked up as Jess bounced over to get it. They had been receiving packages and cards off and on since Vivian's arrival at the homey little cabin they were currently sharing.

After tomorrow she'd have it all to herself when Jess took up official residence in Kismet Cove with her two men. Unofficially she was already moved in, more or less, meaning that Vivian had spent last night alone after Jess had dropped her off and headed out for some personal time with Rory and Evan. Judging by the bags under her eyes this morning, they hadn't wasted their time doing anything as mundane as sleeping.

Jess squealed and bounded back into the cabin with yet another basket of some kind, but when she set it down on the table beside Viv, she handed the card to her instead of opening it.

"It's for you!" she declared in a sing-song voice. "Somebody has an admirer."

Viv didn't need to look at the card to know who had sent it. One look at the basket told her everything she needed to know. There were two highball glasses nested inside, along with an unopened bottle of the same brand of scotch she'd been enjoying with Tucker last night. "Tucker," she said to Jess in explanation.

"Of course it was Tucker. Byron would never send you booze." She peered past the cellophane. "There's something else in there too."

Viv leaned in and realized there was a canister of some kind tucked in behind the bottle. "What the hell is that?"

She tore away the plastic so she could see better, then burst out laughing as she read the label. He'd sent her a canister of bear spray.

"What on earth is that?"

Unable to talk past her giggles, Viv handed it to Jessica without a word and opened the card that had come with it.

For a woman with great taste in scotch. I hope we get to share this bottle someday soon.

T.

P.S. The bear spray is to keep you safe when we're not around.

"Why is he sending you bear spray? I don't understand." Jess handed it back to her with a shake of her blonde head.

"He mentioned there were bears around here and I might have overreacted slightly. City-girl thing." Viv showed Jessica the note.

"That is the weirdest present I have ever seen, but it's sort of sweet too. One thing's for sure, you'll have fun seeing them. "

"Them?" Viv asked. "Them as in both of them, together? Like your guys? You really think that's their plan?"

"Mhmm." Jess nodded as she read the note. The note says when *we're* not around. They're both from triad families, Viv. Are you going to be okay with that?"

43

She thought about it for a minute. "I am. I got that vibe from them last night too. So long as no one gets hurt, I think I'm okay with it, at least in theory. It's certainly done *you* a world of good." She laughed as she picked up the next bit of ribbon. "It'll give me something to do while you three are off on your honeymoon. It isn't likely to be anything serious, anyway." Jess had known her long enough to know that with Vivian, romances were never serious. It was better for everyone if she kept things simple.

"I still feel bad about leaving you alone after inviting you out here," Jess said. "We'll be back before Christmas though, and you are spending it with us. Christmas Eve is apparently a big party. Everyone will be at Rory's parents' place that night, and then we're having a much smaller get-together Christmas Day. It's going to be wonderful!"

"Don't feel guilty! I am going to eat every decadent thing I can lay my hands on, spend hours in your hot tub watching the waves crash on the shore, and apparently I have at least one date to look forward to."

There was a knock at the door and Jess was up before Vivian could even stand. "Want to bet this one's from Byron?" She tossed over her shoulder as she opened the door and squealed. "Oh! Flowers!"

Viv stood up and caught a glimpse of coral and yellow blooms. Jess spun around with an armful of roses, grinning from ear to ear. "Now these look like something Byron would send. Check the card!"

Sure enough, the card was from Byron.
Slim,
Of all the gin joints in all the towns in all the world, you

walked into mine. I'm glad you did. We'll see you at the wedding.

Byron

The roses were gorgeous, their bright petals contrasting with the sprays of cedar that had been used in place of the traditional baby's breath.

"You're going to need to put those in water." Jess headed to the well-appointed kitchen and started opening cupboards until she found a vase large enough to hold them. "Look at you! Here less than three days and already you're getting flowers and gift baskets! You sure you want to go back to Toronto? When was the last time any guy you've dated out there sent you flowers? Oh, wait. I know the answer to that one. Never!"

"All right, all right." Vivian threw up her hands in surrender and then gathered up the flowers, arranging them in the vase Jess had set out on the counter that divided the kitchen from the living space. "I'll admit this is a first. I'll even admit that it's not the same without you back home. But I'm a city girl, and this is about as far as you can get from the city. There are *bears* for fuck's sake, and the tree-to-people ratio is unbelievable." She tucked the last bit of greenery into the vase and gave it a critical once over. They really were stunning flowers.

"Just think about it while I'm gone, okay? The guys and I are planning on heading back to Toronto early next year to get my stuff from storage, you know we could ship yours too while we're out there. That way you'd have your bike and uh…" She frowned. "Do you own anything other than your bed and a dresser?"

"Ha, ha," Viv stuck her tongue out at Jess. "I have stuff!

There just isn't that much of it, and to be honest half of what I do have I don't really need."

"I know. I've helped you move a time or two. I swear everything you own could fit in a half-dozen garbage bags. You have always been a minimalist."

"Oh, a minimalist! I like that description." She headed back to the table to finish up the wedding crafts. The truth was that she had never found a place that felt like home, and without that sense of belonging, she'd never had the urge to clutter up what felt like borrowed space with personal things.

"I've got this." Jess shooed her away from the mess that covered the table. "You're supposed to be relaxing, not working as my personal drudge. "Why don't you hit the hot tub and I'll join you once I've cleaned up and made a few calls?"

"Okay, but you are the one getting hitched tomorrow. You need some downtime too! If you take too long I'll come back up here and drag you away," she warned.

"I won't be long." Jess picked Vivian's phone up and handed it to her. "Take this with you. I think you have some thank you calls to make."

"Yes, Mom."

"Now you're being insulting." Jess began clearing away the ribbon. "Your mother's head would explode at the mere thought of you going out with two men. Kaboom! And then she'd be mad at you for making a mess with her gray matter."

That got Vivian snickering and she didn't stop the whole time she was changing into her bikini.

The walk down to the hot tub was far enough that by the time she got there her bare legs were covered in goose bumps. The cedar-planked walkway led straight from the house to the gazebo, but it was still a chilly trip. The view was worth the chill though, as the hot tub was under a gazebo built at the end of a rocky point.

Jess had told her that even during the worst storms it was set high enough to be safe from the pounding waves. Vivian could happily spend hours soaking as she watched the ocean and occasional wildlife. She shed her borrowed robe and climbed into the hot tub with a sigh that instantly turned into a cloud of frosted breath that swirled around her mouth before fading away.

She left the jets off, and once she was comfortably stretched out she snagged her cell phone to call up Tucker's number. His smoke-and-whisky rumble of a voice answered on the second ring and she grinned. Could he have been waiting for her call?

"Hello, trouble." His voice sent a thrill straight to her clit and she wriggled in water, her thighs clamped together as a rush of desire washed over her.

"Hi. I wanted to say thank you for the scotch, and the uh…anti-animal spray."

"You keep that handy and use on anything that gets too close to you." He was chuckling now.

"Does that include you?" she asked, throwing caution to the wind and turning up the flirt level.

"Nope. I bought it, you're not allowed to use it on me. Those are the rules." He paused and then added. "Besides, I've already been nice and close to you, on the dance floor last night."

"That's right, you were." She let her voice drop to a purr. "So when are we going to open that bottle?"

"Well, I have it on good authority we're both going to

be busy tomorrow, so what about Monday? If the weather holds we'll go for a ride and then maybe grab a bite to eat in town?"

"Does this town have a decent pizza place? If it does, why don't we have dinner delivered and we can enjoy some of that scotch here?"

"As a matter of fact, I know where to get the west coast's best pizza. You're sure that's all you want?"

"After eating wedding food tomorrow I'm going to want simple comfort food. I'm sure. Pizza would be perfect. Then maybe we can go use the hot tub. It's sinful."

"You have access to a hot tub?" She could hear the interest in his voice.

"I'm sitting in it right now, watching the waves hit the rocks," she told him, and laughed softly as he muttered something in a strangled cough she couldn't quite make out.

"Damn. That visual is going to stay with me all day. Now you have to tell me, swimsuit or skinny-dipping?"

"Bikini. It's the middle of the day, Tucker! I'm not going to wander around Jess's backyard naked. Besides, it's cold out here!"

"Fair point," he conceded, and then paused as a new voice spoke in the background. When he came back on the line she couldn't tell if he was laughing or irritated, or both. "Byron would like to know if you got the flowers he sent."

"Byron's there too? Tell him he's my next call and to quit eavesdropping. Your basket came before his flowers, so I'm calling you first." She waited while he covered the receiver and said something in a low growl to Byron.

"He says he'll call you in a minute. He really sent you

something as boring as flowers?" Tucker asked, and Vivian decided it was time to make something clear.

"I'm enjoying all this attention, but I really don't want to come between you two. So if this is going to cause problems—"

Tucker cut her off. "It's not. You're not. I mean, we're fine. We've just never done this before. So if we screw anything up or upset you, tell us." He paused and then added, "Or use the bear spray."

She laughed at that. "I'll consider it. I should go so I can say thanks to Byron and then get off the phone. Jess will be joining me soon and we need a little girl time before her big day. I'll see you tomorrow."

"I'm looking forward to it. Bye for now."

Vivian shut off her phone and it rang again before she could even set it down. She checked the display to be certain, but she knew it would be Byron. "Hi there."

"Hey. I hear you got the flowers." She could almost see his sexy smile when he spoke.

"I did. They're gorgeous, thank you. They're already in a vase, brightening up the cabin."

"I'm glad you like them. Listen, I'm going out of town for a few days, but when I get back I'd like to see you. Nothing fancy, but since Tucker is taking you on a tour of the land, I thought I'd take you out for a boat ride and show you the area from the other side."

She had a moment's unease at the idea of going out on the ocean, but she deliberately set that feeling aside. Life was too short to be slowed down by fears. "That sounds like fun. Do I need to bring anything? Lunch maybe?"

"I've got that covered. You just bring yourself, slim."

"And the bear spray!" She heard Tucker holler in the background.

"What...he bought you bear spray? Holy shit, dude. Way to romance a woman. You are a real piece of work, you know that? Vivian? Leave the bear spray at home. I promise you will not be attacked by anything while you're with me."

"No bear spray, got it."

"Good. We'll see you tomorrow. Tell Jess to knock her men dead."

"I will. Bye, Byron, and thanks again for the roses."

"You're very welcome."

She hung up the phone again and gave in to a fit of giggles that lasted until Jess arrived to join her in the tub. The next few weeks were going to be anything but boring.

CHAPTER FIVE

THE CEREMONY WENT off without a hitch, and Vivian caught herself tearing up several times. Jess looked so happy she was actually glowing, and her men didn't take their eyes off of her from the moment she came into view. The only thing that had marred Vivian's joy was when Jess and her grooms had allowed their palms to be sliced and then linked hands to signify their bond. It seemed barbaric, not to mention messy and unhygienic, but since no one else batted an eyelash it was obviously something of a local tradition. Apparently so were kilts, because more than half the men present were wearing them, including Jess's two men.

Now *that* was a tradition Vivian could get behind.

The hall was crowded enough she hadn't been able to spot Byron or Tucker during the ceremony, which was surprising considering that Tucker was taller than almost everyone present. Once the rites had been concluded she left Jess and the others to their moment of celebration and headed away from the crush converging on the happy trio.

She'd gotten in her congratulations before, and no doubt would have other opportunities throughout the evening. Right now she wanted nothing more than a glass of water and a bit of quiet. It had been an insanely busy and absolutely glorious day.

She got halfway to the bar when a hand touched her shoulder and she turned to find herself staring into Byron's green eyes.

"Hello, gorgeous," he said, his gaze full of admiration. "You looked good in black leather the other night, but now you look incredible." Despite the short notice, Viv had managed to find a backless sheath dress in a shimmering silver fabric that worked with the color theme of the party and looked damned good. Every penny now missing from her savings account felt very well spent as she saw the heat in Byron's eyes.

"You look pretty fine yourself, but I'll confess I'm disappointed you aren't wearing a kilt." The truth was he looked incredible, like he'd walked off a photo shoot for a men's magazine. He was wearing slacks, a pinstriped dress shirt and a tie that was already showing signs of being tugged at more than once. Instantly her head was filled with a dozen wicked ways she could rumple up his outfit even more.

"He doesn't have the legs for it." Tucker's voice rumbled near her ear and his hand touched her back, between her shoulder blades. "Hello, trouble. I have to say, I like your dress even better from this angle." His fingers traced up her spine and she knew he was following the lines of the Celtic-style dragon tattoo that covered her left side. The tail started at her tailbone and the dragon's head rested on her shoulder blade. "Nice ink," he commented as his fingers continued up to the nape of her neck, leaving shimmering tendrils of heat in their wake.

"Hi, Tuck—wow!" Was all she could say as she turned around to greet him and saw what he was wearing. Black wasn't really a wedding color, but in his case she was going to make an exception. Black shoes, black hose that turned over just below his knees, and oh goddess, a black leather kilt. His black silk shirt was made in a flowing, old-fashioned style, complete with laces instead of buttons.

With his tattoos and brow ring he looked like a sexy mash-up of a highlander and a pirate, hitting damned near all Viv's sexual fantasies at the same time. She gathered her wits and tried to think past her suddenly throbbing pussy, but it wasn't easy. She finally took a step back and then eyed him from toes to nose before nodding in approval.

"He dressed up for you," Byron informed her as he stepped to her side and offered her his arm. "He doesn't wear a skirt for just any woman, you know."

Tucker growled under his breath but Vivian cut him off before he could say anything. "You both look very handsome." She took Byron's arm and then laughed as Tucker appeared on her other side and mirrored Byron's gesture. She took his arm too, and they walked toward the bar set up near the back of the hall.

Byron leaned back and whistled low as he spotted the nonexistent back of her dress. "I have to agree with Tucker. That dress looks even better from the back. I'm making the call right now. You are the best-dressed woman here, and that tattoo is very damned sexy."

"Agreed," Tucker chimed in.

"I'm pretty sure that honor is supposed to go to Jess today," Viv argued and both men shook their heads.

"She's now officially off the market. There's no sense wasting compliments on her," Byron explained. "Besides, Rory would tear my head off and use it for a crab float if he heard me say anything even vaguely flirtatious to Jess. He still hasn't forgiven me for giving her two shots of tequila on the house the first time I met her."

"I'm starting to see a pattern with you, Byron. But it won't work tonight. I'm sticking to water. It's been a very long day and Jess and I forgot to eat."

"You haven't eaten?" Tucker frowned and then glanced at Byron. "Your mom's helping with the catering, right? Go see if you can't talk her out of some appetizers. I'll grab us some drinks and meet you…" He glanced around, trying to pick a spot. "We'll meet you in the corner nearest the fire exit."

"You got it." Byron cocked his head at her. "Requests?"

"If I remember the menu right, there are smoked salmon and cream cheese puff pastries. I'm dying to try real west coast smoked salmon."

"You like seafood?" Tucker asked, looking oddly pleased.

"Love it," she confirmed. "Why?"

The two men exchanged a look and then Byron nodded, a slow smile dawning over his face. "Seafood is a favorite of ours. I think I know what Tucker's got in mind, but it'll have to wait until I'm back from Victoria." He released her to Tucker and stepped away from them, heading toward what she assumed was the kitchen.

Tucker escorted her over to the bar and surprised her by asking for two ice waters and a cola. "No drinking tonight?" she asked as he handed her one of the glasses of water and then took her hand as he led her along the wall toward the fire exit he'd pointed out to Byron.

"We're both driving tonight, so no drinking."

"Please tell me you drove your bike, because if you did, I'm going to take you out there right now and get pictures," she told him, her pulse beating a little faster at the mental image she had just conjured up.

"Not a chance! There is nothing pleasant about a cold, wet, winter wind blowing straight up your kilt." His gray eyes gleamed with amusement. "I took the work truck. Byron could have walked, but the weather was dicey so he drove over from his place. If he'd appeared looking like a drowned rat his mom would have torn a strip off him and his dads would have stood back and laughed while it happened."

They found a couple of free chairs and sat down. "So his parents live here, and so does Byron, and you live in town." She tipped her head in query. "Do you have family here?"

His jaw tensed and for a moment she thought he wasn't going to answer, but then he blew out a breath and said, "I've got cousins, like Rory, and my second father is still here, but my mother and my dad left some years ago and haven't been back since."

"That's got to be tough." She made a wry face. "I barely speak to my parents and we live in the same city. Well, half the year we're in the same city. They're in Florida for the winter. So, are you close with your…second father?" She stumbled over the unfamiliar term.

He shook his head and she could almost see the storm clouds gathering around his head even before he said a word. "We don't speak. He's the reason my parents left, and I have nothing to say to him. It's a long story though, and not one I want to talk about during what should be a happy occasion."

"I understand, and I'm sorry. I should have guessed that family trouble came with the black sheep label."

"If you're not speaking to your folks, I'm betting that means you're a black sheep too?"

"Baaa," she bleated at him. "I'm a dues-paying member of that club."

He laughed and his expression softened, the tension she'd seen at the mention of his family fading away as quickly as it had come. "So if you aren't close with your family, what do you normally do for the holidays?"

She noticed the subtle shift in topics and went with it. "Jess and her mom adopted my grandmother and me for holidays years ago. My grandma lived next door to Jess, that's how we met. I spent a lot of time with her because she always had time for me, even when my parents were too busy. This year is Jess's first one alone, and I was worried about her. Now it turns out she's not alone at all. She's got her guys, and grandparents and a whole family she never knew about."

"And you're feeling like the odd man out, huh?" Tucker asked, clearly understanding.

"Exactly. She told me yesterday that I'm invited to some big party Christmas Eve, but I'm not sure I should go." Viv gestured to the crowd around them. "Everyone's been great, but I'm a stranger and the holidays are supposed to be about family and friends. I was thinking of skipping it and staying home to celebrate Yule quietly."

"Yule?" He cocked his brow at that. "Does that mean what I think it does?"

"Depends." Her lips twitched into a smile as she hedged, "What do you think it means?"

"That you're a goddess who follows the Goddess," he murmured and took her hand, threading their fingers together. "You're full of surprises."

"My grandma taught me. My parents didn't approve, but they didn't do anything to stop it, either." She shrugged. "Story of my life, really. But you get bonus points for calling me a goddess."

"I'm more or less a pagan myself, in fact most of the folks here are," he told her. "So you're in good company. And for the record, you are most definitely a goddess."

She squeezed his hand as she felt her cheeks heat. The man had actually made her blush! It had to be because she was still getting over her surprise at finding herself in the company of someone who shared her spirituality. It wasn't something most people understood, never mind had in common with her.

"I'm surprised Jess didn't tell you, given your beliefs."

"I don't know if she actually knows what faith they are. She's been too busy falling for her guys to worry about details like that." Vivian laughed. "Not that she'd care. She's a firm believer in letting people make their own choices. Which I guess is pretty obvious given she just bound herself to two guys."

"She was destined for them, even I can see that."

Vivian turned to look at Tucker. "You believe in that? Destiny? Soul mates?"

"I'm probably risking my man card here, but yeah, I

do. It doesn't happen for everyone, but in their case, I truly think they were meant for each other."

"You think there's someone out there for you?" The words were out of her mouth before her filter could catch them, and she could only pray he didn't laugh at her.

"If you'd asked me that a week ago, I'd have said not a hope in hell. Maybe it's the wedding, or maybe it's the company, but tonight I'm feeling a little more optimistic."

Damn it, she was blushing again! She couldn't believe it. She was not the sort of woman who blushed. She was usually the one causing others to blush, in fact. Feeling more than a little off balance, she went for a fast change of topic. "We got off track somewhere. I was going to ask you about your holiday plans and we ended talking about destiny instead. Do you have anything big going on over Christmas?"

"Not much. I usually work Christmas Eve, and then Byron's family takes pity on me every year and have me over for turkey dinner and save me from my own cooking."

"Speaking of food, I come bearing edibles for the lady." Byron reappeared out of the crowd, holding two plates full of assorted appetizers. "You have no idea how hard it was to get here without being mugged. Everyone's hungry."

"Thank you so much." Viv patted the chair beside her in invitation and once he was settled the three of them organized plates and napkins. "So which of these is the smoked salmon?"

"This one." Byron lifted a delicately puffed bit of pastry off a plate, leaned closer, and offered it to her straight from his fingers. "It's delicious."

She opened her mouth and let him feed her, moaning

softly as the pastry melted against her tongue and the flavors of the filling came through.

"That's really fucking good," she exclaimed as she licked the last traces of it from her lips, and then realized both men were staring, their eyes locked on her mouth. "Guys? You're staring. Did I miss a bit?" She deliberately ran the tip of her tongue over her lips again.

"My turn." Tucker picked up another pastry, this one a different shape, and fed it to her, letting his fingertips brush her face as she took it from him. The taste of warm brie and wild mushrooms filled her mouth and she made another soft noise of enjoyment. Whoever was catering this event was incredibly talented, that was for sure.

Byron curled his fingers around her free hand and drew it off to her side so that she found herself lightly tethered between them. Each of them had one of her hands as they continued feeding her choice morsels from the snacks Byron had liberated from the kitchen. It felt a bit strange being the center of two men's attention, but since no one else seemed to pay any attention to them she tried to let herself relax and enjoy it.

Byron had brought more than enough to take the edge off her hunger, and when the plates were empty they released her hands so she could go back to sipping her water and talking, though Tucker placed an arm around the back of her chair and Byron's hand lay on his thigh, close enough his fingers brushed her knee from time to time as they talked.

They had just about finished telling her their version of the night they had met Jess when Tucker's voice trailed off and she saw him sit bolt upright. The laughing, relaxed man she'd been spending time with vanished in a heartbeat, and in his place was a dark god with anger flashing in his stormy eyes.

"Oh shit," Byron hissed and took Vivian's hand. "What's he even doing here? He's been banned from these events since the last time."

"He knows. He just doesn't care." Tucker stood up and then looked down at Vivian with regret. "I'm sorry, I have to go deal with something. My father's here and he's not supposed to be. I need to get him back to his place before there's a scene. Jess doesn't deserve to have her day ruined by my asshole of a parent."

"Family, I get it." She paused and then added. "Do you want me to go with you?"

Tucker stared at her in obvious surprise. "You'd do that? He's likely drunk and going to be incredibly obnoxious."

"Then you're going to need help getting him out of here quietly. I don't want Jess's day ruined either." She looked at Byron and cocked her head. "You coming?"

He shot her a devilish grin and stood up, taking her hand again. "I'm coming along to make sure you two don't raise too much hell. Someone has to be the adult here. I'm just not sure how I wound up with the short stick."

Tucker led the way and Byron went after him, keeping Vivian behind him despite her quiet protestations she'd be fine.

"I'm sure you can handle yourself just fine. The question is, can you do it in a backless dress while wearing high heels?" he asked and pointed to her stiletto-heeled shoes. "You look amazing, but I'm not sure those are the ideal footwear for handling an intoxicated asshat."

"You'd be amazed what I can do in these shoes," she muttered in response, and Byron gave her a heated look.

"I'm sort of hoping I get to find out one of these days."

She gave him a wicked grin in response, trying to ignore the sizzle of lust that went straight to her pussy. "I'll get back to you on that." She lengthened her stride as she realized Tucker was getting ahead of them. Byron did have a point, she wasn't exactly dressed for this, but the reality was that Tucker was the size of a linebacker and should really be able to deal with things himself. She just didn't want him to have to do it alone.

"There he is!" A voice bellowed, and she winced as she caught the telltale slur of someone who'd already had a few too many. "Knew you'd be here, you ungrateful pup. Won't answer my calls, never come around, so I had to come find you here."

Byron stopped and gripped Vivian's hand tighter. They were near the main doors, and Tucker was staring down at an unkempt, older man who was swaying on his feet while shaking a nicotine-stained finger in Tucker's face.

"You owe me, boy," he brayed, his mouth twisted into an ugly sneer.

"I don't owe you a damned thing, Tobias." Tucker's voice was strained and a single muscle jumped along the side of his jaw. "However, *you* owe Darius and his family the courtesy of not disrupting this day. Go home and sleep it off."

"I raised you, fed you, wiped your sorry ass and took care of you. Damn right you owe me, keep me on a damned allowance like a child! I'm your fucking father!" Tobias jabbed his finger into Tucker's chest to punctuate his last words and Byron breathed a curse.

"Shit."

Tucker moved almost inhumanly fast as he spun Tobias around and locked a powerful forearm across the drunken man's throat. "I warned you never to touch me again," he snarled and lifted Tobias so that his feet barely touched the floor. "You're leaving. Right now."

Tobias thrashed and flailed, but he was clearly outmatched. He finally went still and Tucker lowered him back to the floor before catching hold of his belt and frog-marching him outside. Vivian tugged on Byron's hand and led him along behind. She wanted to make sure things didn't escalate once Tobias didn't have so many witnesses around. He was a twisted, abusive bastard, judging by the way he had just treated Tucker. His reddened cheeks and sickly appearance indicated he was a chronic alcoholic as well.

Tucker let him go when they got to the bottom of the stairway, giving him a light shove so that he staggered away a few feet, out of easy striking distance but still within the area illuminated by the large floodlights that drove back the winter darkness. Tobias regained his balance and turned around, laying into his son yet again.

"Damned arrogant pup! Do you enjoy making me beg? Does it make you feel like a big man?"

"If I gave you any more you'd just drink it away." Tucker shook his head. "The community feeds and shelters you and I cover everything else. I'm not going to give you money just so you can drink yourself to death faster than you already are!"

Tobias snarled like a wounded animal and took a shaky step toward Tucker. "You're just like your fucking mother. She was always judging, convinced she was so much better than me. Her and your father both. Now they've run off and left us with only each other for company." His voice faded briefly into a whine. "And you won't even come see me. You're all I've got, Tucker."

Then his lips twisted into a sneer and his tone grew vicious again. "Do you think they laugh at us both? At least they feared me, boy. You? You, they just scrape off the bottom of their shoes on their way out the door. You need to come back to the colony and do right by me. That's what you need to be doing. I'll make a man out of you yet."

Tucker didn't say another word, but Vivian didn't have to hear him speak to know he was hurting. She could see it in his eyes.

She'd had enough.

"Go home, Tobias. My best friend is celebrating the happiest day of her life right now, and I will not have you poisoning this moment with your anger and your negativity." She ignored Byron's hiss of warning and shook out of his grip when he tried to stop her from descending the stairs.

"Who the hell are you?" Tobias demanded as he turned his focus away from Tucker for the first time.

"I just told you who I was. I'm Jessica's best friend. I was invited today, and you were not. So I suggest you turn around and go back home. You're only embarrassing yourself."

Byron landed at her side and she realized he'd actually jumped down the stairs to catch up to her. He caught her hand, preventing her from getting any closer to Tobias, and this time she didn't resist.

Tobias caught the gesture and scowled, which made him look even nastier than he had before.

"She with you, pansy boy? You should teach her to watch her mouth before someone does it for you. Uppity bitch, telling me—"

He didn't get to finish his sentence before Tucker had him by the front of his shirt, hauling him half off his feet. "You don't touch her. You don't talk to her. You don't even *look* at her. Not now. Not ever!"

Tobias's mouth open and shut several times in rapid succession and then he burst out in broken, ugly laughter.

"Both of you? You finally found one willing to take you, ya sorry excuse for a pup! Will wonders never cease!" He was still dangling from Tucker's fist when he craned his head to look at Vivian again, and then his eyes narrowed and he appeared to draw in a deep breath through his nose.

"She's not even—" The rest of what he was going to say was lost as Tucker shook him hard and then let him go so quickly he staggered back several steps before falling on his ass in the mud.

"Get out of here. Now." Tucker's words were more of a growl than actual speech, and Tobias finally seemed to take the hint. He scrambled back to his feet and limped off, muttering under his breath every unsteady step of the way.

The moment it was clear Tobias wasn't going to turn around, Tucker pivoted on his heel and walked straight over to where she was standing. His expression was as dark and stormy as ever, and she braced herself for impact, convinced he was going to give her an earful for interfering. Instead of yelling, or scolding or even growling at her he just drew her into his arms and held her tightly against him, so tightly she could feel the thundering of his heart against his ribs.

"I knew you were going to be trouble," he finally whispered against her hair. "From the moment I laid eyes on you, I knew it." His arms loosened their hold the slightest bit. "Tobias is mean, drunk and dangerous. Promise me you won't do that again."

"No. I'm not fucking promising any such thing. I won't stand by and have someone I care about be treated that way. That's not who I am."

"And I like that about you. Really, I do. But if he hurt you…" Tucker left the sentence unfinished, but his meaning was clear.

"I've told you before. I can take care of myself," she reminded him. She hadn't realized how cold it was until now, but as he held her she was tempted to burrow deeper into his arms as the winter night sucked the warmth from her body.

He felt her shiver and drew her in closer still, so that she was pressed tight against the powerful expanse of his chest. "I'm sure you can, but that doesn't mean we're never going to step in if you need it. Just like you did for me a minute ago. Friends take care of each other, right?"

"Right," she said, nodding slightly. "Friends do that."

He ran his thumb along the swell of her lower lip and smiled a little. "Thank you for what you did. It means a lot to me."

Butterflies filled her stomach as he stared down at her for a long minute, and she wondered if he was going to kiss her, but in the end he just brushed a kiss to her cheek before gently letting her go.

Disappointment hit her like a physical pain, but she understood why he hadn't kissed her. This wasn't the time, or the place. She hoped they found that time and place soon though, because the thought of his mouth on hers had her toes curling in anticipation.

"I have to go after Tobias and make sure he gets home in one piece. After that, I think I'm heading home. I'm not feeling much like celebrating anymore. Do you mind?"

"You can make it up to me tomorrow," she told him with a smile. It amazed her that after everything she'd just witnessed, Tucker was still going to check up on his abusive father. It made her like him even more.

"You have yourself a deal." Tucker turned to Byron. "Make sure she gets home okay? And tell everyone congratulations from me, will you?"

"You bet. I'll call you when I get to Victoria."

"Drive safe." He bumped fists with Byron and then set off down the road after Tobias, his black-clad form quickly vanishing into the darkness.

Byron offered Viv his arm. "Shall we go report to the others that the monster has been vanquished and the black knight has returned to his castle?"

She had to laugh at that. "I believe we shall."

CHAPTER SIX

IT WASN'T until the party was winding down that Byron discovered Vivian had intended to take a cab home. She and Jess had gotten a ride to the wedding with Jess's grandparents, but they had gone home around ten o'clock after she had assured them she had a ride arranged.

"You're not taking a cab. Hell, I'm not even sure this place actually has an address for them to find even if you did call for one," he told her. "I know where you're staying and I can have you home in no time."

"But you were going home to sleep for a few hours. Aren't you driving down to Victoria tomorrow? That's what, a five-hour drive?"

"More like four the way I drive it, and I'll get a better night's sleep knowing you got home safe and sound." He helped her on with her jacket, taking a moment to admire the elegant lines of the tattoo that flowed down her back and vanished beneath the soft drape of fabric near the small of her back. He wanted to see all of it soon, preferably while she was sleeping beside him, naked and worn out from a long night of life-altering sex.

The guests of honor were saying good-bye to the guests near the door, and he watched as Jess hugged Vivian with tears in her eyes.

"I'm so glad you were here for this," Jess told her. "It wouldn't have been the same without you."

"If you had done this without me I'd have been totally pissed at you," Viv replied.

"Toodles, gator."

"Later, poodle."

"You keep these two out of trouble," Byron said as he hugged Jess good-bye, earning himself a rumbling growl from both Rory and Evan. "Yeah, yeah. She's yours, hands off. I know." He grinned and shook both their hands. "Congratulations. This was a very good day."

He slid an arm around Vivian's waist as they headed outside, enjoying the chance to have her so close. She had impressed them both tonight, standing up to Tobias the way she had. Tobias's reaction to her had also reminded them that some of the older members of the colony were not going to react well to the idea of them being with a human woman. Not that it was going to stop them from trying, but the fact she was strong enough to deal with any resentment had made both of them very happy.

He and Tucker had stayed in contact with each other telepathically after he'd left and they'd agreed that they absolutely wanted to pursue things with Vivian. She was captivating, funny, and sexy as hell. They were going to focus on getting to know her, and hope that when the time came for her to return to Toronto, they'd made enough of an impression that she'd consider staying. That is, if everything worked out. It was way too soon to know how things would go, but he was hopeful.

Vivian's cell phone chirped as they made their way across the parking lot, and he watched as her lips curved into a warm smile when she saw who it was from.

"It's a text from Tucker. He was just wishing me good-night and reminding me he's coming to pick me up around two."

"You're really going to go out on that deathtrap of his?" Byron teased as he unlocked the passenger side door of his SUV.

"You really go surfing in water so cold you have to wear a wetsuit to avoid hypothermia and call it fun?" she sassed back.

"Actually, I call it heaven. Just me and the waves." Instead of opening the door he turned and hauled her into his arms, moving them both around so that her back was pressed up to the vehicle's door. He pinned her lightly with his body and dropped his mouth to hover just above hers, so that the frosted clouds of their breath mingled and he could feel the warmth of her skin on his lips. "Like right now, it's just me and you. This feels a lot like heaven too."

"Such a poet you are," she whispered as her arms twined around his neck, holding him close.

That was all the invitation he needed. As his mouth covered hers he could have sworn he felt a jolt of raw power arc between them. Her lips were soft and lush, and the soft scent of her perfume blended with a honey-sweet flavor that was purely her own. His blood sang through his veins as he took the kiss deeper, so that their tongues tangled and their mouths fused. He speared his fingers into the silky tumble of her hair, drawing her head back so he could plumb the secret depths of her mouth.

She moaned softly and he felt the sting of her fingernails as they bit into his neck. The sensation sent a surge of blood to his cock and he let her feel just how much she was affecting him as he rubbed the hard length of his dick against her soft curves.

The world around them faded away and he let his senses drink her in, imprinting this moment on his memory. The way her hair felt in his hands, the heat of her mouth, the soft sounds of pleasure that rose up from her throat as she wriggled her hips back and forth against his cock, stealing every rational thought from his head.

It wasn't until an icy rain started falling that he finally lifted his head and drew a ragged breath into his burning lungs. He looked down and the sight of her kiss-swollen lips and flushed cheeks had him aching to taste her again, but he resisted. He and Tucker had agreed they were going to court her, not jump her bones the first chance they got. This was new ground for all of them, and they were determined not to push her too fast, no matter how incredibly fucking tempting she was.

He straightened just as a gust of wind sent a drenching wave of rain over them both, effectively dousing his libido and bringing him back to reality.

"I need to get you inside before you catch a cold. If you get the sniffles for your date with Tucker, he's going to kill me."

He let her go reluctantly, and he was glad to note she was just as slow to release him. Whatever was growing between them, it was definitely not one-sided. He helped her inside and pressed a kiss to her hand before closing the door and heading around to the driver's side, taking a moment to shift his still rock-hard cock to a more comfortable angle before he tried to sit down and ended up doing permanent damage to himself.

He barely got the engine started before she turned and asked the question he'd known would come up sooner or later.

"You and Tucker are really okay with me seeing both of you? I told Tucker this, but I want to say it to you too. I don't want to ever come between you two. I know you're friends, and if this…whatever this is causes problems, then we should stop."

"I know what you told Tucker, and I'm going to tell you the same thing he did. We want this. We might stumble a bit from time to time because this isn't something we've done before, but we want to try. We want to try with you." He reached out, wanting to touch her, to try and help her believe in what he was saying. "We've never met anyone like you. You're the first woman who would even consider taking us both on." He squeezed her hand. "And just so we're very clear here, that's what we want to happen. Not just you and me and you and Tucker, but all three of us."

"The way Rory, Evan and Jess are," Vivian murmured. "Got it. Jess has been helping me wrap my head around the idea."

"And you're okay with it?" he asked, needing to be sure.

"I'm attracted to both of you, and what girl wouldn't at least consider saying yes to two hot men who offer her a chance to find out what it would be like to be the filling in a very sexy sandwich? I'm willing to try and see how this goes." She laughed softly in the darkness. "Which I guess is a long-winded way of saying that yes, I'm okay with it."

"Good." He blew out a relieved breath. Neither of them had actually come out and stated their intentions clearly until now, and he had been concerned that despite the evening they'd just spent together, she would balk at the idea of sharing a bed and possibly her life with two men. It wasn't something most women would have even considered. Once again she was proving that she was not most women.

"So you two have never dated the same woman before? I thought that was more or less the norm for your community, or colony. I've heard it called that several times now. It's sort of an archaic name, isn't it?"

"Kismet Cove is sort of an archaic group, and we're certainly a little different." Byron pulled out onto the main road and then turned to look at Vivian. "And yes, triads are the norm, but Tucker's not exactly a good fit with what's normal for Kismet Cove, in case you haven't noticed."

"Tobias," she said his name with contempt and anger. "He's got to be a big part of the reason Tucker doesn't live out here with the rest of you. If I had to face that every day, I'd move too!"

"It's not my story to tell, but yeah, Tobias is a big part of Tucker's problems with the colony. Tucker takes care of Tobias out of duty, but there's no love there, and there never has been."

"Well, if we're going to try this, I'm sort of glad we're all going to be figuring it out together. I don't think I'd like the idea of you two having done this before."

He laughed at that. "You just remember that when we

inevitably screw up. It's bound to happen, we're guys. I'm just aiming for something less catastrophic than the way Jess found out she had family in Kismet Cove. Her guys were eating crow for days after that fiasco."

"Well, I know I don't have any family here, so unless you have some deep dark secrets you're keeping, I think we're safe from that level of communication catastrophe."

"Dark secrets? Nope. Afraid not." Byron drove up to her cabin and was thankful that there wasn't enough light for her to catch the expression on his face as he came uncomfortably close to lying to her. Secrets they had aplenty, and high on the list was the fact she had just agreed to try dating not one, but two seal shapeshifters.

If things starting getting serious with Vivian, they were going to have to tell her the truth, and that meant she would find out that her best friend wasn't human either. This was going to be more than a little tricky.

When she went to open her door he growled and shook his head. "You stay put, I'll come around. My mother would have my ears if I didn't walk you to your door. She tried to instill *some* manners in me. I'm not promising they all took, but she did try."

He hopped down and jogged around the front of the vehicle, getting wetter by the moment. The rain was coming down hard now and he took off his jacket, holding it over his head as a makeshift shield as he opened her door and helped her down.

Unable to resist the temptation he tugged her forward and into his arms to steal another kiss. As the rain poured down around them he felt her wrap her arms around his shoulders. Then she was stretching up to kiss him back, her tongue tracing the seam of his lips and branding his skin with her touch. He forgot about holding up the jacket or shielding them from the weather. He even forgot to breathe as her lips parted and she moaned into his mouth.

He had her lifted into his arms in seconds and he carried her the last few feet to her door. She had managed to catch hold of his jacket with one hand, and her other was still clinging to him as she kissed him between peals of laughter. They were wet, laughing and breathless by the time he finally set her back on her feet.

As she dug in her purse for her keys, he was suddenly struck by how much he would miss her in the few days he'd be gone. Normally he looked forward to his business trips to Victoria to meet with their various suppliers and find out the latest in microbrews, but not this time. This time he had a reason to keep it short and get back home, to her.

"I'll call you while I'm gone," he promised. "If you had your pick of beers, which is your favorite? Pale ale? Amber? A stout?"

"Uh, Molson?" she said and gave him a confused look. "What the hell is an amber?"

"So you know your scotch, but I bet you drink your beer out of a can. Barbaric. We're going to have to fix that. You leave it to me. I'll give you a lesson in decent brews when I get back and I'll pick up a few specialty brews for you to try."

"That sounds good." She found her keys and unlocked the door before turning back to him. "Thank you for driving me home." He leaned in and kissed her cheek, hovering close enough to inhale the warm scent of vanilla one last time before stepping back.

"Thank you for the most enjoyable evening I've had in a long time. I'll see you in a few days, slim."

He headed back to the car, the coat back over his head and a goofy smile on his face.

"Good-night," she called back, and she stayed there in her doorway, silhouetted by the lights of her cabin until he drove around a bend and lost sight of her.

ONCE SHE COULDN'T SEE his taillights any longer, Vivian closed the door and kicked off her shoes with a sigh of relief. Despite the lateness of the hour she wasn't tired yet, and so she opted for a long, hot shower to help her relax. One of the cabin's nicest features was a fully modernized bathroom, complete with a decadent, river-rock-tiled shower.

She had her earrings off before she reached her bedroom, and dropped them on the dresser as she shed her clothes and headed to the bathroom. She needed to process the events of the day, and right now they were tearing around the inside of her skull at high speed. Jess's ceremony, the fight between Tucker and Tobias, the kisses she'd shared with Byron were all tangled up in her head. She needed some time to think about everything before she'd be able to sleep.

The moment the hot water started to fall from the rainwater showerhead, she was reminded of the incredible kisses Byron had given her out in the rain. Was she really okay with what he and Tucker wanted from her? If she wasn't she needed to tell them, and soon.

She closed her eyes and breathed in the steam-filled air,

drawing every breath in through her nose and out through her mouth. She forced herself to relax and focus on that one thought. With each breath she became more certain that this was what she wanted. What few doubts she had crumbled under such close scrutiny, all of them ultimately proving to be worries about what other people would think or feel if they learned of her choices.

She had always made her own choices. Always tried to do what was best for her and not what would appease everyone else. She wanted to try and be with both men and see where it led them. If it didn't work out, she'd be gone soon enough, and if it did…She put that thought aside for now. There was no sense thinking too far ahead, not when she'd yet to have a proper date with either of them.

Thoughts of leaving brought up thoughts of going back to Toronto without Jess, and that made her heart ache. Jess was here to stay, with two men who adored her and loved her in a way Vivian hadn't believed possible. More questions filled her mind. Should she stay here and start over again? Was it time to take the money she had inherited from her grandmother and find a way to make her dreams happen? Would she want to stay if things didn't work out with Tucker and Byron?

Her sense of calm faltered, then vanished, and she shut off the shower with a curse of frustration. She had too many questions and not enough answers, and she knew it was time to get a little guidance.

After a quick toweling she ducked into her bedroom just long enough to snag a velvet bag out of her suitcase. She didn't bother to dress, she just finger combed her hair back from her face and turned on the gas fireplace that dominated one wall of the living room. She picked a spot near the hearth and sat cross-legged in front of it.

The rain splattered against the windows and the wind howled beyond the walls, but the little cabin had been made to defeat the elements. Inside its walls she felt snug and comfortable. This place was full of good energy, clean, bright and restful. It was doing her soul good just to be here. She drew her tarot cards out of the bag and held them for a moment, letting her energy flow around them and through them before shuffling them slowly. When she was ready, she laid them out facedown in a line in front of her and then stared into the flames until her mind was clear. Only then did she ask a single question.

"If I stay here, what will that choice bring me?" She held that question in her mind and repeated it aloud as she drew five cards from the deck and laid them face down in a simple cross shape in front of her. Taking another cleansing breath, she turned them over and read them in turn. Past, present and future, all laid out for her. The Death card was there, representing change, and she rolled her eyes at the universe's knack for understatement. The other cards were an interesting mix. Her past was mostly Pentacles, the cards showing a life of hard work with little reward as well as financial frustration. Her future, though, was entirely made up of Cups, cards that represented the element of water. They suggested that if she stayed, there could be an abundance of joy and emotional satisfaction to be found, along with love and a unity of spirit.

She stared at the cards a long time, until her legs were falling asleep and her back ached from lack of movement. Never in all the years she had worked with tarot cards had she been given a reading that was so very clear. It worried her she was missing something. Had she worded the question incorrectly? Was she falling victim to the ever-present danger of projecting her hopes into the interpretation of the cards?

"Well, shit. I get an answer and I'm still second-guessing myself," she muttered and picked up the cards, reshuffling them into the deck and tucking it back into its velvet bag. She got up slowly as pins and needles filled her lower legs, and she jigged from foot to foot until the feeling went away. "Full of doubt and getting old."

For a moment she was certain she could hear her grandma laughing off in the distance, and it brought a smile to her face. Grandma would have been quick to remind her that thirty was hardly old and then she'd have told her to follow her instincts and stop second-guessing herself.

If she wanted to stay, then she should stay. If she wanted Tucker and Byron, then she should go get them and stop dithering about it. "All right, Grandma. Message received." She patted the cards. "I guess I'll stick around and see how this plays out."

CHAPTER SEVEN

THOUGH THE RAIN and wind continued all night, by morning it had blown itself out and the sky was clear for the first time since she'd arrived. She had slept in after the night before, and felt more refreshed and clearheaded for both the rest and the uneventful hours before Tucker's arrival.

She had cleaned up, made a note of what groceries would be needed soon, and even finished unpacking, a step she hadn't had the time or inclination to do since her arrival. As she closed the closet doors she felt a sense of rightness come over her, and she knew she'd made the right call. Next she'd changed her return ticket to an open-ended one and called her roommate to let her know that her life was in flux and she'd let her know soon what her plans were.

That done, she'd sat down on the loveseat, pulled a handmade afghan over her legs and picked up the first book she'd laid her hand on. It turned out to be a dog-eared book all about selkies, a mythical seal shapeshifter legend she vaguely recalled from her grandma's stories. It made for interesting reading, and she wondered why Jess had it. Research for writing some future book, maybe, or something that had been in the cabin when she'd moved in.

As she read she found herself rather intrigued, and soon she was surfing the web on her phone, reading more about them. It was a fun way to pass the time, and before she knew it an alarm on her phone warned her it was time to get ready for her date with Tucker.

She donned boots, jeans and a warm sweater beneath her leather motorcycle jacket, and by the time she heard the familiar growl of a Harley Davidson engine she was waiting by the door, bouncing with anticipation. Not just because she was looking forward to going out for a ride, but because she was going to get to wrap her arms around Tucker and hang on to him for the whole trip while the wind whipped around them and a powerful engine thrummed between her legs. It was shaping up to be a damned good day.

She had the door open before he'd even shut off the bike, and she knew she was wearing an ear-to-ear grin as she stepped out and greeted him with a wave, trying to ignore the throbbing of her clit as her body chimed in with its opinion of his appearance. He was wearing riding leathers, the deep black broken up by slashes of red across the sleeves and chest. She knew they were for visibility, but all she could think about was that they enhanced the width of his chest and made him look even bigger than he had before.

He lifted the visor and then removed his helmet,

hanging it off the handlebars as he stood and swung a long, jean-clad leg over the back of the bike.

"Hey, trouble." He smiled and that dimple appeared back in his cheek, making her itch to kiss it. "You ready to go?"

"Hell, yes," she said and walked over to him, taking a moment to appreciate the sleek lines of the bike she was going to be riding shortly. "Nice ride."

"She's my baby." He patted the seat with affection. "I thought we'd take the Pacific Rim highway as far as the lake, and then swing back into town and put in an order for pizza on our way by. There are some really nice views along the way. Sound good?

"Sounds perfect." She moved in close and stood on tiptoes to kiss his cheek. "I've been looking forward to this."

His arms curved around her and he drew her in close to his body, holding her there for a long moment. "So have I. And before we get going I just wanted to say thank you again for what you did yesterday. It was appreciated."

"Forgive me for saying so, but Tobias is a really nasty piece of work. I can see why you don't want much to do with him."

"You know what they say, we can't pick our families." He shrugged his broad shoulders and for a moment she could have sworn his lips brushed her hair with a kiss, but it was done before she could be sure it wasn't just the wind.

"Well, we can pick our friends, and today my newest friend is going to show me Mother Nature in all her glory."

"That's my plan." He released her gently and then

turned his attention to one of the saddlebags, pulling out a second helmet for her. "This one is for you. The speakers work, so you should be able to hear me just fine, but the mic got broken the last time I talked Byron into coming out with me. I have no idea how he does it, but if you value your electronics, don't let him near them. They come in contact with his aura and self-destruct."

"Oh wow. I'll keep my phone away from him. My life is on that thing!" She slid on the helmet and he did the same, and then she heard his deep voice rumbling in her ears. "Can you hear me all right?"

She nodded. "Loud and clear." Those were the last words she said before she dropped the visor and climbed on behind him. She threw her arms around his chest and positioned herself so that her legs spanned his outer thighs. Her fingers found nothing but muscle anywhere she touched, and she could feel her nipples hardening where they were pressed up against his back. She was grateful for the two layers of leather between them, otherwise there'd be no hiding the effect he was having on her right now.

The second he turned over the engine, her entire pussy clenched as the deep vibrations coursed through her. As she moaned aloud she was thankful that the mic was broken. This whole trip was going to be delicious torture.

They headed out, flying along the road and eating up the miles. When they neared a good viewpoint or pretty bit of scenery, Tucker would slow the bike to a crawl so he could act as her tour guide, his deep voice rumbling in her helmet. He would give her the history of the land or just share details and snippets of a lifetime spent in the area.

The coastline was almost like an alien landscape, gray

and rocky and scoured by the ever-present wind. The force of it twisted the trees and shrubs into stunted, living sculptures, their limbs all forced to grow in the direction of the prevailing wind. At her request they pulled over to the side of the road so she could take a look at a line of pine trees. None of them were more than twelve feet high, and their twisted forms cast strange shadows across the rocks and grass beneath them.

She popped up her visor and pointed to them. "The wind really does that to them. Twists them around like that?"

He nodded and turned to look at her, his gray eyes a match for the waves that rolled onto the shore behind him. "The ones that survive that close to the water all look like that. There aren't enough of them to protect each other." He pointed to a line of normal pines closer to the road, all close together to form a natural windbreak. "These ones have it easier. They have deep soil for their roots and protection from the worst of the wind. It's the seedlings which take root alone that turn out that way."

His gray eyes gleamed with good humor. "And don't start looking for metaphors about black sheep and the perils of going it alone in a couple of twisted trees."

She burst out laughing. "Metaphors? Hell no. Jessica's the bestselling author in the family, I just cut hair."

He grinned and winked at her from behind his visor and his laughter filled her helmet. "All right, shall we get back on the road? I want to show you a few more spots before it starts getting dark and we have to turn back."

She dropped her visor and wrapped her arms around him before giving him the thumbs up. Seconds later they were back on the highway. Soon they left the ocean behind and drove into a tunnel of deep green trees that soared overhead. There was almost no traffic, and she felt like they were the only two people for a hundred miles. It was both peaceful and a little eerie for someone who had grown up in a city with more than two million people living in it. Overall, though, it was a feeling she thought she'd get used to.

That is, she could get used to it, *if* she decided to make this place her home.

HAVING Viv wrapped around him was equal parts joy and brutal torture. By the time they turned back toward Tofino, Tucker's body was humming with lust. He was nearly positive he was going to have a permanent zipper pattern all down his dick too, because every time Vivian's hands had slipped a little lower or she'd shifted on the seat behind him, he'd gone from half-aroused to hard as a rock.

He already knew tonight was going to end with a very cold shower, because he had no intentions of sleeping with her on their first date. He wanted to get to know her better, and that was going to have to take priority over his persistent desire to have her long legs wrapped around his hips as he fucked her until they were both too exhausted to move.

Fuck. Thoughts like that were not going to help him keep his hands off her tonight. He banished the X-rated images to the back of his head and brought his focus back to the moment. As they rounded the next bend the ocean reappeared before them, both sea and sky painted in breathtaking hues by the quickly setting sun. A second later he felt Viv stir behind him and he knew she'd seen it too.

"Want to stop and watch the sunset?" he asked, already mulling over the best vantage point. Vivian lifted her hand from his chest to give him a thumbs-up before wrapping herself around him again and he could swear she'd dropped her hand another inch closer to his aching cock.

"Just up the road there's a good spot. Hang on and I'll make sure we'll get there in time to see it." He gunned the engine, confident that his passenger wouldn't be bothered by the extra speed. They made it just as the glowing orb kissed the Pacific, drawing a line of gold and orange light across the water.

He killed the engine and dropped the kickstand while Vivian let go of him to hop off the bike. She took off her helmet and turned to face the ocean. He came to join her, leaving his helmet on the seat beside hers. He slipped an arm around her waist as they watched the sun drop down behind the waves, and she leaned into him, her hand stealing under his jacket and her head coming to rest on his shoulder.

"I wish I had a camera with me. That's the most incredible sunset I've ever seen," she said as the light faded and the sky turned red and the ocean deepened to a soothing purple.

"We may not have every convenience a city girl might be used to, but living out here does have its perks."

"Yeah, it really does," she agreed with him and then lifted her head to flash him a smile. As their gazes met, every good intention he had shattered and fell to his feet to become paving stones on the road to Hell.

He dropped his head to claim her smiling lips. She

stood on tiptoes to meet him, and her arms tangled around his neck to draw him down into a deeper kiss. Holding her was like holding a live wire. Heat and light seemed to flow between them every place they touched and he craved more. Instinct overrode reason and he stroked his hands down her back to grip the sweet curves of her ass, hauling her tight against him. He could not have said which of them moved first, but as tongues met and danced for the first time he found her in his arms, her legs around his hips and her pussy grinding along his cock.

The sunset was forgotten as he turned away from it and walked them both back to his bike, throwing one leg over the seat so that the handlebars were behind him. She relaxed her legs enough to let her ass rest on the seat, but her legs were still thrown over his thighs and her hands held fast to his shoulders.

He braced his feet on the ground on either side of the bike and speared his hands into her hair, holding her close as he narrowed his focus down to her, and only her. She was like a drug, addictive and heady, the feeling of her in his arms one he was afraid he'd never get enough of. If one kiss felt like this—he kissed her again and she mewled softly and then closed her teeth on his lower lip, sending sparks of raw need coursing through him.

Yep. He was in serious trouble.

The sun was gone and the twilight was fast giving way to full darkness by the time their last kiss ended and they came back to their senses. He lifted his head and glanced around with a rumble of amusement. They'd lost all track of time.

"We missed the sunset," she pointed out, her voice bordering on laughter.

"We did, but the fireworks were worth it."

"Fireworks?" She looked confused for a second and then grinned. "Oh, yeah. They were incredible. I'm hoping we get to see those again soon."

"I think I can arrange that." Tucker felt his heart warm as he stared down at her in all her kiss-tousled glory. "You are so damned beautiful," he told her, surprising them both. Flattery wasn't usually his thing, it was Byron's, but looking at her in the last of the fading light was enough to inspire him. "One day, would you let me draw you?"

Now he wasn't just surprised, he was stunned. He never told anyone about his art. No one had a clue that the murals that graced the walls of Breakers were his own work, and here he was outing himself and asking her to pose for him.

He'd officially lost his fucking mind.

"You draw?" She eased herself carefully backward, untangling their legs and freeing herself as she talked. "What's your preferred medium? Charcoal? Pencil? Do you have a sketch pad? I'd like to see it."

Her enthusiasm was a refreshing change from the norm. The few people who had discovered he was an artist invariably laughed at the idea of a bad boy biker-type trying to paint or draw.

"I'll draw with a stick in the dirt if I have to, but I like charcoal, and I paint too."

She had gotten off the bike and had her hand on her helmet when he said that, and she froze for a moment. When she moved again it was to glower at him like she was suddenly furious. She stepped in close and planted her forefinger firmly against his chest. "You did the murals at Breakers, didn't you? You did those and nobody has a clue. I know, because I asked Jess and she had no idea who the artist was! You're good! You're damned good!" She poked him in the chest in time to her last words. "So why doesn't anyone know that about you?"

"Because badass bar owners with Harleys don't paint landscapes and aren't supposed to see the beauty in the world." He popped the collar on his leather jacket and gave her his best scowl. "It would mess with my image." He knew she wasn't going to buy it for a second, but he just couldn't resist goading her. She was even hot when she was telling him off.

"Your image?" she repeated and then shook her head. "Bullshit. You care less about your image than any man I've ever met. You're good. *Really* good. I should know, I've been to enough gallery showings and have more than my share of artistic friends. I think they come as part of the bohemian lifestyle package I signed up for when I moved out. Before I go, I want to see everything you've done." She kissed him then, hard and sudden and with a fierceness he hadn't seen in her before. "Then, when you've shown me, I'll let you draw me, or paint me, or anything else you want."

"You have yourself a deal." He was tempted to drive home and show it all to her right now, so he could have the excuse to have her in his place, and then he could sketch her, naked and stretched out on the couch…or his bed.

His cock surged to life and he resisted the temptation to haul her back on the bike for another kissing session. What he really wanted to do was take her home and spend the night in bed, fulfilling any one of the other half-dozen fantasies that suddenly came to life in his imagination.

Instead he pulled her close and kissed her until they were both breathless and then gently released her, shooing her back enough that he could stand up and get off the bike. "Let's go order that pizza and then head back to your place. I believe you mentioned something about a hot tub, and I know you have some damned good scotch on hand."

She nodded and tugged on her helmet, and her next words came out muffled from behind her visor. "That all sounds good. Take me home and feed me, lover."

"Lover, huh?" he asked once he had his helmet on and he knew she could hear him via the mic. She got back on behind him and wrapped her arms around his waist in reply, and he started the bike and headed back out onto the highway. "I like the way that sounds, trouble."

As they headed back he couldn't help but wonder if he had the willpower to keep things slow between them for much longer. He was starting to seriously doubt it.

CHAPTER EIGHT

NIGHTFALL BROUGHT with it freezing temperatures, and by the time they pulled up to the cabin Vivian was feeling the cold all the way down to the marrow of her bones. Jess had explained to her that it was the dampness in the air that made it feel so cold. Then she'd confessed that she had started having hot showers or visiting the hot tub before bed to stave off the chill. Right now Vivian was cold enough she was considering sleeping in the damned hot tub. She let go of Tucker and got off the bike, removing the helmet with a wince as the cold bit into her still-warm cheeks.

"It got cold," she muttered and watched as her breath turned to fog around her head.

"Welcome to winter on the west coast. One minute it's almost balmy and the next you're dreaming of hot chocolate and marshmallows."

"Now *that* is a brilliant idea." She handed him her helmet and turned toward the cabin, already tugging her keys out of a pocket. "I'm making us something boozy, hot and chocolaty to drink while we wait for the pizza to get here." She could hear him laughing behind her.

"I like the way you think."

She unlocked the door as she walked inside, turning on the lights and shedding clothes as she went. By the time she got to the kitchen she'd left a trail of boots, gloves and her jacket dropped on whatever was handy along the way. She was on a mission to get warm, and that meant getting the kettle on. Tucker was not far behind her, but he stopped to hang up his leather jacket and leave his heavy boots at the door before coming and looking around.

"This is nice," he said. "When you two kept saying cabin, I had something a lot more rustic in mind. This is cozy. Hey, gas fireplace! Nice. Want me to turn it on?"

"Hell yeah!" I'm chilled to the bone." She pointed to the switch on the wall near him. "Bathroom is down the end of the hall, and grab whatever bit of furniture you want and get comfy. I think we've got a bit before the pizza arrives."

She reached up to snag the cocoa out of the cupboard and came back down to find him standing right behind her. He snagged an arm around her waist and drew her back against his chest, his lips already nibbling a path from her ear down along her neck.

"You said you were cold."

She shivered as his breath fanned over her skin and she burrowed into his arms. "Are you here to warm me up?"

"Mhmm," he hummed an affirmative as he brushed more kisses along her skin. "Is it working?"

"Mhmm," she hummed right back at him and tipped her head to the side, offering him more of her throat. He kissed his way back up to her ear and sucked the lobe into his mouth, toying with the sleeper hoop earring she'd put in that morning. His mouth was hot, a contrast to the cool skin of his cheeks and nose as he nuzzled and nibbled.

"You taste as good as you smell," he told her as he raised his head at last.

"You are clearly starving to death and hallucinating that I am actually a supreme pizza with the works instead of a woman covered in road dust and suffering from a funky case of helmet hair."

"Nope, you don't taste anything like pizza." He pressed an open-mouthed kiss to her neck and stroked over her skin with the tip of his tongue. "You taste much better."

"Thank you...I think." She found herself laughing as she closed her eyes and crossed her arms over his, holding him as he held her. "I'm warmer already."

He held her, sharing his warmth as his mouth drifted over her skin. It was sexy and surprisingly intimate considering they were both fully clothed. Then she realized that this was the first time in memory a man had simply wanted to be with her, asking nothing more than for her to be in the moment with him.

The kettle eventually began to bubble and steam, bringing her out of her reflective mode. "I need to make us those boozy hot chocolates. Why don't you go wash up?"

"Double whipped cream in mine, please." He nipped her neck softly and then retreated. The moment he was gone she missed the warmth of his presence.

She was finishing up their drinks when he came back. "That is the coolest shower I have ever seen. I don't suppose Jess knows who installed it?"

"Why, do you want one too?" she asked and handed

him his drink, piled high with whipped cream and smelling of the shot of Bailey's she'd found in the cupboard. "Jess said Rory and Evan are having the guy who did it come out to renovate their whole bathroom. I think there's talk of a hot tub too. They miss the one here."

"Not for me, for Byron. He's got a house, and he's always going on about renovating it. That bathroom is exactly the sort of thing he wants to put in, if he ever gets around to it." He glanced around. "So what's going to happen with this place now that Jess is living in Kismet Cove?"

She picked up her drink and shooed him out of the kitchen and over to the living room where the fireplace had already warmed the area nicely. "Well, for now, it's mine. Jess has offered to let me live here if I decide to stay. If I go back, I imagine she'll put it back in the rental pool."

He sat down on the loveseat and patted the spot beside him before sipping his drink. "You really could be a bartender, this is good."

"Told ya," she shot back at him, and sat down close enough their thighs touched and she could rest her head against the comfortable bulk of his shoulder.

"Do you think you will?" he asked and then clarified. "I mean, do you think you'll stay?"

"I don't know yet. I'm definitely thinking about it, though." Her gaze strayed to the bag that contained her Tarot deck, and she remembered what the cards had revealed to her. "If I stayed, would that be a problem? I mean, I know you and Byron sort of started this with me thinking I was going to be gone in a few short weeks."

Tucker was silent for a minute and then shook his head. "Honestly? I think I'd be damned happy if you decided to stick around. I'm really enjoying spending time with you. In fact, I think I might make it my mission to give you some reasons for staying."

"Yeah? And what sort of incentives were you thinking of?" She turned her head to look up at him, but his answer was cut off by a sharp knock at the door. "Hold that thought, I do believe dinner has arrived."

She bounced off the couch and went to get their pizzas, which was a simple task given that Tucker had already paid for them before leaving.

When she turned around she spotted him in the kitchen, checking the cupboards for dishes. "The one to the right of the sink," she told him, and brought the two boxes over to the counter that divided the kitchen from the rest of the living area. "I'm still not sure about this pizza you ordered. Banana peppers as a pizza topping?"

"Trust me, you're going to love it." He grinned and his dimple flashed. "I had them go light on the peppers. When Byron and I get it we have it smothered."

She opened both boxes and inhaled the fragrance of fresh, hot pizza. "Now I am *starved*. Let's load up and head back to the couch." She took the plate he offered her and then piled it high with pizza slices, making sure that she had the one with and without banana peppers. She still had her reservations about eating anything electric orange and spicy enough she could smell it over the other ingredients.

She plunked herself down on the loveseat and tucked her feet beneath her, then propped the plate on her knees sank back with a contented sigh.

"I second that emotion," Tucker said as he settled in beside her, moving close enough she could feel the heat from his body even through her jeans. "Try the one with the peppers. I want to know your thoughts."

She picked it up and gave him a dubious look before taking a bite, but as the sweet heat of the peppers hit her tongue she had to admit, it wasn't bad. She took another bite and caught him grinning at her.

"It's good," she managed to mumble.

"Bikes, scotch and banana peppers. You might just be the perfe—" He stopped speaking mid-word, his jaws closing so fast she could have sworn she heard his teeth click.

She swallowed the pizza and winked at him. "I am perfect. Quite right. Thank you for noticing."

He looked slightly sheepish as he leaned over and gave her a light, pizza-flavored kiss. "Believe me, I noticed. So did Byron. We spoke this morning before he took off, and he is looking forward to taking you out on his boat when he gets back."

"It's a big boat, right?" she asked between bites of pizza.

"It's a runabout, twenty feet or so. And it has an engine, he won't make you paddle," Tucker joked but Viv felt a small knot form in her stomach.

"Twenty feet? That's not very big. I've seen the waves out here, they get pretty huge. We're not going to end up capsized or something are we? I've seen *Perfect Storm*."

Tucker laughed and then cut it off when he realized she was serious. "You'll be perfectly safe. He lives to be out on the water, remember? He swims like a seal and has a good weather sense. You might get rained on, but that's it."

"Okay, good." She felt a bit foolish, but she realized she

was going to have to confess something she didn't usually admit to. "I…uh. I can't swim."

He blinked at her, surprised. "You don't swim well? Or you don't swim, period?"

"I can sort of dog paddle, a little." She made a paddling gesture with her free hand. "But mostly I sink."

Tucker laughed again, and he didn't stop until tears were rolling down his cheeks. "I'm sorry, but…I just…I've never met anyone who couldn't swim! This is an island. Most folks around here learn when they're very young."

"My parents didn't see the point in spending money on swimming lessons. They enrolled me in a private school to ensure I had an exemplary education, and then more or less left me alone. They didn't see the point in extracurricular activities. After all, those would just distract me from my studies."

"Private school?" he asked, and she caught the twinkle in his eyes. "Tell me you had a school uniform, one of those little kilts and kneesock combos, and I can die a happy man. I'm sorry about your parents though, sounds like you didn't have the world's greatest childhood."

"It wasn't so bad," she said and made a dismissive flick of her fingers. "I survived. And I should have known not to mention private school." She rolled her eyes at him. "What is it about guys and schoolgirl uniforms? Yes, I wore a uniform. Kilt, socks, even a damned tie and a blazer, and if you ask me if I still have it I will laugh at you." She dropped her voice to a sultry whisper. "And then I'll tell you it's in my closet back home."

Sexual heat flared between them and his eyes turned dark with lust as he groaned low in his throat. "If you stay out here, I hope you plan on packing that. Hell, I'll fly you home just to pick it up."

"What, without even asking what else is in my closet?" she teased, and left him to stew on that as she finished off her slice of pizza.

"That is totally unfair," he grumbled. "Now my head is full of thoughts that are probably illegal in several provinces."

"You did say you were going to give me some reasons to stay. I'm just giving you some incentive to make them *good* reasons."

"Believe me, right now I have a head full of incentives, teasing little witch."

"Flattery will get you nowhere," she informed him with a laugh, and picked up her second slice of pizza.

They finished eating in relative silence, but she was intensely aware of him sitting so close. Just being near him had her panties soaked and her entire body aching with the need to be touched again. She'd always enjoyed sex, but the way she reacted to Tucker and Byron was a whole different kind of connection, hotter and far more volatile.

She cleared away the dishes, telling him to stay seated despite his expressed desire to help. There wasn't much to clear away anyway. When she glanced over at him she noticed he had a book in his hands, the one she'd been reading earlier.

"That's Jessica's. I found it this morning and was reading it for a bit. I haven't a clue where she got it from, but it made for some interesting reading."

He looked up and gave her a strange smile, like he was privy to some secret. "Do you believe in this sort of thing? Shapeshifters and faerie folk?"

She nodded. "My grandmother swore we were descendants of the wee folk. Fae touched, she called us. She was a redhead too." Viv reached up and tweaked a lock of her hair. "I really am a redhead, just not this exotic shade. She used to tell me stories about the faerie, and I seem to recall a few mentions of selkies, but she definitely left out a few choice bits. My teenage self would have been running down to the lake every damned day to see if shedding tears really summoned a sexy seal lover."

He laughed and shook his head. "Selkies are saltwater creatures. You'd have been sorely disappointed."

"You know what a selkie is?" She didn't bother to try and hide her amazement. She was finding out that Tucker was just full of surprises.

"Selkies are a Scottish legend, lass." He spoke with a broad brogue that brought a smile to her lips. "Would ye think I dinna ken what one would be?"

"Holy hell man, that's…damn! I bet you use that on the hot, single tourists."

He threw his head back and laughed. "No comment," he finally managed to get out between chuckles.

"Which is another way of saying yes, you have done that," she crowed in triumph, grinning at him. "And I have to confess, if you used that on me I'd probably go for it too."

"I think I did pretty well getting your attention without it," he said, and winked at her before standing up and stretching, giving her an impressive eyeful of muscles and man.

"You ready to enjoy our scotch in the hot tub?" she asked, suddenly itching to see him shirtless so she could find out just how far down that tattoo went.

"Good idea. My stuff's out with the bike though, so I'll be right back."

"I'll go change. First one back gets to break the seal on the bottle."

"You're on." He jogged for the door and she sprinted down the hall, both of them laughing like loons.

She had her sweater over her head before she hit her bedroom door, and she tossed it on the bed as she kicked the door closed behind her and started shedding her jeans.

That was when the phone rang.

"Shit!" she yelped as she tried to walk over to her phone while hobbled by her pants. She managed an awkward skippity-hop that got her within reaching distance and snagged it. It was Byron.

"Hey there. How was the drive?"

"Good. Did you sprint for the phone or something? You sound out of breath." His tone lowered. "Or does just hearing my voice do that to you?"

"Your voice does all sorts of things to me, but I'm out of breath because I'm racing Tucker to the hot tub and you caught me while I was changing."

There was a moment's pause and then he asked, "So, what are you wearing right now?"

"I cannot believe you are asking me that!" She managed to reach down and tug her jeans off. "I was half dressed...now I'm less than that."

"Fuck!" he swore. "Now I'm going to be thinking of that all night."

"You asked! And since you're already thinking about me, you might as well get the details right. I'm in a black bra with red polka dots, and matching lace underwear."

She heard Byron groan and had to bite back a satisfied snicker as he muttered, "You are not playing fair, slim."

"Who said anything about playing fair? I'm just making sure you're still game to take me out on that date when you get back."

"I can't wait. Speaking of dates, how are things going with you and Tucker?"

"We're having a really good time," she said, trying to ignore the weirdness of discussing her date with the other guy she was seeing. They're okay with this, she reminded herself. Hell. It was their idea!

"Good." He sounded relieved. "So no need for the bear spray?"

"Not yet, anyway." She laughed. "Night's still young though."

He barked with laughter. "Yeah, better keep it handy. I should let you go. I just wanted you to know I'm thinking about you."

Her heart swelled a little at his words. "I miss you too. When are you due back?"

"No later than Thursday. They're actually forecasting heavy snow by that afternoon, so I will be back before the storm hits. That's the plan, anyhow."

"Call me tomorrow?" she asked.

"You bet. I'm off to have a cold shower, Miss Polka-Dot-Bra-and-Panties."

"Good-night, Byron."

"Night, Viv."

She hung up the phone and made quick work of changing. The moment she was done she ducked into the bathroom to brush her teeth and snag her bathrobe off the back of the door, along with a couple of towels. When she reached the end of the short hallway she stopped dead in her tracks and stared.

Usually a guy looked bigger dressed, but not Tucker. Wearing nothing but a pair of swim trunks, he seemed to fill up the cabin. He was standing with his back to her, arranging their drinks on a tray he'd managed to find. So far he hadn't noticed her arrival, so she took a moment to enjoy the view. He was as powerfully built as she had imagined. The tribal tattoo that started below his ear covered his back, shoulders and both arms down to his biceps. The black lines vanished beneath his trunks and reappeared on his right thigh. He was like a living sculpture, and she thanked the goddess and all her faces that he was hers.

At least for now.

When he turned he didn't seem surprised to see her standing there. "Aw, you're covered up already." He gestured to mimic the robe she was wearing. "No fair."

"It's cold out there! I'm not walking down to the gazebo without at least a little cover, I'll get frostbite and then this evening isn't going to end the way I hoped."

His eyes narrowed and a wicked grin played across his lips. "And how are you hoping this ends?"

"With us both being warm and sleepy," she answered, being deliberately vague. "Don't you want a towel or something? You're going to freeze outside."

"Cold doesn't bother me," he shrugged his broad shoulders, and she felt her nipples harden and her pulse race a little faster in response. "And I have no intention of letting you get cold either. I've got the drinks, you bring the towels."

She slipped on a pair of flip-flops and headed out the

back door, cursing softly as the icy chill in the air hit her bare legs. "Just follow the walkway."

There was enough moonlight she could make her way down to the gazebo without bothering with the floodlights. Once she had made it to her destination she flipped on the fairy lights that were hung around the perimeter of the gazebo. They gave off enough light to see without interfering with the views of the Pacific crashing on the rocks a few feet away.

She set down her bundle of towels and took a moment to stare out at the water, unsurprised when Tucker did the same. He slid an arm around her waist and drew her back against him, tucking her head under his chin.

"This is beautiful," he murmured into her hair. "No wonder you like it out here."

"I'm starting to like a lot of things out here," she murmured back to him and covered his hand with hers.

"Good." He started undoing the tie of her robe. "Then my plan is working. Now, let's get this robe off of you so I can see that bikini I've been dreaming about."

CHAPTER NINE

It was all he could do to resist tearing her robe off and spinning her around to kiss those soft lips of hers. He wanted her in his arms so that he could feel her long legs wrapped around his hips again. Standing there holding her was a test of his control, and that was something new.

Tucker had seen uncontrolled rage firsthand, and he had known early on that he would never be like Tobias. He never allowed himself to lose control. Not at any time, not for anyone. At least not until he'd met Vivian.

Viv's soft laughter brought him back into the moment and he slowly peeled back the soft cloth of her robe. Green and gold fabric appeared underneath, barely enough to cover her breasts, and he found himself staring. She really was a rare beauty, soft but lithe, her pale skin gleaming in the dim light. He watched a wave of goosebumps flow over her skin and belatedly remembered that it was freezing outside, at least for a human.

"Sorry, I forgot how chilly it was." He left her robe on and let her go so he could get the lid off the tub and get them both into the warm water. "Does this thing have jets?"

"You get the lid, I'll get the jets." She gave him a soft, sensual smile that made his cock impossibly hard and turned his soul inside out. She was the greatest threat to his control he'd ever had, and right now Tucker wasn't even sure he wanted to keep resisting temptation. Not when she smiled at him like that.

He was still wrestling the awkward bulk of the lid over to one side when the thrum of an engine came on and the water began to swirl and froth. By the time he had the lid secure, Viv had shed the robe completely and was setting the tray with their drinks onto a shelf that ran along the railing near the tub. "Jess said her guys made the shelf so they had a place to rest their drinks. I think it works perfectly."

Tucker knew he should respond, but he didn't have breath in his lungs to speak at that moment. Seeing her in that barely-there green and gold bikini had been like a sucker punch to the gut. Then he'd spied the golden gleam of her navel piercing and he couldn't tear his gaze away. A small red stone was set in the ring, and he knew that he was going to spend hours playing with that tiny bit of jewelry. He loved piercings and ink, and now that he'd discovered she had both...

"Nice bling." He finally managed to say, and then came over to help her step up and into the tub, keeping her hand trapped in his as he joined her.

"What? Oh, right." She grinned at him. "Don't tell Byron, a girl needs to have a few surprises."

"Your secret's safe with me." He settled himself back

into a molded seat and then tugged on her hand, coaxing her into his lap. "C'mere, trouble."

She let herself drift over to him and he drew her in close, the scent of vanilla mingling with the faintly chemical scent of the water as she rested her head against his shoulder and closed her eyes.

"Thank you for one of the nicest dates I've ever had."

"You're welcome. And for the record, today was *the* best date I've ever been on." Her lips turned up into a smile and he dropped his head to kiss her. She turned her head and kissed him back, her tongue teasing at his lips until he parted them and took the kiss deeper. God he loved kissing her. With her curled into his lap there was no hiding his reaction to her either, but she just moaned low in the back of her throat and wriggled her shapely ass back and forth across his dick.

He slid his hands up her ribs and found the soft rise of her breasts. They fit perfectly into his hands and he smiled a little as she arched herself against his touch. He stroked his thumbs across the hard nubs of her nipples until she rewarded him with another soft moan that vibrated against his lips and tongue.

She reached behind her, her fingers brushing his chest as she twisted and squirmed. He was having a difficult time thinking as her bikini-clad bottom bumped and rubbed along his cock, but then her top fell away and he understood what she'd been doing. She lowered her arms and lifted the bit of fabric out of the water, nipping at his lower lip before sitting up and tossing it onto the edge.

"Much better," she murmured, and then twisted in his arms so she was straddling his hips, her bare breasts barely clear of the water as she reached past him to grab the bottle of whiskey. She lingered there to pour them each a glass, and he took full advantage of her pose, palming both breasts in an attempt to distract her. Her skin was slick and hot under his hands as he rolled and teased the tight buds of her nipples.

"You're going to make me spill this really expensive scotch," she chided, her voice husky and low.

"I don't care right now. Right now everything I want in the world is right here, in my lap." She laughed and handed him his glass, which he took with one hand while continuing to caress her with the other.

"So what are we going to drink to this time?" he asked her and then immediately regretted it when he saw the gleam in her eyes.

"Well, last time we drank to new friends." She raised her glass and laughed again, and the sound resonated deep inside him. "This time, I think we should drink to new lovers."

She leaned in and kissed him before he could say another word, and he let go of her breast to curve his free arm around her waist so he could haul her in hard against his chest. Her bare flesh plastered against his, and he kissed her until his lungs burned and she was panting and half-wild. Only then did he tear his lips from hers and take a deep breath of cool air before he remembered the drink in his hand.

He touched his glass to hers as he looked into her eyes, liking the heat he saw gleaming in their depths. "To us," he said simply, and then threw back his head and downed the contents of the glass in one shot. He barely felt the burn as it coursed down his throat because all of his attention was on the woman in front of him.

He managed to set the glass back down without dropping it and then wrapped his arm around her waist again, holding her firmly enough she was stable against the roiling currents of the tub, but loose enough she could enjoy her drink while he enjoyed *her*.

He dropped his mouth to the valley between her breasts, kissing his way over to one pert nipple. He sucked on it until she mewled and rose on her knees to press herself deeper into the heat of his mouth. Back and forth he nibbled and sucked, encouraged every second by her soft cries of need.

She draped one arm around his neck and bucked her hips against his cock in a slow, teasing rhythm. The taste of scotch hit his tongue and he glanced up to see her dribbling the last of her glass over her chest. He licked off every drop as she watched him, laughing.

She leaned in, her breath fanning over his face as she flicked her tongue over his brow ring. Every touch sent another bolt of pure lust sizzling straight to his dick and he couldn't hear anything over the hum of the jets and the blood pounding in his ears. He was too distracted for even his heightened senses to alert him to the fact that they were no longer alone until he heard a piercing whistle followed by someone calling his name.

"Tucker? Hey, Tucker. That *is* you, isn't it?" The beam of a flashlight played over the gazebo, blinding him before he could make out the visitor's face, but he already had a pretty good idea who had dropped by. "It's Trent. Byron said you'd be out back in the..." The voice trailed off as the light caught Vivian slipping off his lap and submerging herself again.

"Trent, kill the flashlight already!"

The light flicked off. "Sorry. I didn't realize you were uh, busy."

"I'll kill him," Tucker muttered under his breath. "If Byron sent the cops out here to break up our evening…"

Vivian snorted with laughter and then said, "If he did, I'll help you hide his body."

"Deal." He growled and moved so that she was shielded behind him and then called up. "What brings you out here, Trent?"

"There's been a bit of a mess at the bar." Trent called back. "You weren't answering your phone, so I called Byron and he told me where to find you. Look, I'll go wait around front, but you're going to want to come back to Breakers and see for yourself. You've got two broken windows and a couple of minor injuries. Staff and customers."

"Fuck!" Tucker snarled and ran a soaking wet hand through his hair. "I'll be there in two minutes, but you're going to need to give me a ride back into town. I just had a drink and I'm not going to drive. Who got hurt, Trent?"

"Nina got caught in the scuffle and was knocked down. She's shaken, but it's nothing serious. I'll get you to the bar and you can see for yourself that she's fine. I'll be out front." There was a moment of silence and then a riff of muffled laughter before Trent added, "Out of sight of you and your lady friend."

"Who was that?" Vivian asked once they were alone again. "And who's Nina?"

"Nina's one of my bartenders, and *that* was RCMP Constable Trent Smith. A very nice guy when he's not shining a light on me in the middle of…what we were in the middle of. Goddamnit, I haven't been caught out like that since I was a teenager!"

She laughed and hugged him. "Me either." She melted into his arms and kissed him gently. Tucker felt a momentary wave of resentment that he was going to have to leave her to go see what had happened at his bar, but he knew he wouldn't be happy until he'd seen for himself that Nina was okay. He had to go.

"If you want, I can bring back your bike tomorrow. That is, If you trust me to ride it," she offered.

"I trust you," he responded without a second's hesitation. "Bring it in tomorrow night and you can keep me company at the bar if you want. Tuesdays are usually pretty quiet, and then I'll give you a ride home afterward."

"Ooh, a second date?" She kissed him again. "I like that idea. Go get dressed, you shouldn't leave Officer Snickerpuss waiting. I'll grab our things and see you inside. I'm sorry you have to go into work, but I understand."

"You aren't the only one who's sorry right now, believe me. When I find out who the fucking idiots were who ruined the best date of my life I am going to hit them with a lifetime ban from my bar."

"Nothing's ruined," she whispered and dropped her lips to his chest, pressing an open-mouthed kiss to his skin. "Just postponed."

"Postponed," he agreed. "Thank you for understanding."

"And you're going to make it all up to me tomorrow night." She let go of him and drifted over to the edge of the tub, getting out without bothering to hide her beautiful body. He admired the Celtic-style dragon tattoo that curved along her spine, and mentally added tracing every line of it with his fingers and tongue to the list of things he wanted to do to her before she left…if she left. If he let her leave. The more he got to know her, the less he even wanted to think about her going back to Toronto. His wilder nature growled somewhere deep in his psyche and he locked it down. Now was not the time to get into a battle of wills with his other half.

"I will make it up to you any way you want, lover," he vowed, and she tossed him a saucy smile.

"I'm going to hold you to that." She grabbed her robe and covered herself, denying him the sight of her beautiful body dripping wet and glowing under the fairy lights while he got out and quickly wrestled the lid back into place. She tossed him a towel and he dried himself off as he headed back up to the house, his anger growing at every step. Who the hell had busted up his bar? Why hadn't Tim been able to handle things? He had a lot of questions and no answers. Not yet.

He was struggling to tug his jeans on over still-damp skin when she came into the cabin. He reined in his fury long enough to haul her against him for one last, hard kiss. "I'll see you tomorrow." He pressed the keys to his bike into her hand and cupped her face for a moment, grateful to see nothing but understanding and a sizzle of sexual frustration in her pretty hazel eyes. He was feeling fucking frustrated himself, and he planned on taking out that frustration on anyone who got in his way for the rest of the night.

"Dream of me," she whispered, and turned to press a kiss to the palm of his hand. He had no doubt that was exactly what he would do. She was going to haunt his dreams, and he wasn't going to get any damned sleep until he had her in bed beside him.

"Good-night."

He headed out the front door and found Trent waiting for him. "Let's go see what the bastards did to my bar."

He was getting into Trent's cruiser when his acute sense of hearing caught the turn of a deadbolt and Vivian grumbling to herself on the far side of the door. "How is it possible that I am seeing two guys and I *still* can't get laid!"

It was going to be a long night for both of them.

That thought gave him a little comfort as Trent filled him in on what had happened in the few hours he'd been gone.

By the time they pulled into the parking lot of Breakers, Tucker was ready to tear Steve Trask a new one. Trent had told him that the fight hadn't even started in his bar. His patrons had been the victims, not the instigators. It had been some of Trask's shit-disturbing buddies who had been hanging out at the T-Spot, drinking and harassing anyone coming or going from the bar. Tucker's bouncer, Big Mike, had tried to get them to go back inside the shop, but Trask himself had gotten in Mike's face and that's when things had gotten ugly.

Trask's buddies had ganged up on Mike, and when he had done the smart thing and retreated, the thugs had taken tire irons to the windows that flanked Breakers's main doors. Petty mischief hadn't been enough to satisfy them though. After that they'd come into the bar looking for a fight. That's when Nina had gotten knocked down and all hell had broken loose.

Someone had already swept up the broken glass into a

pile, and plywood was leaning up against the wall in preparation for boarding up the windows until they could be repaired. Again.

The tattoo shop was dark and silent, which was likely a good thing given Tucker's current mood. Trask had clearly cut bait and run, but he'd be back in the morning and Tucker planned on giving him notice that he wasn't going to be renewing his lease. By the end of January he wanted the son of a bitch and his idiot friends off the property.

The music was still playing and there were a few people drinking and talking, but the mood was subdued. It felt closer to closing time than anything else. Tim glanced up from the bar and gave a wry smile of greeting.

"Hey, boss. Sorry about all this." He gestured around the bar and Tucker noticed there were new dings in a few of the tables near the doorway.

"Trent caught me up on the way over, this wasn't your fault. It was that idiot, Trask. You'll be happy to know I'm not going to be renewing his lease, so this won't be happening again."

"Glad to hear it. Nina's in the kitchen if you want to check in on her."

"Why is she in the kitchen? She shouldn't be working at all!"

"Yeah, I know, but she's one very stubborn woman. I tried to get her to sit her ass down and take it easy, and she suggested I do something biologically impossible to myself and then headed to the kitchen. She said she could sit and still be useful."

"Well, then I guess she's fine." Tucker's tension eased down a notch at that bit of news. "Where's Big Mike?"

"He gave a statement and then did the sensible thing

and went home once he knew you were on your way in. He's coming back after he's cleaned up to drive Nina home. He doesn't want her going outside by herself."

"Neither do I. Phone Mike and tell him to come get her. I'm going to go see Nina and punt her ass out of here."

"Good luck with that," Tim said and then barked out a sharp laugh. "Word of warning, make sure she puts down the knife before you try to talk to her. Last time I checked she was helping prep tomorrow's food."

"Thanks for the warning." Tucker headed into the back to disarm his bartender and send her home. Then he needed to call Byron and talk to him about Trask. He was sure Byron would agree with him, which meant they were about to be short a nice chunk of income. They'd need to come up with a plan for the space, but it would be worth it to get rid of Trask and all the problems that came with him.

CHAPTER TEN

SLEEP HAD NOT COME EASILY for Vivian and when it had, it was accompanied by dreams so erotic she had woken up and been surprised her sheets hadn't been scorched. Memories of both Byron and Tucker's kisses had added fuel to favorite fantasies and created some new ones too.

Whatever her connection was to the two men, it was getting stronger even when she was only seeing one of them. It was as if they were connected for her in some strange way, and she decided to ask Jess if this is how it had been with her and her guys in the beginning. If so, she was starting to understand how three people could live the way Jess, Rory and Evan did. It wasn't just about sex, it was about connections.

She spent the morning doing chores. Catching up on her laundry and generally cleaning up the place before finally making a run into town to restock the kitchen. Cold pizza was great, but not for three meals in a row.

By the time she got back home the sky was full of dark gray clouds and the temperature was starting to drop. It looked like the storm Byron mentioned was arriving a few days early. A little snow didn't worry her, not after growing up in Toronto, but she hoped it didn't mean that Byron would be stuck in Victoria for longer than he'd planned. She was looking forward to seeing him again.

With that thought in her head she grabbed her phone and called him. When it went through to voice mail she left him a message telling him that the weather looked to be getting worse, and she hoped he was snug and safe somewhere.

Making that call left a warm feeling in her heart and she hummed to herself as she unpacked the last of the groceries and finally flaked out on the loveseat for a much-needed rest. She grabbed the book on selkies again and started reading, wondering again why Jess had the book at all. It really wasn't her thing.

At some point she must have dozed off, because she woke up to near darkness, her mind full of strange images from her dreams. There had been two men who had come up out of the sea to make love to her on the sand as the waves had crashed ashore around them. They'd somehow coaxed her to go into the water too, and she had been able to swim easily in the surprisingly warm water as they'd made love to her again.

"Like that's going to happen," she muttered as she eased herself up off the loveseat. "If two hot men tried to fuck me in the water I'd drown before anyone got to have any fun at all."

Bits and pieces of her dreams stayed with her while she got ready, and she found herself continuously distracted by half-remembered sensations of four hands touching her and two mouths kissing her while the waves surged around them all. Clearly, all the sex she'd been dreaming of all night and part of her day was having an effect. Tonight she was hoping that Tucker was as ready to take the next step as she was. She had never felt so sexually charged in her life.

She managed to pull together an outfit that was both fashionable enough to make Tucker look twice and practical enough she wasn't going to freeze to death on the ride in. She turned up the cuffs on her black leather boots so they became thigh-highs, and zipped her motorcycle jacket up over the charcoal gray, V-necked sweater she'd chosen. After some consideration she tossed a few overnight items into her purse, in case things went the way she was hoping and she didn't make it back home tonight.

Home. The thought caught her by surprise. She was already thinking of this place as home.

Riding into town on Tucker's Harley was a blast, and she drove it for an extra few blocks for the joy of the ride before pulling into the parking lot at Breakers.

That was when she realized she hadn't actually asked where to park it. Well, she'd park it out front for now and duck in and ask Tucker where he wanted it. She was still unfastening the helmet when a rough voice sounded from right behind her.

"Hey sweet thing. If you like having something hot and throbbing between your legs, I'm the man for you."

She groaned inwardly and eased the helmet off so she could get a look at her would-be Don Juan.

Why is it always the hideous ones who use the cheesiest lines?

Her admirer had greasy hair, an unkempt beard and a

beer gut that spilled over his belt and out from under his well-worn shirt. She had to hide a grimace when she saw that he was actually licking his lips as he ogled her.

How charming.

"Sorry, I'm spoken for," she said with a disarming shrug, and sidestepped so that she was no longer trapped between the stranger and the motorcycle.

"A real man wouldn't let his old lady ride around on his bike without him. Whoever he is, you need to make an upgrade."

Vivian managed to bite back a laugh at that. This loser wasn't an upgrade from anyone. "I'm pretty happy with him, thanks. If you don't mind, I'd like to go inside now. He's waiting for me."

"Let him wait, sweet thing. You going to tell me your name? Mine's Tony. You're going to need to know that later when you're telling people who gave you the best ride of your life." He licked his lips again and this time she felt a prickle of unease. This guy was as persistent as he was ugly.

"Sorry, Tony. I'm really not interested." She took another step toward the front door of the bar and closed her fingers around the key in her hand so that it was a short, but still effective, weapon.

"Leave her alone, you horny bastard." Another man came to the door and pointed to the bike she'd ridden in on. "That's Pine's bike, which means she's Pine's piece. I'm in enough shit with him right now without you putting your pathetic moves on his bitch. You trying to fuck up the deal before I even get a chance to sell him on it?"

Whoever the newcomer was, Tony took the point and

moved out of her way. "Your loss," he grumbled as he sauntered back into the shop beside Breakers. She didn't waste her chance and headed indoors. Warmth and noise greeted her and she was surprised to find the place relatively busy. There was a woman she didn't recognize behind the bar and no sign of Tucker, so she decided to head over to ask for his whereabouts when a hand came down on her shoulder.

Again? What is with people tonight?

She grabbed the offending hand and tossed it off her shoulder with practiced ease, then spun around in a single, fluid motion to give whoever it was a piece of her mind.

Before she could open her mouth a deep voice barked. "You can head right back outside and tell your shit-disturbing buddies that sending a woman in here isn't going to change the rules."

"First of all, hands off!" she snapped, and tipped her head back to glower up at her newest problem. "Second of all, I have no idea what you're talking about. And thirdly, if this is the way you treat customers then I'm going to tell Tucker to fire your ass. And where is he anyway? I'm here to see him and you're in my way."

"You're wearing bike leathers and carrying a helmet, so don't tell me you're here to see the boss. You're part of those slimeballs next door, and you're *all* banned." The big lug crossed his arms over his chest. "So get out before I call the cops and get you arrested for trespassing."

She ground her teeth together and struggled to find her sense of calm. "I am carrying Tucker's helmet, because I brought his bike back. I'm his…girlfriend."

"Oh yeah. Now I know you're lying. The boss doesn't have a girlfriend."

"Actually, he does. And he'd really like to know why you're pissing her off right now, Big Mike." Tucker appeared beside them. Viv didn't know whether to hug him or groan over the fact she'd called herself his girlfriend and he'd confirmed it - publicly. This evening was already going off the rails. "Hey, trouble. What's going on?" He wrapped a strong arm around her waist and drew her into his side, and she went for option number one.

"Hey, lover." She stood on tiptoes and brushed a kiss to his lips as his eyes widened with surprise and pleasure. "Your boy grabbed me and then tried to throw me out. Is this a new policy? Because I'm pretty sure it's going to get you in a heap of trouble."

"He grabbed you?" Tucker tensed and his next words came out in the darkest tones she'd ever heard him utter. "If you touch her again, Mike, you're done."

"I thought she was with Trask's bunch!" he defended himself.

"You don't lay a finger on a customer until there's no other option. You know that, man! Don't let what happened last night get to you."

"Sorry."

"Don't apologize to me, apologize to Vivian. "

Mike looked sheepish. "I'm really sorry. I thought you looked like a biker chick and after last night..." He cleared his throat and glanced over at Nina. "They hurt someone I care about, and I thought you were with them. I'm really sorry." He grinned a little. "And I didn't know Tucker was dating anyone. He never tells us anything."

"I didn't have time to! I was with her last night when all hell broke loose, which is why she's bringing my bike back tonight. Vivian Waverly, this is my head bouncer, Big Mike. Mike, this is Vivian." Tucker glanced down at her outfit and grinned. "Man. Look at her! Does she look like she belongs to one of those sad sacks next door?"

Viv laughed. "Be very careful how you answer that, Mike. Our future friendship depends on your answer. I think I had a run-in with some of the guys you're referring to, and I'm considering taking offense."

The smile left Mike's face and Tucker's arm hauled her in tight to his side. "What happened?" Tucker demanded. "What did they do?"

"Some guy tossed some cheesy pickup lines at me and didn't want to take no for an answer. Then some other guy came to the door and told him to back off, I was clearly riding your bike…and that meant I must be your bitch and he's in enough trouble with you already."

"Did he touch you?" Tucker's voice was bordering on a feral snarl now, and Vivian turned in to face him. "No, he didn't." She splayed a comforting hand across his chest. Under her fingers she could feel that his heart was pounding hard with barely checked anger.

"And where the fuck were you when this was happening?" Tucker snapped at Mike.

"I do a parking lot check every five minutes like we talked about. I must have just missed her."

"Tomorrow I'm hiring a guard to patrol the lot. This shit has got to stop. Byron is going to lose his mind when he hears about this."

"Mike, new policy. Any female guest gets an escort to her vehicle tonight. Hell, anyone who wants an escort gets one. No one goes outside alone, and that includes staff." He looked down at her and frowned. "And you too, trouble. You look way too damned good to be wandering out there alone after last night."

"What happened last night? I think this is a story I need to hear. Oh, and I have to go back out there. Your bike is still out front. I didn't think to ask where you wanted it parked."

"Not a chance." He held out his hand. "Keys."

"You're not going out there without me, either," she told him as she handed over the keys. "I have plans for you tonight, and they don't involve you getting into a brawl."

"I don't brawl, sweetheart. Fighting isn't a sport, it's a final resort. And so we're clear? I too, have plans for tonight, and they don't include you getting harassed by my soon-to-be-ex-tenant or his scumbag friends." He loosened his hold on her but she stayed stuck to his side for no other reason than it felt good to be there.

"I think that's the sweetest thing I've ever heard him say," Big Mike snickered and then nodded at Vivian. "I really am sorry, Vivian."

"It's okay. I get that you were being protective. I think I'm going to be flattered you thought I could be a threat and leave it at that."

"Yeah, I don't know what he was thinking there," Tucker drawled and tweaked her leather collar as his gaze dropped to her boot-clad legs. "You're clearly a candy striper who got lost on the way to the hospital."

"Jeez, first schoolgirls and now nurses, I'm starting to suspect you're seriously into role-playing," she teased and Mike groaned in horror.

"Oh god, my ears. I don't want to know. I'm going to patrol the parking lot!" Mike clapped his hands over his ears. "La-la-la I can't hear this," was the last thing she heard as the big man headed toward the door.

"I think you may have scarred him for life," Tucker said with a grin big enough to show his dimple. "Come on, we can both go move the bike around back and then I'll give you the nickel tour. You can drop your stuff off upstairs at my place. That way you don't have to watch your purse or jacket all night."

"That is the smoothest 'let's go to my place' line I have ever heard!" she said and wrinkled her nose at him. "Does that work?"

"I don't know, I've never used it before." He cocked his brow at her and she melted a little inside. "So you tell me."

"I'm not sure if it's the line or the fact that you're drop-dead sexy when you do that eyebrow thing, but yeah, I'm all yours. Take me to your man cave."

He took her hand and headed outside, not even bothering with a jacket. When they passed Big Mike he told him, "Mike, I'm moving the bike. You watch the door and make sure Nina's good in there until I get back."

"Got it, boss."

Tucker didn't bother with the helmet, he hopped on the bike, started it, and then patted the seat behind him. "Come on, the man cave is this way."

She got on, the helmet in one hand and the other thrown around his chest for balance as he drove around to the back and pulled into a carport wide enough for at least three cars. He got things settled, took her by the hand, and led her past a loading bay to a barely discernible doorway. He took a second to punch in a key code, but then he had her inside a dimly lit stairwell and up against the wall. His hard body pinned her in place, and his hands were on either side of her, caging her in as his mouth covered hers in a hard, breath-stealing kiss.

Moving away from him was the last thing on her mind. She gripped his shoulders tight as the world spun out from beneath her. She loved the way his unshaven skin rasped against hers and his woodsy scent struck her nose, filling her senses. His tongue swiped over her lower lip and she opened her mouth to his. Tongues dueling, their bodies pressed together until her pussy was drenched with the proof of her desire. He kissed her again, still hungry for more.

She decided to give it to him.

Fumbling fingers found the button of his jeans and managed to pop it open, sliding her hand beneath to wrap her fingers around the silk-clad length of his cock. He was as big as she'd imagined, and he was still swelling in her hand as she milked him with strong, firm tugs.

He lifted his mouth from hers and groaned. "We don't have time for this."

"For everything I want to do to you? No. But we do have time for *this*." She released his shoulders, letting her purse fall to the floor as she pushed at his chest. She guided his big body backward until he bumped into the far wall of the small stairwell. She kissed her way down his body until she was on her knees in front of him, her hands still on his fly. When she tipped her head back to gaze up at him she found him staring down at her, his eyes shimmering with molten heat.

He nodded once, a muscle in his jaw jumping as he put himself in her hands. She leaned in and nuzzled his cock as she tugged his jeans down, the warm silk of his briefs caressing her lips and cheek. His dick twitched and she felt him lean back, bracing himself against the wall with a low groan. She moved with him, tracing every steel-and-velvet inch with her tongue before freeing his cock from the fabric and doing it all over again. She stroked her fingertips from crown to root and then down to his balls before fisting him firmly as her tongue traced over his glans. The salty tang of his pre-cum filled her mouth and she spent several slow seconds lapping it up, encouraged by the shaky groans coming from above her.

He tangled his fingers into her hair, coaxing her forward, and she took his hint with a soft laugh she knew he'd be able to feel all the way down to his balls. She took his cock deep, working him with her tongue as she slowly increased the suction until his thighs shook and his balls tightened.

He finally broke the silence. "Oh damn, that feels good! I like watching you suck me off, seeing your pretty lips wrapped around my dick. Viv, sugar you're going to turn me inside out if you don't stop soon. Fuck! So good!" He rocked his hips against her mouth and she knew he was on the verge of losing control, which was exactly what she wanted. "Just like that. Fuck yes!" He groaned again as words escaped him and then she pushed him over the edge, swallowing his seed as he came and came until he was spent.

He stroked her bangs out of her eyes as she finally lifted her head to grin at him. "I've been thinking about doing that since you left last night."

"Goddamn, if I had known that I would have come back." He helped her up off her knees and wrapped his arms around her, holding her close as he showered her face and hair with tender kisses. "I wanted you, but I wanted our first date to be more than just me trying to get you naked. At least that was my plan…as I recall I was failing miserably before we got interrupted."

His confession made her smile, and she was glad that fate had made them wait at least one more day. "It's a good thing it's our second date then, because I'm hoping to get you naked tonight," she admitted. "And if we lock all the doors there's no chance we're going to get interrupted again."

"No chance," he agreed. "Which is good, because I don't think I'm going to get a good night's sleep until I've got you in bed beside me, naked and very thoroughly fucked."

His blunt declaration made her wish they could go upstairs and get started right away, but they had hours left to go, not to mention a bar to get back to. She reined in her libido after one last kiss and then eased out of his arms. "So, show me the rest of your bachelor pad. Then we need to get you back to work. I believe you promised me food and drink, barkeep!"

"The tour starts now." He reached out and flipped several light switches at once, bathing the stairway in light. Once her eyes adjusted she found herself staring and a soft gasp escaped her throat. He'd painted the entire stairway as one incredible mural.

CHAPTER ELEVEN

THE PAINTING CREATED the illusion that she was standing between the ocean and a rainforest at dawn, but as the stairs ascended the scene shifted to full daylight and then back to dusk as the mural ended at another door.

"This is incredible!" She reached out to touch the wall, her fingertips skimming over the ridges of oil paint that added depth to what she was seeing. "How long did this take you?"

"Almost a year." He pointed upward and she tipped her head back to see that the ceiling was painted to represent the sky, tying the two scenes together. "That took me the longest, and I nearly broke my neck a few times getting up and down the scaffolding." Tucker bent down and picked up her purse, tucking it under his arm before heading up the stairs.

Viv lingered at the bottom for a minute longer, still taking in the details of his work. "I can't believe no one knows you can paint like this," she finally exclaimed, and jogged up the stairs behind him.

"A few people do, but not many. You might have noticed by now, I like my privacy."

She snickered. "You mean you use your big, badass vibe to keep people at arm's length." Viv stepped up behind him on the landing and pressed herself against his back, resting her cheek against his shoulder blade. "I'm sort of an expert at that tactic myself."

"I noticed. Byron's going to have his work cut out for him. He's always bitching I'm not social enough, and now he's going to have you to deal with too..." he trailed off. "I mean, if you stay here and if you're really good with this and...fuck. You made me babble. I don't babble!"

He set her purse down on a table covered in papers and hauled her into his arms while she laughed. She was getting more okay with the entire idea by the minute, but before she could say so he cut her off with a kiss that short-circuited her brain and made her toes curl. Thought was impossible for a long time as she seized the moment and showed him without words how good she was with everything that was happening.

Finally she broke the kiss and leaned back far enough she could catch her breath. "You know we are never going to get back downstairs if you don't stop doing that."

"I know. Right now I really don't care."

She reached around and swatted him playfully on his denim-clad ass. "That's no way for the boss to talk!"

"Hey, I just discovered I have a girlfriend. I think I'm allowed to celebrate a little." He cocked his brow at her as he tipped his head a little to one side. "Or did you think I'd forgotten about that?"

"To be honest I was sort of hoping the blow job had blanked that from your memory."

"Not a chance." His smile faded into a more serious expression and he stroked a feather-light finger down her cheek. "Whatever we have between us, I want it. I want you. I won't promise you forever, because it's too soon for that. But you have my complete and undivided attention. I don't see that changing anytime soon. As far as I am concerned you *are* my girlfriend, okay?"

She nodded silently, unable to speak past the lump in her throat.

"Good." His expression warmed again. "And when Byron gets back, I hope you wrap him around your finger as tightly as you've got me."

"I'll do my best." She found her voice again.

"Then he's royally screwed. Thank the gods. I'll feel better if he's in this with me."

That made her laugh long and hard. There were tears in her eyes when she finally got herself back under control. "You make it sound like you're facing the apocalypse!"

"Maybe I am. You are an amazing woman, Viv. And you *are* a fucking force of nature."

"Damn right I am."

He showed her around his place after that, which didn't take very long at all given that it was all one big space, apart from the bathroom. Canvases that were four feet to a side were everywhere, some finished with more in various states of completion. Drop cloths covered large portions of the hardwood floor and there were painting and art supplies everywhere. Skylights overhead clearly provided most of the light during the day, but there were enough lights to make it almost painfully bright even during the darkest night. The walls were a simple off-white color, and all the furniture she could see was comfortable, well used and varying shades of blue. His place was not exactly elegant, but it was definitely a well-functioning man cave.

His kitchen area was small and she could see there were a handful of dishes in the sink, and a pizza box with a familiar logo was sitting with the recycling. His king-sized bed took up one section of the space, the dark blue sheets turned back neatly. She eyed it with amused suspicion. "All this chaos, and you made the bed? Really?"

Tucker shrugged. "I didn't have time to tidy up. I figured that way you'd know I made an effort to do at least one thing."

"And it had to be the bed." She snickered and shrugged out of her jacket, tossing it onto the corner of the bed in question.

"No comment." He stood in the middle of the room and began pointing. "Kitchen, bathroom, bedroom, living room." He ended by pointing at a couple of blue leather couches facing a massive flat-screen television that was mounted on the wall. "And that concludes our tour. Please visit the gift shop on your way out."

"Later on you're going to show me all of these." She gestured to the paintings that were scattered around the space.

"I'll show you after breakfast tomorrow."

"You've got yourself a deal."

He took her hand again and led her to another door with yet another keypad. "This one leads down to the storeroom. It saves me having to go around the building to go to work. He drew her in close as he keyed in the access code. "6-9-0-0," he gave her the numbers as he keyed them in. "Now you can come and go as you please."

"Wow. Our second date and you gave me the proverbial key to your apartment?"

"Trust me. My bathroom is much nicer than the ladies' room downstairs." He grinned at her. "You're welcome."

He started through the door, leading her with him. "And here I thought the first thing you were going to comment on was my choice in codes."

"Sixty-nine, oh, oh?" she sniggered. "I'm still sorting through smart-ass comments. I'll let you know when I've picked one."

"That's what I figured."

They headed back down to the bar after that, and Tucker set Vivian up on a stool down near the end so they could talk as he worked. There were fewer customers now, but the ones still there seemed rooted to their chairs. They only moved to order more drinks if the waitress was too slow coming around.

As he made drinks and worked on various bits of paperwork, he updated her on what had happened the night before. The fight, the damage, all of it.

Then he told her that during his meeting with Trask today he'd made it clear that the lease was not being renewed at the end of next month. He hadn't taken the news well. Instead he'd offered Tucker a laughable amount to buy out the two of them and take over as the owner of Breakers. Trask had some insane idea about turning Breakers into a hangout for his biker buddies, meaning that the scum that had accosted her in the parking lot and caused the fight last night would become the main clientele. Tucker said no.

"I think you and Byron were right to refuse to renew the lease. You don't need the headaches or the broken glass. That guy Trask and his friends would be nothing but an ongoing problem."

"Byron was ready to drive back up here last night and change the locks on the doors. You wouldn't know it to look at him with that goofy grin and surfer attitude, but that guy has a serious temper, and last night he was *pissed*."

"So you're saying you're not the scary one?" she teased, and had another sip of her diet cola.

"No, sugar. I'm saying I'm not the *only* scary one."

"Please. You two aren't scary, you're just big, snuggly sweethearts."

Nina made a noise like someone was strangling an asthmatic cat as she passed close enough to hear them.

"Something you need to say?" Tucker challenged her and the other bartender threw up a hand and shook her head.

"Me? No. Not a thing, snuggly-wuggles."

"Insubordinate brat! Just for that I'm going to have Big Mike drive you home again tonight." He chucked a wet bar rag at Nina's retreating back, ignoring the one-fingered salute she tossed him as the cloth sailed over her shoulder.

"Speaking of Mike, where is he? I haven't seen him in a few." Viv glanced around the bar in case she'd missed the big guy, but he was nowhere to be found.

"He's probably escorting someone to their car, but I'll go check out front to be sure. I don't trust Trask's buddies not to be pulling more shit tonight. They're not happy about the ban."

He ducked out from behind the bar and Vivian fell in behind him. She ignored the disgruntled look he shot her when he glanced back and found her two steps behind him. Like she was going to sit at the bar, waiting for him to come back? Not bloody likely.

They weren't even to the door yet when both of them heard shouting and angry voices. Tucker broke into a run and Viv turned around and called to Nina. "If we're not back in five minutes, call the cops!" With that she charged out the still-open door and into the night.

Wet snow was falling hard outside, but the cold weather was doing nothing to cool the tempers flaring among the men yelling at each other outside. She recognized Tony and Trask standing in the company of several other rough-looking characters. Trask was standing toe-to-toe with Tucker, and judging by the look on Tucker's face, he wasn't enjoying anything the smaller man had to say. Big Mike stood behind his boss, arms crossed as he glared daggers at the other men.

"...being unreasonable! There's money to be made here for everyone if you would quit being so fucking shortsighted. It's time for a change, Pine."

"Oh I agree. Changes are coming. Which is why you have until the end of January to get the fuck off my property, Trask. Those are the only changes my partner and I are making. We're not selling the bar, or changing anything else about it. That's final. Furthermore, if you wanted to talk business, you should have done it during business hours, not brought your gang over to my door to harass my employees when you knew you were not going to be allowed inside! The ban stands, and so does everything else we discussed today."

Tucker's voice dropped to a dangerous rumble. "Now get back to your shop before I start thinking about early eviction." He glanced over at Vivian and then pointed in her direction. "One more thing. If I find out any of you so much as looked sideways at my girlfriend, I will end you. We clear?"

"Yeah, sure. Your old lady is off limits. Got it." Trask sneered in her direction. "She's not my type anyway."

"Glad to hear it. Now go."

Tucker came back inside, followed by Mike. Both men were soaked to the skin, and Viv couldn't help but admire the way his shirt clung to every contoured muscle of Tucker's torso as she followed him back to the bar.

"You two look like you went swimming with your clothes on," Nina observed.

Tucker ran a hand through his sopping hair and grimaced. "Welcome to winter. I'd guess in a few hours we're going to have a few inches of snow on the ground. I think we're closing things down early tonight. Everyone should be getting home before the roads get sloppy and slick." He gave Viv a sly grin. "Looks like even Mother Nature is on our side tonight."

"And that's my cue to start cashing out. Whatever's infected you two snuggle bunnies, I don't want to catch it," Nina said, and headed back down toward the register.

As she retreated Viv caught Nina glancing over at Mike and grinned. "Methinks the lady doth protest too much." She flicked her gaze from Mike to Nina and Tucker nodded.

"He's been trying to get her to go out with him for almost a year now. I think he's finally making progress. Don't let on though, or she'll lead him on another six-month chase, and I don't think he deserves that."

"I won't say a word." She pressed a finger to her lips and mimed turning a key in a lock.

"Mike will be grateful for your silence. Now, grab a seat and I'll go let everyone know that it's closing time."

There were some grumblings at first, but as the guests headed outside into the snowy night the grumbles faded. In next to no time everyone made a hasty exit, none of them apparently wanting to cope with driving in snow. It was a reaction that seemed downright strange to Vivian.

"So what's with the panic over a few inches of white stuff?" she asked as the last of the customers headed out for their cab and Mike locked the door behind them.

"We hardly ever get snow up here, which means no one gets much practice driving in it. It's wet, icy stuff too. Hard to drive in, especially if you don't have snow tires," Tucker explained as he started cleaning up behind the bar.

"Do you think Byron will be okay driving back? He figured he could leave tomorrow and beat the storm."

Tucker looked pleased with her question. "He'll be fine. He's got the work truck, which is a four-wheel-drive beast. Plus he's got snow chains with him. It just means he'll have to actually take his time heading back instead of treating the drive like his own personal speedway."

Someone turned the music down and Nina appeared beside them. "Mike and I are headed out. The kitchen staff took off like the place was on fire, so I do believe you two are the last ones here. Don't do anything I wouldn't do." She waved and grabbed her coat from behind the bar. "Night, snuggly-wuggles."

"You call me that again, you're fired!" Tucker called after her, laughing.

"Yeah, yeah, you keep saying shit like that, but you keep paying me."

"Great, once Patricia gets back to work tomorrow night

the whole damned bar is going to be calling me snuggly-wuggles." He groaned. "I'm blaming you for that."

"Who's Patricia?"

"She's my head waitress. She and Tim have different days off. That way there's always someone with the authority to get things done around here. You'll likely meet her the next time you're here. Now that they've discovered I have a girlfriend, they are all going to be dying to meet you. Be warned, you're going to get grilled for details, and if you give them any I will take it out of your hide."

"Did you just threaten to spank me if I tattled? Because that's more of an incentive than a threat," she sassed back, and was rewarded with a panty-meltingly hot look.

"I'm going to remember you said that."

"I hope so!" She hopped off the barstool she'd claimed earlier in the evening and started putting up chairs and stools so the cleaning staff could do the floors when they came in. The bar felt different now that it was empty, as though the entire place was at rest until the doors were opened again.

She was only partially done with the chairs when the lights dimmed and the first strains of Foreigner's *I Want to Know What Love Is* came over the speakers. She turned around to say something to Tucker and found herself swept up into his arms as he half walked and half carried her to the middle of the dance floor. He'd left the dance lights on, bathing them in a rainbow of slowly shifting colors.

"They're playing our song," he murmured near her ear as he drew her in close and nuzzled her throat, sending a shiver of desire chasing down her spine.

"I'm impressed you remembered."

"You made a lasting impression that night," he whispered before lifting his head to stare down into her eyes. "If you're not sure about this, then say so right now, because this is the last chance you have to change your mind. By tomorrow morning I'm pretty damned sure I'm going to be addicted to you."

"You're not already? Then I'm not doing this right." She rose on the points of her toes to reach his mouth, silencing him with a kiss that flooded her with heat and a need so powerful she felt her knees tremble. The music still played, but their bodies began to move to another rhythm, swaying and touching in a prelude to the lovemaking to come.

His tongue played tag with hers as his hands stroked over her possessively, fueling her passion. Her clit throbbed and ached, needing attention to ease the desire raging through her. She straddled his thigh, riding it hard in an attempt to take the edge off, but it only made her hotter, craving more.

He cupped her ass and lifted her, using his thigh to boost her higher so she could wrap her legs around his hips. His groan of approval mixed with her moans and she clung to him like a limpet as he carried her off the dance floor.

She assumed they were headed upstairs, but instead she found herself perched on the edge of the bar. Their height difference was reversed this way, and she had to bow her head to continue kissing him. She framed his face with her hands and tightened her legs around him, keeping him close while he slid his hands under her sweater, working it up her body with practiced skill.

She lifted her head and raised her hands so he could peel it off, gasping in surprise as he dropped his head to her stomach and ran his tongue over her navel ring.

"I really like this," he muttered as he nuzzled her tummy, the unshaven roughness of his skin making her squirm as it tickled. Every tug and touch of his mouth on her piercing sent a sizzling bolt of energy straight to her clit, pouring more fuel on the bonfire raging inside her.

"Upstairs?" she gasped as he swirled his tongue over her navel again.

"Too far." His growled response was muffled against her skin. She undid her bra and slipped it off, dropping it somewhere in the general vicinity of her sweater. Then she reached for his shirt, taking two handfuls of the still wet fabric and tugging upward.

"If we're staying here, then you're wearing too many clothes," she said and tugged harder.

He stopped what he was doing long enough to tear his shirt off. Then he leaned over her again, dusting open-mouthed kisses from her belly button to her breasts before drawing one tight nub into the heat of his mouth.

She buried her fingers in his hair and dipped her head so she could reach the gold ring in his brow, running her tongue across it. He groaned and nipped at her breast hard enough to sting a little.

"What, you're the only one allowed to have a thing for piercings?" she muttered, and then tightened her lips on the brow ring, giving it another light tug.

"Fuck!" He released her breast with a curse, rising up to kiss her hard. His mouth almost brutal as he claimed her lips, and he ground his cock along the seam of her jeans, making her clit pulse. "Jeans," he said when he finally lifted his head, his fingers already fumbling to open her pants. "Jeans need to come off now."

She laughed and released her legs from around his waist. "You're speaking in monosyllables!"

"I do that when I'm fixated on something I want," he told her, and then moved around to her side, one hand between her shoulder blades and one on her shoulder as he guided her back until she was lying stretched out on the bar top. Her legs dangled over the end and he grabbed his shirt to tuck under her head as a makeshift pillow.

"And what do you want?" She knew she was teasing him, but she couldn't help herself. It was intoxicating being the focus of Tucker's world, and she was riding high.

"You. In every way I can think of. But for right now, I want to return the favor you did for me earlier tonight."

"Believe me, that was no favor, but feel free to do anything you want. Just promise me you locked every damned door."

"Locked and double checked them all. No one is going to interrupt us this time."

"That's what I wanted to hear, lover." She unzipped her jeans and then burst out laughing as she lifted up her foot and stared at it. "I think we got ahead of ourselves. Boots first."

Tucker ran a hand down her thigh all the way to her toes, leaving a trail of fire in its wake. "When I sketch you, I want you to wear those. Nothing else, just those damn sexy boots."

"Anyone ever mention you're hot when you get all bossy?"

His lips curved up into a grin and his dimple flashed. "Not until tonight."

"Well you are." She relaxed as he tugged off her boots, enjoying having someone undress her. Warm hands touched her waist and she arched her back, wriggling her hips as he skinned her jeans down her legs and off. She lifted her head to find him staring at her, his big body between her thighs and his hands resting on her knees as he stared at her naked body with raw hunger.

"You're not wearing panties."

"I thought it might save time."

He laughed at that and bent over to brush a kiss to her navel, working his way slowly down to her soaking wet pussy. He lifted her legs up over his shoulders and parted her labia with his thumbs, blowing a stream of warm air over her throbbing clit.

"Tucker, please!" She wiggled her hips, trying to get him to touch her and relieve the ache. He stroked his thumb alongside her clitoris without connecting and she mewled in need and frustration.

"That's the sound I was waiting for," he said. Then he was feasting on her pussy, sucking and licking her so thoroughly that her vision greyed and she keened until there was no air left in her lungs.

He was relentless, tonguing her clit over and over again until she was shaking with the need to come. He kept her at the brink, holding her at the edge of the abyss, until finally he plunged two fingers inside her and pressed down on her clit with his tongue, sending her hurtling into the most incredible orgasm she'd ever had.

She was still trying to get her breath back when something tingled at the edge of her awareness. It was a sense of familiarity that hadn't been there before, and then she heard footsteps. Her legs were still draped over Tucker's shoulders, which meant he wasn't the one walking across the room...so who was watching? The odd sense of familiarity grew stronger and she felt Tucker straighten up, easing her legs back down to the bar, but he didn't seem agitated. She turned her head and opened her eyes as the new arrival finally spoke, revealing his identity.

"Holy shit. Am I glad I came home early so I could see that."

Byron was back. She sat up and snatched up Tucker's damp shirt, covering herself even as her cheeks heated with embarrassment.

How long had he been watching them?

CHAPTER TWELVE

Byron had been watching the weather reports closely, so when Environment Canada announced a heavy snow warning for the mid and northern island, he knew right away it was time to pack up and head home. He canceled the last of his meetings, made his apologies and hit the highway just as the sky filled with storm clouds.

He'd tried to call Tucker to let him know he was coming home, but his phone had gone the way of so many others and refused to turn on. Perfect timing.

It had taken him longer than he'd hoped to get back, but the snow was only starting to fall by the time he was on the last stretch. That was when he felt his connection to Tucker kick in. It was an almost overwhelming sense of lust combined with flashes of Vivian's face and body that nearly sent him skidding off the road into the ditch.

He couldn't tell if Tucker had partially opened the link on purpose or if he was simply so caught up in what he was doing with Vivian that his control had slipped. Of course, Tucker also thought Byron was more than a hundred and fifty miles away, too far for their connection to work save in case of death or dire injury.

No matter the reason, the feelings grew stronger with every passing mile, and Byron found himself driving to Breakers instead of to his house in Kismet Cove. Both the selkie and the man were in agreement. Whatever was happening between his blood-brother and their woman, he had to be there. He had to be a part of it.

He pulled into the parking lot and frowned as he noticed that the signs were dark and the parking lot was empty. It was only eleven o'clock, the bar should have been open for another three hours, but it was clearly closed. That explained why Tucker had time to be getting it on with Vivian, but there was no way he shut down their business early just to get laid.

The snow was starting to come down hard by the time he had the truck parked and gotten inside, barely able to think past the incredibly hot images pouring into his mind. He dropped his bags off in the kitchen and headed through the doors to the main bar, already knowing exactly what he'd see when he got there. His dick was straining at his zipper as he stepped around the corner to spot Vivian stretched out on the bar, naked and beautiful. Her face was a mask of ecstasy and her long legs were wrapped around Tucker's shoulders.

"I'm here." Byron eased the link open a little wider and groaned as the connection to Tucker's mind flooded his with a barrage of sexual thoughts.

"Where?" Tucker threw the query at him so hard it was physically painful.

"Dial it back, will you? I'm standing by the kitchen door, watching you make our pretty redhead scream."

"Pervert."

"Dude, I'm not the one currently having sex on a bar."

"Jealous?" Tucker sent the thought at him and then closed the connection, leaving Byron with only his own rapidly growing desires to deal with.

He stayed near the door, watching his best friend take the woman they were both dating to the brink and then finally sending her flying right over it. Her breathless cries filled the room and he had to clench his hands into fists to ensure he didn't start jerking off to the scene playing out in front of him.

She was beautiful and sensual, and he knew if she saw him jerking off in the shadows like a freak she was likely to cut off a body part or two. Watching her with Tucker was the most erotic thing he'd ever seen in his life. He wanted to see it again, and that wouldn't happen if he didn't handle this next bit right. Clearly, things between Vivian and Tucker had heated up while he was gone, and that gave him hope that maybe there was a future for the three of them.

Now all he had to do was figure out where he fit into all this. That is, if Viv was still interested in exploring the idea of the three of them together.

I guess I'm going to have the answer to that any second now.

As her soft cries of pleasure faded to greedy gasps for air, he straightened up and slowly walked over to them and announced his presence.

"Holy shit. Am I glad I came home early so I could see that."

Vivian's head turned and her big hazel eyes went wide as she spotted him standing there. She looked flushed and deliciously rumpled, and it was all he could do not to cover the last few feet between them and kiss her swollen lips.

"You're home early," she said as she scrambled to cover herself with what looked to be one of Tucker's shirts, denying him the pleasure of her naked body. "How long have you been here?" she demanded.

He scrubbed a hand through his curls and gave her his best puppy dog look. "Long enough I should be apologizing for not announcing my presence, but frankly, slim, I'm not at all sorry I got to see that."

She glanced at Tucker, her carefully schooled expression giving away no sign of what she was thinking. "How long did you know he was there?"

"Not long. Let's say by that point I had absolutely no intention of stopping what I was doing. Not when you were so close." Tucker came around the bar and held out his arms to her, but she ignored him and hopped down unassisted on the far side, using it to shield her from their gaze as she pulled the shirt over her head so she was at least nominally covered.

Shit. She isn't happy.

"When I agreed to date both of you, that didn't mean I gave up all expectations of privacy or basic courtesy." She crossed her arms across her chest, looking from one to the other with agitation.

"No, you didn't," Byron said, choosing his words with care. He'd screwed this up enough already. He didn't want to make it worse. Not when what he wanted more than anything else was finally within his reach.

"I'm sorry. I came home early because of the storm and decided to check in. When I saw the place was already closed I was a little worried so I came in to check on things and well, uh…wow. I forgot my manners. Hell, I pretty much forgot to breathe. That was the hottest thing I've ever seen."

"Mhmm." She gave him an irritated look, but there was a hint of a smile on her lips as she turned to Tucker. "Next time it's a question of letting me know we have company or giving me an orgasm, which choice are you going to make?"

Tucker gave her a sheepish grin. "The one that doesn't piss you off?"

She bit back a laugh at that. "Okay, I'll give you half marks for that. The correct answer was the first one. If we have surprise company, let me know so I can decide if I want to be on display or not."

"Got it."

Tucker came around the bar and opened his arms to her. "I'm sorry, Viv. I wasn't thinking straight. In fact, I wasn't thinking at all. I should have considered your feelings."

Byron watched as she went into Tucker's arms and laid her head on his chest. That small act made it very clear that their relationship had deepened despite the fact he'd only been gone a few short days, and a part of him wondered if he was about to be left behind.

"You're forgiven. This time. "

"Thank you. I really am sorry. I hate that we embarrassed you." Tucker's arms closed around her.

"I'm sorry too." Byron said, but he stayed right where he was, rooted to the floor by growing uncertainty.

Viv lifted her head from Tucker's chest to look at him, a myriad of emotions in her beautiful eyes. "I'm not with you two to be some kind of sex toy. If this is going to work, we're going to have to work on trusting each other."

"You are not a sex toy. Neither of us thinks of you that way. I screwed up, slim. I'm sorry. This is all new territory for all of us."

"Apology accepted," she finally spoke as her tiny smile grew warmer. "So, now we have that dealt with, does anyone have a clue what happens now?" she asked, and both he and Tucker chuckled.

"That all depends on you," Byron opted to cut straight to the heart of the matter. "If you tell me to go, I'll be out of here in two minutes. I'll call you tomorrow and we can talk then. Or I can stay and we can start figuring out how this is going to work for us. The *three* of us."

Tucker nodded in agreement and then chimed in with his thoughts. "I'll take you any way I can get you, sugar, but I'm still hoping you're crazy-brave enough to consider taking on both of us."

"So this is really okay? You're not going to beat on each other now?"

Byron let go of the breath he'd been holding since he'd said his piece, grateful that she was going to give them a chance. "We've had years to get used to this idea. It's just that we've never met a woman we wanted to share. Someone who wanted to *be* shared. So, no. We're not going to beat on each other."

He lifted a hand and reached out to her then. "What's your call, slim? Am I staying or leaving?"

She glanced over at Tucker one last time and then threw her hands in the air. "I've got to be fucking insane, but I don't want you to go. I have no idea how this is going to work, but I'm willing to at least try and see what happens." She paused and gave them each a stern look. "But only if you both promise to be respectful of me and my feelings. If something like this happens again, I'll be gone."

She crossed the floor between them and took his outreached hand. Then she led him back to where Tucker was standing, looking slightly bemused as she took his hand as well.

"I think we should head upstairs and talk," Tucker suggested. "But as much as I like holding your hand, I'm going to need to stop and grab your clothes on the way up. I don't need the cleaning staff discovering your bra draped over the beer taps come morning."

The look on Viv's face was enough to make Byron crack up and then double over with laughter. "Charlie would have a heart attack if he found that! Best we take it with us."

"Oh goddess," she groaned, and bowed her head as her cheeks turned crimson. "How many health code regulations did we break?"

"Oh, one or two," he teased, and she groaned again as Tucker gathered her things off the bar and rejoined them.

"Come on, let's get you upstairs before I'm tempted to add a few more violations to the list." Tucker grabbed her hand again and the three of them headed out. It was time for them to talk.

HER THIGHS WERE STILL sticky from the incredible orgasm Tucker had given her, but having both men in close proximity for the first time since Jess's wedding had Vivian's libido revving back up in record time.

Her body knew what it wanted. The trouble was in her head. She was struggling to silence a nagging voice that sounded a lot like her mother. It was currently calling her a shameless disgrace to the family for even considering getting involved with two men at once, and it was getting louder with every step she took. She wanted them, there was no denying that. But every relationship she'd ever been in had turned into a complete train wreck. If this went sideways there'd be enough explosions and destruction that Michael Bay would have to direct the movie version.

By the time they reached the top of the stairs, tiny tendrils of doubt were starting to take hold, tearing away at the happiness she'd felt only minutes before. As they walked back into Tucker's apartment, Byron spoke her name in a tender tone, tugging on her hand to draw her back against his chest. He wrapped his arms around her and held her, his breath tickling her ear as he nuzzled her hair.

Tucker turned around, dropping her clothes so he could cup a hand against her cheek. "It's going to be fine," he promised her. "I know you believe in fate, and so do we. I think this is supposed to happen."

"Fate's all fine and good, but what I'd like is a damned instruction manual," she grumbled. "All I have to go on here are romance novels and the advice of my best friend, who happens to be incommunicado while on her honeymoon."

Byron laughed and hugged her. "I think we can figure this out without a how-to guide."

She wrinkled her nose at that. "Of course you do. You're a man. Men never read instructions."

"We're going to have to try things out, and if something isn't working, we all have to agree to speak up. None of us is the type to suffer in silence, so…" Byron blew across the shell of her ear and she shivered in response. "I think we need to see how this goes. Less talk, more do."

"Less talk, more do?" Tucker repeated, shaking his head. "Man, we need to get you some new lines."

"Lines are for single guys," she pointed out. "If this is happening, then neither one of you is single anymore, and neither am I. Well, Tucker and I sort of worked that out earlier tonight, but now it applies to you too, Byron."

"I'm good with that." She could tell he was smiling by the tone of his voice.

"You should have seen Big Mike's face. He tried to stop her from entering the bar and she got up in his grill and told him she was my girlfriend," Tucker said with a grin and leaned in to kiss her. As their mouths met she could taste herself on his lips, and it was an erotic reminder of what they'd been doing not long ago.

"Wait until we tell him she's *our* girlfriend," Byron murmured in a voice ripe with satisfaction.

Vivian's inner voices started to chatter again and she slammed a heavy door on their negative mutterings. She'd made her decision. She was not going to regret it now. She'd never let other people's opinions affect her happiness before. She'd be damned if she was going to start now.

"You still owe me a first date though, Byron. We may be doing this out of order, but I still intend to collect."

"You got it," Byron said, and then loosened his hold enough that he could turn her around without letting go of her. When they were face-to-face he smiled and pressed a kiss to the tip of her nose. "Now, can I please have a kiss hello? I've been dreaming about our last kiss since I left you at the cabin that night."

"I'm glad you're home," she said, curling her hands into his sweater as she rose up to kiss him. Byron's mouth crashed down on hers and she found herself locked in his embrace. His kiss was heated, hard, and demanding, and the last of her doubts were burned away to ashes and dust as he showed her how much he needed her.

He kept kissing her until she was panting and dizzy. Her fingers tightened their grip on his sweater, needing the support to keep her balance. Only then did he lift his head and smile down at her, his green eyes as bright as sunlit emeralds.

"That was even better than I remembered." He slipped a hand down her back to lightly swat her ass. "And I have to say that knowing you're naked under that T-shirt is definitely enhancing the experience."

"Yeah, I noticed that I'm the only one not wearing pants. I think I'm at a distinct disadvantage." She cocked a brow at Byron in challenge. "Care to level the playing field here? At least Tucker's shirtless."

"Anything you want, slim." His smile morphed into a devilish grin as he let go of her to skin his sweater over his head, baring his chest. He was fit but not bulky, and the dusting of blond hairs that covered his chest dwindled to a treasure trail that led her eye down to the waistband of his broken-in jeans.

Temptation won out over everything else, and she

brushed her fingers down his trim stomach to graze the top of his pants before reversing course and stroking back up to his chest again. Desire blossomed again, sending out tendrils of heat that had her pussy throbbing and her fingers tingling as they stroked over bare skin.

"Much better," she told him.

"I think Tucker got tired of standing." Byron inclined his head in the direction of the couch. Viv turned to find her dark-haired lover seated, his big body settled comfortably with his arms behind his head as he watched them together. His gaze met hers and he patted his lap in silent invitation.

And this is where things get interesting.

Byron gave her a gentle nudge toward Tucker and she took the hint, crossing the room to the couch and settling herself sideways in his lap so that her legs crossed his thighs. The moment she was comfortable he captured her lips with his, giving her a slow, leisurely kiss that sent lust spiraling outward from deep in her core.

She expected Byron to sit down beside them, but instead he knelt on the floor by Tucker's feet, his hand stroking up her bare thigh. No words were said, but Tucker seemed to understand what Byron intended. He lifted and shifted her so that she was facing more or less forward as Byron arranged her legs so she was straddling Tucker's thighs. When they were done she was sitting with her legs parted and her pussy barely hidden by the hem of her borrowed shirt. Tucker's mouth was still on hers and Byron's fingers were tracing lazy circles across the tops of her thighs.

"I want to taste you," Byron told her as his hands stilled. "Will you let me do that?"

She broke her kiss with Tucker and looked down to where Byron was kneeling between her legs with an expression of raw hunger on his face.

"Yes," she whispered, feeling a rush of power at being able to control him with a single word. If she had denied him then he wouldn't have touched her. That knowledge gave her a sense of security and comfort. Safe in the arms of one lover with another at her feet, she tried to let it all go, freeing herself to enjoy this moment.

"Thank you," he murmured and then bowed his head to place several butterfly kisses along the inside of her knee. He kissed his way higher, an inch at a time, and Tucker spread his legs, taking hers with him until she was spread out between them like an offering.

"So pretty," Tucker whispered in her ear. "I want to see all of you, sugar. Are you ready for me to take this shirt off of you?"

She nodded and he groaned in approval before grabbing the shirt and whipping it off her so quickly she barely had time to raise her arms. He had his hands on her breasts before the shirt hit the floor. Byron lifted his head to stare at her, his eyes gleaming and his mouth quirked into a lopsided grin.

"I think we need to start a new theme at the bar. Topless Tuesdays. I'm willing to go shirtless if you are, Viv."

"I'm certain that's not legal," she managed to talk despite the fact Tucker was expertly fondling her breasts, lightly teasing her nipples until they were aching and hard.

"And *I'm* certain no one else gets to see her naked.

Period," Tucker grumbled. "I don't share well, and neither do you, bro."

That made Vivian laugh out loud, and she kept laughing until both men stopped what they were doing to stare at her. When she finally got her breath back to speak she gestured to the three of them before snickering again. "Sorry. It's just that you two seem to be doing a great job of sharing right now. At least from where I'm sitting."

"Glad you're enjoying it," Byron said and then dipped his head again, kissing his way ever closer to her now dripping pussy. His fingers stroked along the seam of her labia and her comeback was lost in a guttural moan of pleasure.

"Is he making you feel good, sugar?" Tucker's voice was a low, sensual whisper. "Are you going to come for him the way you came for me earlier?" His words short-circuited her brain and she turned her head to kiss him, too turned on to form a coherent thought. His tongue twined with hers, making her whimper against his mouth as Byron's fingers pressed into her folds and worked slow circles around her throbbing clit.

The sensation of having two men's hands touching her and two mouths tasting her at once was making her hotter than she had been in her life. She knew that if Byron would just touch her clit she'd come hard and fast. She squirmed in Tucker's lap, trying to get what she needed, but Byron would not be rushed.

"Not yet. I haven't gotten to taste you." He moved in close enough that his shoulders were brushing her knees and he could nuzzle the neatly trimmed curls of her pussy. His breath fanned over her wet skin while his fingers kept up their steady, teasing strokes, making her wriggle again.

Tucker tweaked her nipples and she nearly came out of his lap at the added stimulus. Before she could refill her lungs, Byron parted her labia with his thumbs and finally gave her what she needed, drawing her clit into his mouth and lashing it with the tip of his tongue until she was once again on the jagged edge of release.

Tucker ended their kiss, moving his mouth a few inches away from hers. "Fuck, I never thought I'd like watching, but I do. I like watching your face as Byron eats that pretty pussy. You're so tasty, I know he's loving it. Loving making you feel good. Are you going to come for us?

Tucker kissed her again before she could answer. Her muscles trembled and her breath was coming in ragged gasps between the moans that flowed into Tucker's mouth as he kissed and stroked her. Sensation piled onto sensation until she finally flew apart with a muffled cry. Her orgasm tore through her like a brutal storm, leaving her gasping and limp when it finally passed.

"You are glorious when you come," Tucker murmured as he lifted his head and let her breathe unobstructed.

"She's fucking glorious, period," Byron chimed in as he drew the back of his hand across his mouth and grinned up at her. "Glorious, gorgeous and all ours."

"You two are going to give me an inflated ego saying things like that." She stirred in Tucker's lap and he moved his legs so she was no longer stretched out on display. Feeling brazen, she turned her head to kiss Tucker, nipping at his lips before reaching out and tousling Byron's blond curls. "Thank you for making me feel like a goddess."

"You are a goddess," Tucker informed her.

"*Our* goddess," Byron added.

"Well then." She drew in a quick breath and decided to embrace whatever the fates had planned for her. "Your goddess wants to know if her devoted servants would like to take her to bed now."

Byron was up off the floor in seconds, eagerly helping her out of Tucker's lap.

"All you had to do was ask."

CHAPTER THIRTEEN

TUCKER WATCHED as Byron drew Vivian to her feet. He felt a brief pang of jealousy as she left his arms to fall into Byron's, but it passed quickly. Sharing her body and her heart was going to take some getting used to. There was an undeniable sense of rightness to things, though. The more he explored his reactions the clearer it got that the part of him he thought of as his selkie half had already accepted the situation without complaint or question. In fact, that part of his psyche was downright content. The smug bastard was happy to have Tucker acknowledging his true nature.

I'm still not turning into a damned seal for you.

He hadn't altered form in years. It was a petty act of defiance and he knew it. That didn't matter though, because it was one of the few ways he could set himself apart from the colony whose rules had made his life hellish and eventually torn his family to shreds.

He got up off the couch and gave himself a mental shake. This was not the time for thinking about his past.

Not when there was a beautiful woman heading for his bed…without him. That thought spurred him to action and he covered the space between them in a few long strides. When he caught up to Vivian he simply scooped her into his arms, ignoring her startled yelp as he carried her the rest of the way, tossing her into the middle of his king-sized bed.

"Subtle," Byron snickered.

"You were moving too slowly," he shot back, and headed for the near side of the bed as Byron circled around to the far side.

"Says the guy who was still on the couch last time I looked back." Viv was laughing as she cocked her head in question. "What's got you all fired up?"

"You do." He hardly recognized his own voice it was so distorted by desire. He stopped at the edge of the bed, his hands on the waistband of his jeans, not moving. He sent a warning flicker of thought to Byron that pulled his blood-brother up short. They'd been communicating telepathically since they'd entered his apartment, using their link to coordinate their seduction.

"She needs to make the first move."

Byron caught his meaning and gave a brief nod, then said, "Viv, I think you should help Tucker out of those jeans. Is that what you want? Because once we're naked, we're not going to let you out of here until morning at the very least."

She gave them both a cocky grin and a nod before reaching for Tucker, brushing his hands out of her way as she began undoing his jeans for the second time that day. Memories of the first time brought his already half-hard dick surging to life behind the zipper. He would love to experience her sweet mouth again, but he wanted to claim her pussy even more.

He forced himself to stay still as she undressed him. His hands were clenched at his sides to keep himself from touching her. By the time she had his pants and briefs tugged to his calves she'd reached as far as she could from her position at the edge of the bed, so he toed off his shoes and stripped off his jeans himself. He was completely out of patience and all he wanted was to finally have her in his arms, skin to skin.

It didn't matter that she'd already made him come tonight, or that he'd had her naked and screaming on his bar and couch. She was his addiction, and he needed her so badly he wasn't sure he'd ever get her out of his system.

The second he kicked clear of his clothes he joined Viv on the bed, hands in her hair and her soft body tugged up hard against his. Her tits were pressed flat against his chest and he felt the vibrations of her laughter as he cut her off with a kiss.

He felt the mattress dip and the small part of his brain that was still able to function properly knew that Byron had joined them. Even if he hadn't there was no missing Vivian's reaction to the other man's presence. Her joyful laughter morphed into a throaty moan and she arched herself into Tucker, her stomach rubbing along the hard shaft of his cock. She squirmed against him again and his eyes nearly rolled back into his head with pleasure. She was so fucking responsive that he knew that making love to her was going to be like riding the edge of an oncoming typhoon.

He kissed her one last time before releasing her so she could turn to Byron. She lingered in his arms for a moment, kissing him again before rolling off of him and into his best friend's embrace. That maneuver exposed her back to him, so he took advantage of her preoccupation to enjoy her tattoo. He ran his hands and mouth over the elegant lines of her Celtic-style dragon, starting at the base of her spine and working his way upward.

It took a delicious age for him to explore every line and curve until finally he was nibbling the soft skin at the nape of her neck as she writhed and twisted between them.

His link to Byron was still open so they could communicate, and that meant they were both getting glimmers of each other's physical and emotional state. Their bond had always been exceptionally strong, but until today they had always shielded themselves when either of them was with a woman. Now things were different, and as the lines between his pleasure and Byron's blurred he wondered if they would ever be able to go back to the way things had been before.

"We can't go back." Byron's thoughts touched his. *"So we better figure out a way to keep her."*

"With our track records? We're going to need divine intervention."

Vivian's skin felt like it was bathed in flames and she couldn't seem to catch her breath. Every kiss, every caress heightened the sensation until she was nearly feverish with need. When Byron eased her up onto her hands and knees she followed his cues eagerly. They were now long past doubt or second thoughts. All three of them were working toward the same goal, mutual pleasure.

Fingers swept through her hair, drawing her head back and she found herself staring into Byron's eyes. The lust she saw there mirroring her own.

"Are you ready for us?" he asked, his hand working the thick length of his cock as he settled on his knees in front of her. "I want to feel your mouth on my dick while Tucker fucks you."

"She has the hottest mouth. You're never going to want her to stop," Tucker warned him from somewhere behind her. She started to look back but Byron tightened his fingers a little, holding her gaze on him.

"Eyes on me, sweetheart. I want to see your face when he buries his cock inside you."

"It's always the quiet ones," she muttered, grinning up at him. "I never pegged you for a dirty talker."

"I'm full of surprises, slim." His words held a wealth of wicked promises, and she licked her lips as a flurry of erotic thoughts filled her head. The X-rated images made her pussy clench and pulse, needing something to fill her empty channel.

She felt the mattress bow and then Tucker's thighs were pressed up against hers, his fingers stroking down her hips to the curve of her ass. She spread her legs wider, inviting him to take her, but instead of his cock she felt his fingers brush against her soaking folds. She knew he was teasing her deliberately, so she bit her lip and refused to give him any sign. It would have worked too, except that Byron was watching her, his green eyes laser bright.

"Whatever you did to her, do it again." He trailed a finger along the top of her ear. "That's really sexy, the way you're biting your lower lip to stay quiet."

"Bastard," she grumbled, her next words lost in a

keening wail as Tucker slid two fingers into her pussy and started slowly fucking her with them.

"Oh yeah, she likes that. I wish you could see her face right now, Tucker. She's so turned on I think she'd cream if you touched her clit." He glanced up and gave his friend a wicked smirk. "So be careful not to. I think she needs to wait before she gets to come again."

"Safety tip." Tucker drawled as he kept pumping his fingers in and out of her cunt. "You may want to quit teasing her. Any minute she's going to have her teeth around your dick, and payback's a bitch."

"She wouldn't do that to me," Byron said and winked at her. "Would you?"

"If you keep telling him not to let me come? I might consider it," she said, baring her teeth and clicking them together to make her point. "And quit talking about me like I'm not in the room. I'm here too."

"Sorry." He apologized. "I'm new to dirty talking with more than one person present." He stroked her hair again. "And sweetheart, I know you're not going to hurt me, just like we're not going to hurt you."

"Never," Tucker grunted in agreement as he withdrew his fingers. She moaned in protest and rocked backward, following his hand. "I need both hands for a second here, sugar."

She heard the crinkle of foil tearing and knew he was putting on a condom. As the anticipation grew she turned her attention to Byron, dropping her gaze so she could enjoy a proper look. She'd barely gotten to see him fully naked. Now he was tantalizingly close. The blond treasure trail she'd seen earlier led all the way to his cock. Hard, dark and thick enough she knew she'd feel every inch of him filling her when it came time for him to claim her pussy the way Tucker was about to.

Byron kept one hand on her head and dropped the other to his cock, giving it an idle stroke. "Is this what you want?"

She licked her lips and leaned forward enough she could nuzzle his hand. "I want to be connected to both of you."

"Exactly," Tucker murmured and she felt him move in tight behind her, the thick head of his dick coming to rest at the entrance to her pussy. "That's exactly what we want too." With that he started to move, breaching her body in short, shallow strokes that teased them both and left her aching for more.

"Look at me," Byron directed her, tugging at her again.

She stared up at him as Tucker kept up his teasing thrusts, her entire body screaming for him to take her and fuck her hard.

"Are you ready for us? Please say yes, I don't think I can wait any longer." Byron's voice was thick with lust. His hold on her hair tightened just enough the tingling bite blended with the pleasure flooding her as Tucker finally drove himself all the way home, groaning her name as he bottomed out inside her.

"Yes," she whispered.

"Ignore him. He lives under the delusion he's the one in charge." Tucker stroked a hand down her back, following the lines of her tattoo.

"I think I know of a way to shut him up. Don't stop what you're doing, Tucker." She pushed back against him, making both of them gasp and then reached out to wrap her hand around Byron's cock. She drew him in and swirled her tongue over the tip, using a delicate touch to entice and tease until she knew she had his complete attention. He loosened his grip on her hair and groaned low in his throat when she finally took him deep. As she eased him into her mouth she purred, letting the vibrations reverberate up his shaft and into his balls.

"Fuck yes!" Byron exclaimed.

She kept him deep in her mouth, using her tongue to caress him in time to the slow, rolling rhythm of Tucker's hips. The world faded away, leaving her in a place where only pleasure existed. The three of them were intertwined and forming ties between them that she suspected would remain long after this night was done. It had the feel of magic, and she let the energy of their lovemaking fill her until she was overflowing with it.

Tucker's hands gripped her hips, pulling her in closer as he started moving faster. Each thrust was deeper and stronger than the one before it, and soon she was caught up in the power of his passion. She rode his every movement, letting him push her forward onto Byron's cock and then drawing her back again. Byron's thighs were rigid and she knew he was fighting her, resisting his need to come. She sucked harder, hollows forming in her cheeks as she lightly raked her teeth across his glans.

He gave a shuddering groan and she did it again and then again, pushing him to his limits. His cock swelled in her mouth and he growled her name in warning, releasing her hair so she could pull away from him if she wished. Instead she let Tucker's next thrust push her so far forward that Byron's cock touched the back of her throat as he started to come. His seed jetted into her, hot and salty, and she used her tongue to milk him dry.

Tucker chose that moment to reach between her legs, his fingers pinpointing her swollen clit with breathtaking accuracy. He rolled the delicate bundle of nerves between his fingers as he shifted his hips, changing the angle of his thrusts so that the head of his cock was stroking her sweet spot. That was more than her body could take, and she cried out as her orgasm erupted, tearing through her like a hurricane. He came only seconds later, his cries blending with hers as the three of them crumpled in slow motion onto the bed.

Byron withdrew from her mouth and fell sideways onto the quilt while she collapsed face first with Tucker atop her.

"I'm dead," Byron muttered a little while longer. "I have to be dead, because I heard angels singing and then there was a bright light."

She giggled softly and cracked open one eye to stare up at him. "Are you always this dramatic?"

"Only right after earth-shattering events," Byron said as he reached out to take her hand, interlacing their fingers.

"Earth-shattering is a good word for it." Tucker's smoke-and-whisky voice sounded even rougher than usual. He kissed her bare shoulder before easing himself off and away from her. "Are you okay? That got a little more intense than I expected for our first try."

"I am better than okay." Vivian rolled onto her back and stretched, no longer at all concerned about anything as incidental as modesty after what they'd experienced together.

Tucker leaned over and kissed the corner of her mouth.

"Glad to hear it." Then he rose from the bed and she guessed he was heading for the bathroom.

Byron drew their joined hands to his mouth, brushing kisses to her fingers. "I have never been so thankful for a snowstorm in my life. Being here for this was...amazing."

"I'm glad you were here too."

He let his gaze slide over her body and she could tell the moment he spotted her navel ring, because his mouth curved up into a devilish grin. "I bet Tucker went nuts when he saw this." He touched the piercing with his free hand and she quivered as that simple caress sent sparks dancing along her skin. Byron's eyes darkened with lust and he traced his fingertip around her navel, watching as a wave of goosebumps chased across her skin.

"He likes it, yeah." She lifted her head to look pointedly at his hand. "Apparently so do you."

"I've never dated a woman who had one, so I didn't know I would."

"Had one what? A brain?" Tucker reappeared with a smirk on his handsome face. "He's right, you're the first woman he's gone out with who could count past ten without kicking off her shoes. He has a thing for beach bunnies. Really kind of sad in a man his age."

"No, smart ass. We weren't talking about Viv's brain, we were talking about her belly button ring. I like it. You're quite the package, Viv. Sexy, smart...you might be the perfect girl for us."

"Not quite perfect." Tucker was chuckling as he settled on the bed beside her. "She can't swim."

"What? Everyone swims!" Byron looked totally dumbfounded as he stared at her. "Tell me he's kidding."

"Well, I can doggie paddle a little, but that's it," she

confessed. "So when we go out on the boat, I am literally putting my life in your hands. If I drown, I'm going to come back and haunt your ass as a very soggy ghost."

"You really can't swim." Byron was looking stunned. "Well, the weather is going to suck for a couple of days anyway, so I think I have a new plan for our date. Tomorrow I'm going to teach you how to swim."

"Good idea. I don't think Darius would have a problem with that."

"Why would Jess's father-in-law have a problem with me learning how to swim?"

"He wouldn't. It's just that there isn't actually a community pool in town. There is one in Kismet Cove though, a really nice, heated, indoor one. It's for the residents only."

Vivian wondered again what exactly the deal was with Kismet Cove. Vivian hadn't really explained why they lived apart from everyone. They seemed nice and normal, not at all cultish or anything, but they were *very* protective of their privacy. "So you'd need permission for me to swim there? Your families sure take their privacy seriously."

Both men went silent and she caught a look pass between them. A look she didn't like very much. "I'm not a big fan of secrets, guys. Is there something about your home I should be aware of?"

"Kismet Cove was created to give our families a haven. It's a place where we can live according to our traditions without interference," Byron explained.

"They've got some outdated ways of thinking, which is why I don't live there. They're not really open to outsiders.

It takes some time for them to trust someone new," Tucker added.

"Uh huh." She let her gaze flick between them. "So, if I'm an outsider, how are they going to feel about you two dating me?"

"My parents will be thrilled." Byron grinned at her. "You have no idea how hard I had to work to keep Mom away from you during the wedding reception. She wanted to ask you a hundred questions, and that was just because someone told her you were holding my hand. When I tell them you're with us I won't be able to save you from her interrogation. They don't care if you're from around here or not. They just hope you'll take pity on the two of us and save us from bachelorhood. Billy's too young to care, he still thinks all girls are gross."

"Wait, back up. Who is Billy?" she asked, confused.

"My baby bro. He's eleven and his only concerns these days are surfing and video games." Byron's voice was full of pride and affection as he talked about his brother.

"Your mom had two boys twenty years apart? I bet that was a surprise."

"After my mom found out she was pregnant she didn't speak to either of my dads for a week!" Byron laughed at the memory. "You'll meet them all at the Christmas Eve party."

"About that," Tucker said as he took her other hand in his. "I know you've been invited to go as Jess's guest, but what would you say to coming as our date instead?"

Byron squeezed her fingers. "I'd like that. I'm not going to lie, there will be a few people there who won't be thrilled to see us with a stranger, but we'll ignore them. I'd like everyone to know we've got someone amazing in our lives."

"I haven't been in a few years," Tucker said, and Byron snickered.

"A few years? Try nearly a decade."

"Quit nagging me, we're trying to convince her to come with us, not scare her off." Tucker lifted her hand to his lips and drifted several light kisses to her knuckles. "I'd take the night off from the bar and we'd do this up properly. It's been a long time since I've had a reason to celebrate the holidays. What do you say?"

She mulled over their offer, her heart swelling at the idea that these two men both wanted to tell the world that she was theirs. "You two have yourselves a date for Christmas Eve."

"Great!" Byron cheered.

"Thank you," Tucker murmured and drew her slowly into his arms. "I think I know how to celebrate this." His mouth claimed hers in a searing kiss.

Byron's moved in behind her, nibbling his way down her throat, and Vivian happily gave herself over to their attentions. After all, they had a lot to celebrate.

CHAPTER FOURTEEN

*T*HIS IS DEFINITELY *the best idea for a date I've ever had.*

Byron watched as Vivian stripped off her clothes to reveal the green and gold bikini she was wearing underneath. It didn't matter that he'd spent half the night and a good part of the morning making love to her. Just the sight of her long legs and soft skin had him hard as a rock again.

There were windows high up for light, but the walls around the pool were solid and tiled in soothing blues and greens, allowing complete privacy for the swimmers. The air inside the swimming area was almost tropical compared to the weather outside, and he was looking forward to the two hours he'd managed to talk Darius into giving him alone with Viv.

Thankfully the snowfall was heavy enough to have almost everyone staying indoors, so he didn't feel guilty when he locked the door behind him and put up the "Closed for Maintenance" sign. The last thing he needed was for one of the residents to arrive and transform before he could wave them off. There were some things that they weren't ready to have Vivian know, and at the top of the list was the fact she was dating a pair of shapeshifters.

He tugged off his own clothes, dropping them on one of the lounge chairs scattered around the pool deck before joining her at the shallow end of the pool. He didn't bother trying to hide the effect she was having on him as he waded into the water and held out a hand to her. "Come on in. It's not as warm as your hot tub, but it's pretty comfortable."

The saltwater pool was kept on the warmer side so that even the youngest pups and the seniors could enjoy it for long stretches at a time. It was a haven for them all, a safe place to change to their seal form and swim without any risk of being seen. It was especially important for the young ones to have a secure location where they could learn to control their transformations.

For the younger pups, just being submerged could be enough to trip the change to their seal form, and so every family made use of the saltwater pool to practice, and to enjoy themselves without fear of being spotted.

"I feel a bit silly," she confessed as she took his hand and waded in. "Are you sure this is really necessary?"

"Necessary? No. But you'll feel a lot safer out there if you know the basics of staying afloat and can swim at least a little. Jess isn't the first person who has ended up caught by a rogue wave up here. If she hadn't been such a strong swimmer she'd have gone under before Rory and Evan could have gotten to her."

"I read her account of it. Terrifying." Viv lowered herself into the water and took a seat on the bottom stair so that the water was up to her shoulders. "So you're saying I'm not even safe on the beach? I may need to reconsider staying here if that's the case."

"Well, you're fine on the beach. Jess was standing on the rocks, during a storm. And pretty soon you're going to be able to swim just fine."

"Uh huh. I did mention I can barely doggie-paddle, right?"

"We're going to start a little more basic than that. I'm going to teach you how to float."

She gave him an amused look. "I think this is all an elaborate ploy for you to get to me mostly naked in a locked room. How is floating going to save me if I fall off this boat of yours?"

"Floating beats sinking," he pointed out and tugged at her hand. "And while it is very likely I'm going to enjoy this next bit immensely, you are going to learn to swim while I get to hold your mostly naked, very sexy body. I consider this a win-win situation." Not to mention that his kind spent a lot of time on or in the water, and if she was going to be a part of his world, he wanted to know she was comfortable in the water. Hell, maybe she could finally coax Tucker back into his seal form.

He led her down the length of the pool until the water was chest high and lapping at the top of her shoulders. "Now comes the fun part." He let go of her hand and scooped her into his arms without warning, enjoying this chance to have her all to himself. She shrieked with laughter and kicked her feet, sending water flying in all directions. The sounds of her merriment bounced off the tiled walls, echoing around the large space. It was such a contagious noise that he found himself laughing with her. Somehow they went from laughing to kissing and the echoes faded to silence. Warm, wet arms twined themselves around his neck while her mouth parted beneath his in an invitation to play.

Their tongues tangled and he shifted her in his arms, letting her slick skin slide along his as he forgot everything else but the sensual creature in his arms. He wanted her with every cell of his being, and he walked her over to the side of the pool, determined to have her.

"She doesn't need a lesson in that," Tucker's thought popped into his head accompanied by a sense of laughter. *"And for fuck's sake, shield your thoughts better. I'm trying to work here!"*

"Sorry, I thought I was." They'd never had a problem shielding their minds from each other before, but Vivian seemed to affect both of them the same way. Neither one of them could completely shut off the link when they were with her, not without more effort than it should have taken.

Byron stopped walking and lifted his head to give Viv a mock glower. "Are you trying to distract me from this lesson?"

"Maybe…was it working?" she asked with a wicked laugh.

"Yes, it was. But that's not going to help you learn to swim. I think you need some incentive. How about if I promise to make you come once for every assignment you pass?"

"That sounds like this is going to be the raunchiest swimming lesson ever given. Consider me your eager student." She waggled her brows at him. "Oh, does this mean we can play naughty lifeguard and sexy beach bunny later? I always liked *Baywatch*…"

He groaned and carried her back to the center of the pool. "Lessons first, sexy time later."

"Yes, mister big, strong lifeguard." He caught her fluttering her lashes at him and burst out laughing again.

"If you keep stalling we're going to be out of time before we get to the incentives."

She went still in his arms, her lips quirking into a barely suppressed grin. "Okay. I'm listening. So how do I float?"

"Relax and don't panic when I move my hands away from you. I'll only let go of you a little, I'll stop you if you start to sink. The trick is to pick a spot on the ceiling and stare at it. Then take a deep breath and hold it. The air will help make you buoyant."

He lowered her into the water, coaching her every step of the way. It was humbling to have her trust him enough that she relaxed completely on her first try. When he moved his hands away an inch or so she barely reacted. Soon she was able to float on her back with ease, and as she bobbed in the water in front of him she turned to him and gave him a slow wink.

"That's one."

IT WASN'T easy keeping her mind on her swimming lessons when Byron was close enough she could feel the heat from his bare skin warming the water between them. He was so patient and kind that no matter how frustrated she got he kept coaching her in that calm, sexy voice of his. She'd managed to dunk herself half a dozen times already learning to tread water, but she was finally getting the hang of it.

Sort of.

"Slower. You keep trying to make yourself stay up by kicking hard and fast, and that isn't going to work. Relax and only move as fast as you have to." Easy for him to say, he was treading water beside her with the ease of long practice, his arms and legs moving in slow, easy patterns which made her frantic kicking seem almost cartoonish by comparison.

"It's hard to relax when if you stop, you go under," she sputtered and fought her own instincts, forcing herself to slow everything down another notch.

"Better. But I think that's enough of that for now. You're going to tire yourself out." He slipped an arm around her waist, drawing her into his chest. She stopped paddling, letting him pull her along until they reached the shallow end again.

"So did I pass?" she asked, and he rocked a hand from side to side.

"I'd say you did pretty well for someone who couldn't float when she got into the water today, but you're not ready for the Olympics quite yet."

She blinked some of the salty water out of her eyes and blew a raspberry at him. "I'll do better next time."

"I'm sure you will, but for now I'm going to show you how your lifejacket functions if you went overboard. You'll feel a whole lot safer once you know how well it works.

He waded over to the edge and hauled himself out, giving her a chance to enjoy the way his wet swim trunks clung to the curve of his ass and the nicely toned muscles of his thighs. He came back a moment later with a bulky looking, red-orange vest in his hand and tossed it so it landed with a flat slap on the water in front of her.

"It's not fashionable, but it will save your life. Go ahead, grab it and try to push it under the water. You'll see what I mean."

Viv did just that, but the vest was so buoyant it took a fair amount of force to push it under and keep it there. "Okay, I'm impressed."

He hopped back in and showed her how to unbuckle it so she could get the awkward contraption on. Then he zipped and cinched it onto her so that it was snug. "That's how it'll feel when we're out on the boat. Consider it an incentive plan for you to learn to swim so we can upgrade you to something like a floater coat. Those are a lot less bulky."

"Do they come in something besides retina-burning red?"

"Yes, they do. But that color you're wearing is a lot easier to spot in the water."

"Oh sure, be logical. I'm not sure my personal safety is worth this sort of fashion nightmare." She tugged at the strap. "It is *really* ugly."

"Yep, but it works." Without warning he grabbed the sides of her vest and tossed her up out of the water and backward several feet.

She screamed and threw out her arms, caught totally off guard. When she hit the water she expected to go under, but the life vest held her head above the surface and she found herself bobbing along.

"Byron! What the fuck was that?" she demanded, trying to regain her feet and fight the buoyancy of the vest at the same time.

"It was a demonstration. You fell overboard, and see? You're safe and sound."

"I may be, but you're going to be battered and bruised when I get to you!" She flailed in the water, making no headway. "And how the hell do you swim in one of these? I can't even touch the bottom anymore!"

Byron was laughing so hard he couldn't answer her for a moment, and she took advantage of his distracted state to catch him in the face with a handful of water.

"Quit laughing and help me! What kind of teacher throws his students into the water and then laughs at them?"

"Sorry about laughing at you," he said, and flashed a smile that made her blood heat. "But you looked so damned cute I couldn't help myself." He made his way to her and grabbed her outreached hand, pulling her back into the shallows until she could stand on her own again.

"You chucked me into the drink!" she reminded him as she gave him a playful smack to the shoulder.

"It was that, or have you get out of the pool, walk around to the deep end and jump. I figured this way would be easier for you."

"Interesting logic. I'm glad you were never actually a swim instructor, I'm pretty sure you'd have gotten fired for that sort of thinking."

"I will have you know that until we opened Breakers, I worked as a surf instructor. I was good at it!"

"Clearly you never threw any of them into a wave and yelled 'good luck' as they flailed in panic." She started working at the triple set of straps that held her into her vest. "Can I get out of this thing now?"

"That depends on if you want two orgasms or three."

Well shit.

She pouted at him for a second and then let go of the buckles. "Three please. So, what do I need to do to earn the last one?"

"That's easy. Tuck your hands under your arms and draw your legs up to your chest. Then, float."

It wasn't the most comfortable she'd ever been, but she managed to follow instructions. "Now what?"

"That's it. If you ever go overboard with a lifejacket on, that's what you do to stay warm until you get fished out." He tugged her back into his arms and kissed her. "You are now cleared to go boating with me any time you like. We'll have you swimming like a fish by the time summer rolls around, and then I'm going to teach you to surf."

"That sounds like fun, but only if you swear to me you won't throw me into an oncoming wave!"

He caught her chin in his hand and tipped her head up so she was looking him squarely in the eyes. "I would never do anything to risk your safety. Never. You're precious to me. To both of us. You're a gift, Vivian, and we're grateful to have you in our lives."

A bit more of the wall of reservations around her heart crumbled at his words, and she kissed him before either of them could speak. They had only known each other a few days, but here they were making summer plans, talking about being in each other's lives. She knew if she looked past the lust and the chemistry there were deep feelings growing for both of her men, the kind of feelings that would lead to a broken heart if she didn't start being more careful. Trust needed to be earned over time, and there hadn't been enough of that, not yet.

Byron had been walking them to the edge of the pool

while her thoughts had been tumbling and her tongue had been dancing with his. He lifted her out of the water without breaking their kiss, and he managed to undo the life vest without looking down even once. He pushed it off her shoulders and reached around to undo her bikini, dropping it onto the deck with a wet *plop* the second he got it off her.

Powerful arms curved around her body as he buried his face between her breasts, his unshaven jaw rasping lightly against the sensitive skin. Her nipples puckered into diamond-hard nubs and her clit began to throb as he dragged his tongue down the valley of her breasts and then moved his hand to capture one taut nubbin in his mouth.

She buried her hands in his hair, holding him close while she tried to clasp her legs around his middle. She was seated back too far to reach completely so she shimmied herself closer, rubbing her breasts against his face with every move she made.

Byron growled and nipped at her breast, the noise he made feral and fierce against her flesh. The pain morphed into pleasure as he ran his tongue where he'd bitten her, drawing a low moan from her lips. He lifted her back into the water, lowering her gently until the water was lapping at her breasts before he finally released her.

"Hang onto the ledge," he told her and waited until she had done so before moving again. He stepped back, drawing her body with him until she was stretched out perpendicular to the edge of the pool, her heels resting in the palms of his hand as he let his gaze wander over her. "Goddamn, you are stunning," he murmured before moving to one side and tugging loose the knot on her hip that held her bikini bottoms in place. He swept them away from her with a wave of his hand and then untied the other side so they drifted down to the bottom.

Her head was resting at an angle against the lip of the pool so she could watch as he moved again, this time holding up her legs as he walked between them, crouching down until the backs of her knees came to rest on his shoulders.

"Perfect," he exclaimed as he rose up out of the water again, far enough her legs were clear of the water and only her hold in the concrete and tile lip stopped her from slipping under the surface. Strong hands cupped her ass and lifted her so that with a simple dip of his head his breath fanned over the lips of her cunt. She could do to nothing but hang on and watch as he dipped his head further to brush his mouth over her sopping curls. Every touch and breath teased her without giving any satisfaction, and Vivian's patience was wearing thin. She flexed her calves, digging her heels into his back, forcing him closer.

"Pay up," she demanded.

Byron shifted his grip slightly, moving his thumbs between her thighs to part her labia and expose her aching, swollen clit to view. He ran his tongue over the sensitive pearl and she keened loudly as shimmering coils of desire began to unfurl deep inside her. Her eagerness spurred him on and he pressed deeper, his mouth and tongue working in unison to push her up the scales of pleasure so quickly she could barely catch her breath.

He was relentless in his attentions, and when he drew her entire clit into his mouth and bit down lightly it was as if a bolt of lightning shot up her spine. White-hot need poured through her and she came hard, barely remembering to hang on to the edge as she lost herself to her pleasure.

She was still catching her breath when he lowered her under the surface again and she mewled as the water washed over her hypersensitive clitoris. She heard him chuckle and opened her eyes to see him fishing her bikini bottom off the floor of the pool while she floated, too relaxed to move yet.

"That's one," he said, coaxing one of her hands to let go of the edge. "Come with me and we'll see about two and three."

Byron led her to where they'd left their things and picked up a towel. Instead of drying himself off he shook it out and began drying her, starting at the top of her head and working his way down her naked body. He even dried her feet, making her feel like a pampered princess as he knelt in front of her and drew each foot onto his thigh in turn.

Inspired, she returned the favor, toweling every delicious inch of him as he stood and watched with ever-intensifying heat gleaming in his green eyes. She peeled away his wet trunks to complete her task, and by the time she was done his cock was standing at attention. There was no denying the hunger in his expression as he hauled her into his arms for a scorching kiss, pressing their bodies together so that they were joined from mouth to thigh. Her pussy was slick with need and she made an impatient noise in the back of her throat as she reached between them to stroke his cock.

He was laughing as he broke their kiss, rocking his hips so that his dick slid between her fingers again. "Is there something you want from me?" he asked, doing his best to feign confusion.

"You. I want you inside me, right now." She tightened her grip on his shaft and pumped his length several times.

His breath hissed across his teeth and he nodded sharply. "Whatever my goddess wishes."

He nearly tripped in his hurry to get to the nearest lounge chair, sprawling out on it with enough force that it creaked in protest.

"You sure that's going to hold us?"

"Positive." He dropped a hand to the clothes he'd left on the floor and rummaged through them until he found what he'd been looking for, a foil-wrapped condom. Once it was in place he held out his hands to her. "Come here and ride me, sexy. I want to watch your face when you come."

She settled herself atop him, knees by his hips and the hot length of his cock pressed along the seam of her pussy. She leaned down and kissed him, letting her breasts brush his chest as she rolled her hips slowly, teasing them both. His tongue speared into her mouth at the same time that he surged his body upward, sliding his cock along her swollen clit. Fresh honey gushed from her channel, coating her pussy and soaking his cock and balls as he slid back and forth beneath her.

His teasing strokes ignited a firestorm of needs and wants, and Vivian sat back before rising up on her knees. She reached between them, guiding the wide head of his cock to her entrance before stopping, letting the anticipation build even higher. He tried to thrust upward and she rose with him, denying him what he craved.

Being in control of their pleasure was an aphrodisiac all

by itself. Her entire being thrummed and sizzled as she eased herself down, experiencing each exquisite sensation as her body slowly gave way to his. They were both trembling, barely able to restrain themselves by the time she had taken him in. The moment she flexed her inner walls around his cock the last threads of their control snapped and they moved as one.

"I love being inside you. You feel like you were made for me. Well, me and Tucker. Watching you with him is almost as good as having you myself." His hands were on her hips, offering her support as she rode him hard. She rolled her hips again and shuddered as his cock stroked over her g-spot, making her entire body shudder as raw pleasure slammed through her. She fell forward, hands braced on either side of his head and their mouths fused together once more as she rode him like a galloping stallion.

Her next orgasm came on hard and fast, crashing through her with almost no warning. Stars danced in her vision and she screamed her pleasure against Byron's lips as her world exploded in a rush of light and sensations.

Before she could catch her breath Byron was sitting up, bringing her with him as he tipped her back into his lap and took control. He released her hips and did something to the chair, bringing them back up so that he could lean against it for support, and then hauled her close, slowing their lovemaking down to a more leisurely pace. She wrapped her arms around his shoulders and held on as he led her in this second dance, making love to her with gentle thrusts until the lines between his body and hers seemed to blend and finally vanish. For one perfect moment it felt as though they had merged, their bodies and souls as one.

His kisses were sweet, tender and loving, giving her everything and asking for nothing in return. When she came again it was a gentle pulse that rippled outward, filling her with wondrous pleasure. She came back to herself slowly, surprised to find there were tears in her eyes. She blinked them away before Byron could see them, not yet ready to reveal how deep her feelings for him ran.

He kissed her again and then dropped his head to the crook of her neck. "That was...unforgettable," he finally murmured. "Thank you."

She didn't have the words to say all she wanted to say, so instead she nuzzled his hair and held him until it was time for them to go. There wasn't any doubt in her mind now. She was dangerously close to falling for both of them.

CHAPTER FIFTEEN

VIVIAN'S DAYS passed in a pleasant jumble of passion and laughter as she spent more and more time in Byron and Tucker's company. When Jess returned from her honeymoon Viv filled her in on all that had happened in the few days she had been away. Jessica had squealed with earsplitting glee upon learning that Vivian had decided to stay for at least the immediate future and see how things went with the guys.

As it got close to Christmas, the girls made plans for a day trip to Nanaimo to get their holiday shopping done. Unsure what to buy the guys, Viv had been at a bit of a loss until lunch, when they'd had a martini-induced brainwave. They'd spent the next two hours picking out lingerie and other sexy extravagances, giggling at some of the more outrageous outfits and daring each other to buy them for their men. It had been an amazing, fun-filled day and she was finally feeling the holiday spirit.

It had been a long time since she'd felt this happy.

Viv had her dearest friend with her, as well as new

friends and a pair of lovers who were all making her feel as if she might have finally found a place where she was truly welcome. Jess's Jeep was stuffed to the rooftop with their purchases, and they sang off-key Christmas carols for the entire journey home. As Jess pulled into the driveway of the cabin they were met by a wonderland of lights, and for a moment Viv thought she was dreaming.

Cheery holiday lights had been strung along the cabin's roofline and framed every window, while tiny nets of multicolored lights covered every shrub that lined the short walkway to the front door.

"What the hell?" were the first words out of her mouth as she gawked at the transformation. "Did you hire Santa's entire pointy-eared staff to decorate while we were out?"

"Nope," Jess parked the Jeep and killed the engine. "I had nothing to do with planning this." She grinned and hopped out. "This was all their idea. I just gave them a spare set of keys."

"All *whose* idea?" Viv demanded, but she already knew the answer even before the front door opened. Tucker and Byron stood there grinning at her like a pair of lunatics, despite the fact they should have been working tonight. The revelation that they'd taken the night off to do this for her brought a lump to her throat, and she had to blink hard to stop the tears that welled up in her eyes.

"I think they're waiting for you to say something." Jess nudged her elbow into Viv's ribs. "So quit staring and go see the rest of it."

"The rest of what?" Viv walked toward the cabin and that's when she saw what Jess meant. Behind the guys the entire interior of the cabin was aglow. She could see more lights and candles and even a pine tree, its boughs heavily laden with gleaming ornaments. It was like Hollywood's vision of the holidays had been transported into her cabin. She ran the last few steps and threw herself into Tucker's arms, burying her head against his shoulder before either of them could see the tears she could no longer hold back.

"Thank you," she murmured past a throat thick with emotion. "Thank you both so much."

"Blessed Yule," Tucker whispered as he wrapped her in his arms and drew back from the doorway.

She let herself be led into the cabin, making sure her eyes were dry before she lifted her head to look around. They had really outdone themselves. A variety of delicious aromas were teasing at her nose, alerting her to the fact that not only had they decorated, they had cooked!

"Blessed Yule to you too," she finally managed to respond. She kissed Tucker hard, showing him how pleased she was with her actions since words seemed to be failing her. He kissed her back and then handed her off to Byron, who brushed several kisses to her cheeks before twirling her around in his arms.

"No tears," he whispered so softly no one else could hear him, and then added in a louder voice, "I missed you today."

"When did you have time to miss me?" She waved absently at the decorations. "You two must have worked all day to pull this off! I love it, thank you."

"You're welcome, gorgeous. And for the record, I always have time to miss you." He gave her a tender kiss that evolved into a heated tangling of tongues.

"Uh...guys? I need to break this up for a second," Jess interrupted, her voice laced with amusement. "Viv's got a ton of stuff to bring in, and you two can't see it, so..."

Vivian turned her head to see Jess flapping her hands toward the kitchen. "You see to whatever incredible things you're cooking and we'll go grab the goods."

Byron lowered her back down to the ground with a reluctant grumble and stole one last kiss before releasing her completely. "Go on, we need to go check on dinner, anyway."

"What exactly *is* for dinner?"

Tucker beamed. "Seafood. A lot of it, so I hope you're hungry."

"Starved!" she confirmed and headed back outside with Jess, who was bouncing around and bubbling over with happiness.

"Did you like the surprise? I thought that was incredibly sweet of them! How did you find ones that can actually cook?" The comments and questions continued all the way back to the Jeep, and Vivian finally gave up trying to answer and let her friend's joy wash over her. They unloaded her share of the bags and parcels and lugged it all back indoors, making various threats if either of the men dared to so much as peek over their shoulders.

They managed to get it all stacked up on Vivian's bed, completely burying it. That was when Jess turned around, her hands on her hips and a frown on her face. "Wait a second. Your stuff is still in this room? This is the spare bedroom, and *that* is a single bed! It's been days and days. You should have moved into the master suite by now."

"Well, I sort of felt weird about that, and to be honest I've spent almost every night at Tucker's."

"Mhmm." Jess didn't sound convinced. "Tomorrow I'm going to help you move into the other bedroom. For tonight, I'd suggest you sleep there...because there is no way three of you are sleeping in that." She pointed to the small bed and Vivian fell into a fit of giggles.

Jess was right, there was no way they were going to fit, and there was not a chance in hell she was going to sleep alone by choice. Falling asleep snuggled in between her men had become a luxury she wasn't willing to give up without a fight. Not tonight, and if she was being honest with herself, likely not ever.

"Tomorrow we're going to be busy getting ready for the Christmas Eve party. After today's haul, we both have a mountain of wrapping to do! I promise I'll move everything over once the holidays are done."

"You better! This place is yours now, for as long as you want it. You might as well get yourself properly settled." Jess cast an eye to the doorway. "At least until those two get smart and realize you're the best thing that's ever happened to them."

Viv threw up her hands and shook her head adamantly. "Whoa, woman! Just because you've discovered marital bliss doesn't mean you need to drag me along with you. You know I'm not a big believer in happily ever after, at least not when it comes to my own life." She found herself glancing out the doorway as she thought about the two men cooking her dinner a few feet down the hall. "They're amazing, I'm really happy, and that's enough for now." She reached out for Jess and gave her a surprise hug. "Blessed Yule, my friend. Thank you for inviting me out here."

Jess returned the hug with enthusiasm. "I think you should start rethinking your attitude on happily ever after. Those two seem pretty perfect for you." She let go of Viv and then gave her an oddly intent look. "Just promise me you'll keep your mind and your heart open, okay?"

That request set the hairs on the back her neck quivering. "Why would you say that?"

"Because I know you, and if you think this is getting too serious then you'll start looking for reasons it isn't going to work. All I'm saying is give them a chance. Give all of this a chance."

"Is there something you're not telling me?" Viv had the strange sense there was more going on here than just her tendency to shy away from serious relationships. The only person Viv truly loved and trusted was Jessica, at least until fate had thrown Tucker and Byron into her life. They were rapidly taking up permanent space in her heart, despite what she had told Jess.

"There's some stuff about Kismet Cove that you'll learn later on, that's all. They're a bit different, and some of it might take a little getting used to. I want to see you happy, like you are right now. You deserve that more than anyone else I know."

"I feel the same way about you. I'm glad you found your guys, and a place where you belong." Viv stepped back, deliberately putting a bit of space between them. "That doesn't mean I'm going to be as lucky as you. You know me. I'm a leaf on the winds of fate." She fluttered her hands in the air between them.

Jess shook her blonde head and laughed. "You're a leaf...right. You're a nut is what you are! Just remember what I said, okay? I'm going to take off so your guys can have you all to themselves. I think I need to go home and tell mine that Tucker and Byron are making them look bad. We don't even have a tree yet!"

"That's probably because they've been too busy sexing you up to even remember it's Christmas time," Viv teased. "You go on, and tell them I say hi and thank you for letting me have my best friend back for the day. Toodles, gator." She waved Jess out into the hall.

"Later, poodle!" Jess responded, and bounced down the hall and out, waving good-bye to the guys as she left.

Viv closed the door behind her and then turned around to find both men closing in on her, identical expressions of desire on both their faces. Goddess, it would be easy to come home to that every day. She opened her arms to them and Byron claimed her lips as Tucker moved around behind her, pinning her between their hard bodies.

Hands caressed her and she didn't know who they belonged to, nor did she care. Tucker was forging lines of fire across her neck with his kisses while Byron's tongue played tag with hers, and she could feel the hard evidence of their arousal pressing into her stomach and back. Someone drew her leather jacket off her shoulders and sent it flying to land on the couch, and then strong hands were kneading at her breasts.

They stayed like that, standing in a tangle of lust and limbs until a timer went off and an irritating buzz filled the cabin. "Fuck!" Byron muttered as he lifted his head with a rueful groan. "That would be dinner."

"You deal with that, bro. I've decided that I'm having dessert first."

"Oh, no. We made a deal, remember?" Byron snickered and reached over to cuff Tucker lightly on the side of his head. "Dinner first! Hell, Viv hasn't even had time to look around and see what we did yet."

"I want you two to show me everything. I can't believe you pulled it all off in the few hours we were gone."

Byron retreated back to the kitchen and Tucker released her slowly so she could finally look around. "We wanted you to have a real holiday this year," Tucker explained as he took her hand and led her over to the tree. "And I know that you are invited to spend Christmas Day with Jess..." He paused and Byron picked up the conversation.

"But we'd like to invite you to have dinner with us at my parents' house. It would be really laid back, just my family and you and Tucker."

"You guys are inviting me to Christmas dinner?" A slender tendril of panic slithered down her spine and curled itself in a tight ball around her gut. No. She wasn't going to panic. She forced herself to remember what Jess had said only minutes before. She needed to stay calm and not start looking for reasons to run. "Would your parents be okay with that? I mean, we've only been dating a couple of weeks."

"I checked in with Mom already, because I knew you'd ask that. She would be very happy to have you join us."

"And so would we," Tucker rejoined the conversation. "Jess already knows we were going to ask you, and she's given her blessing to you spending the evening with us...if that's what you want to do."

"I think you lot have all been in cahoots!" she murmured, brushing a finger over one of the delicate glass ornaments that hung from the branches of the first Christmas tree she'd had in years.

Her head and her heart were waging a silent but brutal battle as she struggled to make her choice. Her head screamed at her to take the safe path and spend the holiday with Jess, but her heart wanted more. No wonder Jess had asked her to keep an open mind. She'd known what the guys were planning. Tucker squeezed her fingers, drawing her attention back to the fact she had not yet given them an answer.

With Jess's words still echoing in her head, she took a leap of faith and went with her heart. "I would love to have dinner with the both of you and Byron's family. If you're really sure that's what you two want?"

"We're very sure," Tucker whispered before turning her into his arms and kissing her thoroughly.

"Okay, that's enough of that," Byron called from the kitchen. "Clearly she's not going to get a good look at the decorations until after we've eaten, so unhand the guest of honor and let's get dinner on the table!"

Dinner turned out to be a feast of local seafood and several of Byron's favorite brews for her to try. From stuffed salmon to breaded oysters, everything she could possibly have thought of was present, along with a few things she'd never heard of, like halibut cheeks and fried sea cucumber.

"So where did you find all of this? Not all of this is even in season, is it?" she asked as they were putting away the leftovers.

"There's a great seafood shop in Duncan I hit on the way back up here, Mad Dog's, and then I got a few things from the local markets. The rest, I caught myself." Byron gave her a triumphant smirk. "Behold the spoils of the mighty hunter!"

They all laughed at that, and soon her fridge was stuffed with the remains of their meal and the kitchen was devoid of the wreckage that always accompanied preparing so many dishes. As she hit the start button on the dishwasher, Byron's arms snaked around her waist, drawing her back against his chest.

"*Now* it's time for dessert."

"I still haven't gotten to look at all the work you guys did!" she argued, waving her hands at the evergreen boughs and holly that filled the cabin. That wasn't really true, since she'd been admiring it all through dinner, but she saw no reason to give in without any resistance. After all, they had all night.

She let out a squeal of surprise when Byron swept her up into his arms and carried her around the cabin. He sounded like a tour guide as he pointed out various items. "Well, over here we have evergreen boughs from your own backyard, nicely highlighted with a collection of holly and pine cones that were purchased by Mr. Tucker Pine over there. The candles are from a local craft fair, hand-dipped and guaranteed to smell nice for hours on end. Over here we have the pièce de résistance, your very much alive and will be planted out back after the holidays, Christmas-slash-Yule tree. All decorations on said tree are locally made, handcrafted and individually hung by two men who are absolutely crazy about you." He turned around and headed toward the hallway, with Tucker right behind him. "There you go. You saw everything. Tour concluded."

"So if the tour's over, why am I still being carried around?" she asked, wriggling enough to make her point.

"Efficiency," Tucker said simply. "If he puts you down before we get where we're going, you'll ask questions. We're on a mission, and it doesn't allow time for questions."

"I still have one question," she persisted. "What's the mission?"

"You are." Both men answered at once and the hungry edge to their voices had her pussy instantly slick with need. Byron carried her into the master bedroom and lowered her to the bed so that she was lying across it, his hands already busy tugging at the clasp on her jeans. They worked in tandem, stripping her bare as she stretched out between them, laughing and enjoying their attentions.

What else was she going to do?

"Close your eyes, slim." She closed them, only to reopen them immediately afterward when something touched her face. She jerked her head away and found herself staring up at Byron, who was holding a length of soft fabric in his hands.

"What are you doing?" she demanded, and both men went still.

"It's only a blindfold," he held up the fabric for her to see.

"Great, which one of you is wearing it?" she shot back.

"Uh…you are?" Byron said, looking uncertain. "Or not. I mean, you don't have to if you don't want to."

She didn't usually go for anything that left her vulnerable, especially not when it came to sex. Giving that much trust to someone else wasn't something she did easily, but she also couldn't deny the fact that the idea was making her hot. Images of the two of them teasing and pleasuring her while she couldn't see them made her heart race and her mouth go suddenly dry.

"If you don't want this, just say so. We're in this together," Tucker said, and she felt the weight of his words press down on her heart. They had done nothing but treat her like a goddess from the moment they'd walked into her life. Once again, Jess's words came back to her and she decided to take this chance.

"Yes, I do." She gave them each a soft smile and then closed her eyes.

"We'd never hurt you," Tucker vowed.

"We're crazy about you," Byron affirmed as he carefully placed the blindfold across her face. "Lift up your head," he coaxed, and as soon as she did he fastened it in place. "Comfy? Not too tight?"

"All good," she said, and opened her eyes to find that she couldn't see even a glimmer of light peeking through. "So what happens—"

Her words got caught in her throat as one of them ran his hands up her inner thighs, urging them apart as her other lover captured a nipple with his hot mouth. She reached out blindly and someone snagged her hands by the wrists, drawing them back over her head in a light grip she knew she could break out of easily enough.

The hands on her thighs reached her pussy and slid between her already soaking folds. They stroked and teased, avoiding contact with the one place she ached to be touched. Fingers swirled in slow circles and she bucked her hips in frustration, needing more than they were giving her.

Instead of giving her what she craved, the fingers stroking her pussy withdrew completely, leaving her frustrated. When the mouth on her breast also withdrew she mewled in protest and tugged lightly at the hands restraining her.

"This is going to happen on our schedule, not yours, sugar," Tucker purred as a hand stroked up her inner thigh again. This time she felt the cool slide of gel on his fingers and she parted her legs wider, inviting him to touch her again.

When something cool and slick slid over her clit she nearly came off the bed. "Cold!"

"Sorry. Should have warned you about that." Byron spoke this time, but she still couldn't tell which one was doing what to her.

"So what—" One of them stopped her question with another kiss as a humming noise hit her ears and a low vibration thrummed over her clit. Oh goddess above, a vibrator. She moaned as it was moved slowly around and over her now throbbing clitoris, her hips rising off the bed so she could gain more contact with the source of so much pleasure.

"Do you like that?" one of them murmured in a voice so low she couldn't be sure which one had spoken.

"Yes. More." She gasped out the words and both men chuckled.

"More. Gotcha."

That was all the warning she got before one vibrating end was slipped into her pussy while something else pressed up against her clitoris. Wicked pulses of sensation flowed through her clit and g-spot at the same time, bringing on an impossibly quick orgasm that left her keening and trembling in its wake.

"What the hell did you two do to me?" She asked when she could manage to string together words into a semi-coherent sentence. Not easy to do considering the vibrator was still turned on, and so was she.

"It's called a couples' vibrator, and I am going to buy us one of everything Lelo carries if that's how well they work," Tucker said, too distracted to remember to disguise his voice, revealing he was the one controlling the toy inside her. "And the best part is that it can stay right there while we fuck you. How's that sound?"

"It sounds like one of you needs to give me a hands-on demonstration," she challenged, and Tucker moved away from her side. He wasn't gone long, and when he returned he was tugging her down to the edge of the bed, the vibrator making every movement into a delicious torment.

"Take the blindfold off, now, I want to see you," she said, and Byron removed it gently. She smiled up at him and then cocked a brow at Tucker, standing with his condom-sheathed cock already poised at her entrance. "I'm ready when you are, lover."

CHAPTER SIXTEEN

TUCKER REALIZED QUICKLY that he should have paid more attention to how fast Viv had come when they'd used the vibrator on her. Then maybe he'd have been prepared for the incredible sensation of sliding inside her tight, hot body while the slender, U-shaped vibrator was still working its magic.

"Fuck!" he grunted the single word as the vibrations travelled the length of his dick and made his balls tighten. "Is this okay for you, Viv?"

"I am very, very fine," She clamped her inner muscles around him and he saw stars flash in his vision.

"Do that again and I'm going to be coming before we even get started," he warned her.

"That good?" Byron asked, his hands on Viv's breasts, toying with the hardened peaks of her nipples as he watched them.

"Better than you can believe, bro."

Vivian moaned and shifted beneath him, slamming him with another wave of raw lust. "I think we should show him," she murmured, and for a moment Tucker wasn't sure what she meant, but then understanding dawned and he had to bite back a groan.

"You sure you're ready for that?" he asked, needing to be sure.

"As I'll ever be."

"Sweet mercy, yes." Byron crowed softly. "We'll be gentle, but…damn I want to try this. I can't wait to see you filled by both of us, together."

Tucker rocked his hips a few more times and then withdrew as Byron touched the remote and the vibrator inside her body stilled.

The three of them had talked about the day the men would be able to fulfill their greatest desire, claiming Vivian's body at the same time. They had prepared her mind and her body for this moment, but neither of them had expected it to come so soon. She was truly amazing, and it was clear to Tucker that she was the one they'd always dreamed of finding.

She had to be.

She kissed them both as they rearranged themselves, her soft lips and gentle touches reminding him not to rush. This was an important step for all of them, more important than Vivian could know.

Byron stood at the foot of the bed while Tucker stretched out in the middle, his beautiful Vivian perched above him. Her legs straddled his hips and her sweet pussy was bare inches from his cock. Her kiss-swollen lips turned up into a smile that melted his heart.

This glorious, incredible woman was giving them her complete trust, a gift Tucker wasn't sure he was worthy of. Not when there were still secrets between them.

Returning his thoughts to the here and now, Tucker reached down and settled the U-shaped vibrator back into place, her pussy so soaked and slick that it took no effort at all. "Ready?"

She nodded, only the faintest hint of uncertainty in her lovely eyes. She lowered herself slowly, impaling herself on his cock with a soft moan before leaning forward so that their chests were touching and their gazes were locked together. As her lips brushed his she activated the remote they'd given to her, and he lost the ability to breathe as a rippling wave shivered through them both.

"Oh hell, it's even better this time!" Viv moaned again, and began rolling her hips in experimental circles.

The bed dipped at his feet and he knew Byron had moved in behind Vivian. She moaned again, moving backward so she could connect with Byron too.

Tucker speared his fingers into her hair, kissing her hard as he fought a desperate battle to stay still. Byron needed time to prepare her for what was to come. The link between them told him what his blood-brother was doing, and how eager he was to get inside their sexy lover.

She moaned as Byron stroked and kneaded her ass, then shivered when the lube hit her overheated skin. Tucker didn't need to be in contact to know the moment Byron's fingers began to work inside her body. She hissed softly into Tucker's mouth, her body tensing slightly.

"Just breathe," Tucker whispered against her lips. "We have all the time in the world." He coaxed her forward enough he could suck and nibble on her breasts, loving the honey-sweet taste of her skin in his mouth. The distraction worked and Viv began to relax a bit at a time. Eventually her body softened against his and she moaned in sultry bliss.

She rode his cock with tiny thrusts and movements of her hips, and he could see her getting lost in the world of pleasure he and Byron were weaving around her. Time slowed and every sensation seemed magnified. Touch, taste, smell, the purr of the vibrator became the only things in his awareness. Her pussy was hot and quivering around his cock, her inner muscles pulsing in response to the vibrations that were keeping him aroused almost to the point of pain.

Byron touched their link, telling him she was ready, and the bed shifted again as he moved up behind her, kneeling between Tucker's legs. Viv gasped once as Byron breached her body and Tucker stroked her cheek. "You are so beautiful," he said. He felt his cock being squeezed as Byron pushed himself deeper.

"I love your ass," Byron told her, and Viv blew out a breath with something like a strangled laugh. She responded by turning up the power of the vibrator and Tucker's cock went harder than he had even been in his life. Behind her Byron groaned wildly and then he felt his blood-brother touch the link between them.

"You withdraw and I'll move in, I don't want to hurt her." Byron sent the simple message and Tucker sent back a mental nod. He stroked his hands down Viv's body, letting them settle on her hips. He coaxed her to rise up as he pushed downward, giving Byron the space he needed within Viv's body.

"This is fucking incredible," Byron groaned. "You feel so tight around me, I can feel everything. The vibrations, your body. Fuck. I never imagined…Tell me I'm not hurting you, Viv."

"No hurting." She panted and rocked herself backward, changing the angle of both penetrations and tearing a groan from Tucker's needs. His blood was on the verge of boiling, and coils of fiery need were looped around the base of his spine. Viv moved her hand again and the vibrations changed to a low, rolling pulse. He gritted his teeth to stop himself from coming then and there. The subtle changes were pushing him to the brink of his control, and judging by Viv's expression she was right there with him.

This was not going to last long.

"You take over, sugar. You lead and we'll follow." He lifted his head to kiss her, his tongue swiping the seam of her lips to savor the sweet taste of her mouth.

She began to move between them, small movements at first, but as the fires blazed ever higher in her hazel eyes she grew bolder. Every roll of her hips and pulse of the vibrator fueled his need until the pleasure was almost a torment. Adding to the experience were the flashes from Byron's mind, the link between them so strong that at this moment there was no way to completely block the other one out.

Their experiences were so tangled that it was impossible to know who was truly feeling what, and Tucker no longer cared. All that mattered was the impossible pleasure of the moment as they were both humbled by the glory of the beauty between them.

The pace she set grew faster, rocking her body back and forth between he and Byron until all three of them were panting. She pushed them further than they would have dared, her passion fierce and her desire hot and demanding.

Vivian's control went first and she came with a wild cry, her entire body shuddering hard. His dick was caught in a velvet vise that milked him until he too went over the edge into the abyss. Someone called her name in a hoarse voice but he couldn't have said if it was him or Byron who did it, he was too far gone. The world went gray for a time, and when he came back to his senses there was a sensual goddess sprawled across his chest.

Byron groaned and Tucker felt the connection between them close as his blood-brother withdrew from his mind and Viv's body at the same time. Byron hit the mattress beside them with another groan, and Vivian finally stirred enough to turn off the vibrator before slumping back across Tucker's chest.

"Next time we do that, someone have the paramedics on stand by. In case we need them," Viv muttered.

"There's going to be a next time? Hot damn." Byron cheered weakly from his side of the bed.

"Definitely," Viv confirmed, and Tucker felt himself fall a little deeper in love with her. He couldn't even pretend that it wasn't love anymore. He'd passed that point sometime in the last few days, and there was no reason to deny it. She had taken hold of his heart in a way that he would not have believed possible, and he knew she was the one. Because she wasn't a selkie she didn't know that the act of both lovers taking a woman at once was only done between mates, but as far as he and Byron were concerned, she was theirs.

Tomorrow night they were going to have to talk to Darius. It was time to tell her the truth about who, and what, they were, and for that they needed the permission of the colony's leader.

Byron rose first, and as he headed to the bathroom he sent a single mental image to Tucker. It was of a gold necklace supporting an intricately woven Celtic knot. A necklace like that was the traditional gift given to a selkie woman when she agreed to become a bonded mate. The only problem was he and Byron had never had one made.

"I had one made a few years ago. I never gave up hope we'd find someone." There was a hint of laughter interwoven with deeper emotions in Byron's message.

"I never really believed she was out there."

"Nice to know you can be wrong, bro."

"Since you're so prepared, any idea how the hell we're going to break the news to her that we're not human?" Tucker shot back.

"Not a fucking clue. I thinking booze and having Jessica on speed dial are both going to be required."

"Yeah, I had the same thought."

Tucker stroked his fingers through Viv's soft hair and silently prayed that fate would not be so cruel as to finally bring the perfect women into their lives and then whisk her away again. He wasn't worried that she'd betray their secret, not when doing so would expose her best friend along with the rest of them. He feared that she wouldn't be able to forgive them for lying to her, or that learning the truth about them all would kill whatever feelings she had for himself and Byron. If that happened...he didn't allow himself to go down that path. Vivian would know the truth soon enough. They'd just have to deal with where that led when the time came.

~

THEY TOOK turns cleaning up and returning to bed, but eventually all three of them were burrowed under the duvet with Vivian nestled in the middle. She had always enjoyed sleeping alone, but now she couldn't imagine trying to fall asleep without the warm, comforting presence of her two lovers flanking her. Byron's hand rested possessively on her hip, while she had her head pillowed on Tucker's chest, the steady beat of his heart acting like a lullaby to her senses.

The last few weeks had been some of the happiest she could remember. There was so much living energy flowing through the land here, it had replenished her spirit in ways she never expected. After a lifetime of city living the slower pace of Tofino was a welcome change, and she was finding the idea of living here more and more appealing. All these thoughts drifted through her mind as she lay spooned between her men, and as her thoughts flowed she came to an undeniable realization. She loved them.

As revelations went, it wasn't a dramatic one. There was no crash of thunder, no sudden illumination that things were a certain way. It crept over her slowly but surely, seeping into her consciousness as subtly as sleep. One minute she was simply content, and the next she was content and in love. It came upon her so gently that she didn't have her usual reaction of denial or panic. It simply was, and she accepted the truth with a smile.

"I love you both." The words came straight from her heart, and both men moved closer, holding her tight between them.

"I love you too," Byron told her, and she caught the

undertone of amazement in his voice that exactly matched the way she was feeling.

"Me too," Tucker joined in, nuzzling his lips to her hairline. "I mean, I love you too."

All three of them went quiet after that, and the silence stretched on until Vivian asked, "Well, lightning didn't strike the bed and the world didn't end, so now what do we do?"

"Now? Now we celebrate!" Byron rolled her onto her back and grinned down at her. "You realize now that you've said it, we're never going to let you go?"

"Never," Tucker repeated, his voice rumbling deep in his chest. "You're ours now, sugar."

"Which means you two belong to me, right? I think I have discovered the best two-for-one deal of all time."

"Remember, all sales are final. No refunds or exchanges," Byron said, and then sealed her mouth with a mind-scorching kiss that seared away any other thoughts she might have had on the matter. Byron was right, tonight was a celebration. Tomorrow she'd worry about the details.

CHAPTER SEVENTEEN

VIVIAN'S final hours before the Christmas Eve party flew past in a blur of gift wrapping, last-minute planning and an unexpected attack of nerves. She changed outfits three times, redid her makeup and was still second-guessing her choices as they pulled up outside their destination.

Her usual confidence had abandoned her when she'd been struck by the realization that tonight she'd be attending not as Jess's guest, but as Tucker and Byron's girlfriend. She hadn't even met Byron's family yet, and that thought was enough to make her feel slightly queasy as she got her first look at the house.

It was an impressive log cabin, nestled into the forest on a bluff overlooking Kismet Cove. The building and grounds had been done up with festive lights that cast bright shards of color across the waters of the cove below, and through the windows she could see a great many guests had already arrived.

Byron squeezed her hand as he helped her down out of the truck, and they waited for Tucker to join them before heading up to the front door, arm in arm. Tucker looked as uneasy as she felt, and she remembered that he usually avoided these types of gatherings. Knowing that she wasn't going to be the only one feeling on edge made her feel a little better.

"Anyone else think that maybe we should get back in the truck and go hide at the bar until Santa comes?" she asked, only half joking.

"Tempting as that may be, we should at least make an appearance. We want everyone to see what a gorgeous woman we landed." Tucker flashed her a lopsided grin that showed his dimple.

"Not to mention the fact my mother will kill us if we don't introduce you to her. She missed you at the wedding since she was doing the catering, and she is dying to meet you."

"Mothers don't usually react well to me. I think it's the hair…and the tattoo."

"You've got nothing to worry about, Viv. Dana's used to tattoos and piercings, she's had to look at mine for years," Tucker pointed out. "All she's going to care about is if you make her little boy happy."

"Hey! Who are you calling *little*?"

"Neither of you are little, but I don't think the nice people inside need to know that personal detail. Do you?" Viv pointed to the window where several of the guests had turned their heads at Byron's outburst.

"Very smooth, bro. We're not even through the door yet and people are staring. I'm starting to think Viv might be onto something with her idea to head back to the bar."

"Oh no you don't. There will be no backing out now. We're going in there and going to make nice while showing off our sexy girlfriend. That's the plan and we're sticking to it."

They were saved from any further discussion as the front door flew open and Jess bounded down the stairs to hug Vivian. "You made it. Great! Come on in and meet everyone again." She lowered her voice. "Please, don't make me go back in there alone. Everyone wants to know when I'm going to produce the next heir…" She stopped dead and blinked as Byron made a choking noise in the back of his throat. "Oh lord, see how flustered I am? I'm babbling! Everyone keeps asking me when we're going to start having kids! Please come in and distract them."

"They've already started the baby talk, huh?" Viv hugged her friend back and tried to resist the urge to laugh at her babbling. "I guess this means I'm going to have to suck it up and go in there to save you from their baby bullying." She wagged a finger at Jess. "But just so we're clear? You owe me big time!"

"What, don't I get at least partial credit for introducing you to your guys?" she asked as she hauled Viv into the lion's den, leaving Tucker and Byron to follow behind her.

Vivian was quickly surrounded by somewhat familiar faces, as many of the people she'd met at the wedding came by to greet her. She could see the curious glances and caught several whispers, all signs that word was spreading that she'd arrived with two of the odd little community's bachelors and not with Jessica. Her two men took up flanking positions and were helping her put names to faces while deflecting some of the more determined busybodies. Jess made sure to keep her glass of eggnog topped up.

"Oh, there you are! I swear I haven't seen so many

people at this party in years! Everyone is feeling social this year." A woman with a tumble of curly blonde hair popped up beside Byron and captured him in a familiar hug before turning her attention to Vivian.

"Hello there, I'm Dana, Byron's mom. I saw you at the wedding but never got a chance to introduce myself." She shot a look of maternal irritation at Byron. "Someone forgot he was supposed to bring you around to say hello."

"Don't blame me, blame Tobias. He's the one who showed up and distracted us," Byron protested with a sheepish grin.

"I don't believe you for a moment," Dana dismissed Byron with a smile and a flick of her fingers. "Now, you two can go mingle, I want to have a moment alone with Vivian."

"I'm not sure that Viv wants us to—" Tucker started to speak, but Dana tipped her head back to look him in the eyes and he stopped talking mid-sentence. "Yes ma'am. We've got something we need to speak to Darius about, now seems a good time."

"I thought it might be," Dana beamed as both guys stopped to brush a kiss to Viv's cheek. They muttered vague promises about being back soon and then vanished into the crowd, leaving Viv alone with Byron's mother. Vivian made a note to get back at them later for bailing on her. Dana clearly had them both well trained.

"Thank you for inviting me for dinner tomorrow night. It was really nice of you to include me." She decided the best way to deal with being abandoned by her bodyguards was to resort to small talk.

"You're very welcome. To be honest I wasn't sure you'd accept. You've only been with my son and Tucker for a few weeks, I wouldn't have blamed you if the whole "meet the parents" element was too much."

Vivian had to laugh at that. "I might have panicked slightly," she admitted. "I'm not really the sort of girl who gets taken home for Christmas dinner. This will be a new experience for me."

"For me too. I thought you might like to know that my son has never brought anyone home before now."

For a moment Viv was too surprised to speak for a second. Byron had *never* brought a woman home? "Never?" The single word came out in a startled bleat.

"Not a one. Not until you came along." Dana smiled at her and there was nothing but welcome acceptance in her warm brown eyes. "You can make both of them happy, and that's something no other woman has ever managed. "

"And it really doesn't bother you that your son and his best friend are both dating me?" She hadn't meant to ask that question, but it had tumbled out of her mouth before her internal filter could stop it.

Dana shook her head. "It really doesn't bother me. After all, I have two husbands, and at one point so did every woman here, though some of them have lost one of their loves along the way. I know this will take some getting used to, but for us, this is normal." She waved around the room. "We chose to live and love this way. You may get some odd looks from the rest of the world, but here? You will find a place for yourself here, if you decide that this is what you truly want."

Dana leaned in and whispered. "There will be a few busybodies who will try to get under your skin because you're not born to our ways, but you just ignore them.

Better yet, you point them out to me and *I'll* deal with them." Her eyes gleamed with mischief. "I'd enjoy taking a few of them down a peg or two."

"She has that look again, Chris."

"She does, doesn't she? What trouble are you plotting, wife?" Two men joined them, each of them taking one of Dana's hands.

"I'm not plotting anything! I was warning Vivian here that if any of the old hens start pecking at her about her being an outsider, she's to let me know."

"Ah, so this is Vivian!" A tall, rangy man with green eyes like Byron's smiled in greeting. "I'm Chris and this is Chad. We're Byron's dads."

"Nice to meet you both." She was looking at two very attractive, mature men and part of her wondered if Tucker and Byron would age as well as these two had. It took a moment for her to register that she was thinking decades into their future.

Holy shit. When did I start thinking of this as a forever thing?

"The pleasure is all ours." Chad took her hand and lifted it to her mouth, stopping short of kissing her knuckles as Dana rolled her eyes and Chris laughed.

"Well, I see who taught Byron to be so charming." She withdrew her hand with a soft smile, trying to ignore the blush that heated her cheeks.

"Don't encourage him, he only gets worse if you do." Dana bumped Chad with her shoulder and then looked around with a distracted frown. "Where's Billy? You two didn't leave him unsupervised did you?"

"Uh, define unsupervised. He was with some of the other kids. I think they were planning a raid on the dessert table." Chris pointed vaguely to another part of the house.

"Unbelievable. Two mates and neither of them have a brain in their heads," Dana muttered. "I'm terribly sorry. I need to go find my youngest before he goes into sugar shock. We'll talk later, dear."

With that she headed off, both of her men still grasped firmly in her hands as she dragged them after her.

"Nice to meet you!" Chris called back over his shoulder while Chad waved with his free hand.

Well, that went better than expected, she thought to herself as she went in search of the guys. After a complete lap of the lower floor she still couldn't find Byron or Tucker, but she had found two groups of people whose sly whispers and pointed looks marked them as being the busybodies Dana had warned her about.

She could feel their eyes on her as she moved through the room, making her tension ratchet higher and higher. Finally she gave up looking for the guys and headed for the front door, snagging her winter jacket on her way out. She needed a minute away from everyone to clear her head. Meeting everyone, getting introduced to Byron's family and then dealing with the various reactions of this tight-knit community was giving her a headache.

Outside, the holiday lights cast a cheery glow over everything, while overhead the soaring evergreen trees creaked and swayed in the wind that blew up from the ocean. She zipped her coat up to her chin and jammed her hands into the pockets as the chill of the air sank into her body right down to the marrow of her bones. The silence was welcome though, giving her the much-needed reprieve she'd come out here to find.

She wandered over to the edge of the bluff and glanced down, surprised to see that there was a stone staircase of sorts leading down to the water and a small jetty. Not ready to return to the party, yet, Vivian picked her way carefully down, gripping the driftwood railing tightly every step of the way. Down at the jetty the scent of the cedar trees and the loam of the forest mixed with the tang of the sea, while the only sound she could hear was the lap of the waves washing up against the wharf.

A sense of peace slowly filled her, soothing nerves rubbed raw by the unfamiliar feeling of uncertainty that had dogged her heels all night. She took several more long, slow breaths as she let the peace of the evening flow around her, letting it restore her calm and helping her find her emotional balance.

The scrape of a shoe on stone rasped loudly in the near silence and Viv spun around to see who was disturbing her moment of peace. She'd been expecting Tucker or Byron, but the shadowy form making his unsteady way down to the jetty was no one she wanted to see.

"Saw you duck out and thought we could have a quick word, you 'n me." Tobias slurred as he made his way onto the rain-slick wood of the jetty.

"I don't think we've got anything to discuss," Vivian stated as she tried to estimate if she had room enough to get around him and back to the stairs.

"Oh, but we do." He waggled a finger in her direction. "My boy's got royal blood in his veins, see? Married me an uppity bitch with a real nice bloodline, related to the royals I was! Shoulda had me a boy with the right blood ta make him special, but that bitch got knocked up by

Geoffrey first and they had that big sonofbitch instead 'n wrecked her for more kids."

"You mean Tucker?"

"Tucker, fucker...yeah I mean Tucker," Tobias was rambling as he took a few steps closer to Vivian, who moved back until she was almost to the edge of the jetty. "Ungrateful pup's what he is. He needs to come back to the colony and take care of me. He owes me better'n this. But no, his bitch of a mother runs off with that jellyfish Geoffrey and Tucker up and leaves the colony. Takes all his mother's money and sinks it into that goddamned bar! I'm his kin and I'm not even allowed to set foot in the place! Gratitude, bah! Little fucker's got no sense of honor. Now Trask, he sees the way of things. Smart man. But my boy can't see the writing on the wall. He loves his bar more 'n he loves his father. Goddamn place is full of human girls. Trash like you, just aching to get fucked by a selkie stud. He's so busy banging his whores he's not taking care of his own blood!"

He moved in closer and she caught the stink of stale booze on his fetid breath. "I saw you tonight, arm and arm with those boys. You think they're gonna be allowed to claim a human mate? You think I'm going to let that happen!" Flecks of spittle sprayed her cheeks as he railed at her.

Tucker's dad wasn't just drunk, he was insane. That was the only explanation Vivian's racing mind could come up with. As he lurched toward her she threw up her hands to stop him and his temper ignited like a string of cheap firecrackers.

"Don't you touch me!" he shrieked in drunken fury. "You're not good enough to touch me, you're just trash!

Human trash! You're going to try and ruin everything, but I won't let ya! You can't stop us from putting things to right! He's got a duty to take care of me! I'm kin!"

Viv shifted to one side as he made a grab for her, years of Tai Chi making her movements fluid as she deflected his grasping hands. He cursed and went for her again as she tried to dart past him. The slick surface of the jetty made it impossible to move quickly and Tobias's drunken flailing was almost impossible to predict. She batted his hands aside again and again but he kept coming, a constant babble of curses flowing from his mouth.

She had almost worked herself around him when he made a final, desperate lunge. She managed to dodge and he overshot her, careening straight for the edge. Adrenaline pumped through her veins and time slowed to a crawl as Vivian turned to make a run back to the house. She never made it. Tobias managed to grasp hold of the sleeve of her coat as he tumbled into the water, dragging her with him into the icy waters of the Pacific.

She screamed as she hit the inky surface, and in those first seconds everything that Byron had taught her about water safety was forgotten. The dark water closed over her head, cutting her off from the world and sending her into a wild panic.

The cold was terrible, cutting into her like a thousand tiny, frozen teeth as she thrashed and kicked her way toward the surface. At least, she hoped she was heading for the surface, in the darkness it was impossible to be sure. Her jacket grew heavier by the second as it absorbed more and more water, making it nearly impossible to use her arms. Her lungs were burning and every part of her hurt from the cold by the time she got her head above water again.

She dragged in a lungful of air, half gagging on the sea water she'd swallowed when she'd gone under the first time. She fumbled at the zipper of her jacket, knowing that she needed to get rid of its bulky weight. Before she could get it off something slammed her into her back, pushing her underwater again.

What the fuck?

She fought hard against whatever had her as images of the shark from *Jaws* and every other horror movie she'd ever seen flashed through her head. She hit the surface and gasped for breath, only to get hit again. This time whatever it was took hold of her jacket and shook hard enough her teeth snapped together.

"No!" she shrieked, doing everything she could to keep her head above the waves. She kicked and punched wildly, finally managing to connect with something solid. She lashed out again and got in another blow, making whatever was attacking her finally let go.

"And don't come back!" she yelled into the night, but her voice sounded weak to her own ears and she started to feel the true cost of the battle she'd fought. The cold was leeching the last of her strength, her teeth were chattering, and her limbs felt like they were full of wet sand.

She turned herself around and her heart sank as she saw how far away she was from the jetty. Already freezing cold and exhausted, she knew she'd never be able to swim that far. Byron's instructions came back to her and she pulled in her legs and crossed her arms over her chest, trying to slow down the rapid heat loss that would lead to hypothermia. Now if the local sea monsters would leave her the hell alone, maybe she could stay alive long enough for help to come. Maybe.

"Help!" she screamed, putting all her strength into her voice.

"Vivian!"

"Where are you, Viv?"

"Down here!" she called out as relief flooded through her. They'd found her.

"Fuck! She's in the water!"

"She can't swim!" She thought that last statement came from Tucker, but she couldn't be sure. The cold was sapping her strength so quickly it was getting hard to think.

Someone ran down onto the jetty, moving too quickly for her to see properly. They ran to the edge and then whoever it was dove in a high arc off the side, disappearing into the black water.

She waited for them to come up, but as the seconds ticked past she wondered what could have happened. When a dark head broke the surface she reached toward it and then let loose with a shriek as she came face-to-face with something large and furry.

"No!" The thing that had attacked her before had come back! She tried to lash out at it but she was too slow and it ducked under her arm. The sudden move unbalanced her and she went under again. Before she could claw her way back up to the surface she felt something nudge her side and she tried to shove it away, but instead of the attack she was expecting she found herself being pushed firmly upward, eventually popping up out of the water like a cork.

When it came at her again she was too exhausted to

even scream. Fear turned to confusion as the creature swam up beside her and guided her carefully back to the jetty. It didn't make any sense to Vivian's exhausted brain. Why attack her and then save her? And where was the person who had jumped in? Where was Tobias? Questions filled her mind as she found herself being hauled out of the water by several pairs of hands.

She was shaking so hard from the cold she could barely form words, but she managed to stutter Tobias's name and wave frantically at the water. "To-Tobias went in too. And someone else…"

"Tobias was here?" Byron's question cut through the rest of the babble and she hurled herself toward the sound of his voice.

"I got you, slim." Strong arms wrapped around her, gathering her into the welcome warmth of his embrace before he lifted his head and snarled, "Someone find that son of a bitch. Now! He's got a lot to answer for."

The crowd thinned out and Vivian assumed they'd gone off to find their missing neighbor.

"Tuck–Tucker?" she asked as someone finally found the light switch. The jetty was flooded with bright light and Viv vision was suddenly obscured by dancing blobs and spots.

"I'm right here." Tucker's deep voice rumbled from behind her and another set of arms closed around her. "Are you hurt? Do you need a doctor?"

"Not hurt, or if I am I'm too cold to feel it yet." Viv muttered. "Something might have bitten me."

"What? What bit you? What happened?"

"Your asshole father happened." Someone draped a dry jacket around her and she burrowed into it gratefully.

"He freaked out, started screaming at me and then he attacked. He lost his balance and went over the edge and took me with him."

"If you don't kill him for this, I will," Byron's voice was thick with rage as he looked over her head at Tucker.

"You mean, if he's not already dead," Viv interjected. "I never saw him come back up. I'm s–sorry, Tucker."

"He's not dead. He's far too good a swimmer to ever drown." Tucker dismissed her concerns. "I'm just glad you're okay. When I heard you scream…"

She twisted around so she could see Tucker and then frowned in confusion. He was dripping wet. His shirt was plastered to his chest and trickles of water were tracking down his face.

"Why are you soaked?" she asked as she reached over to wipe away a droplet that was about to fall into his eyes.

"Because I went in after you."

"No, there was no one. I mean…I thought I saw someone dive in, but then that thing that attacked me before came back. At least I think it was the same thing. It must have been, but why did it help me to the jetty? You guys did see it, right? There was something in the water with me!"

"It was a seal," Byron murmured so softly she could barely hear him. "He got you close enough we could pull you out. Tell us more about the other creature, the one that attacked you."

Tucker let go of her to turn his hands over her body. "Where did he bite you?"

"I don't know if he actually bit me or just my jacket. After I hit the water something…the seal I guess. It smacked into the back of me and dragged me further away from the jetty. I was screaming and fighting and it was shaking me and pulling. It was like a nightmare. I couldn't see it, but I knew something was in the water with me. Do seals attack people? I thought maybe it was a shark or something."

"He attacked you after you went into the water?" Tucker's voice was as dark and deadly as the water all around them.

"And Viv, there aren't any sharks up here. It was a seal. Two seals, actually."

"If you say so. I wouldn't know a seal from a Wookiee. But why would a seal be there, and why didn't I see you?" she demanded of Tucker. "And why would a seal attack me?"

She was so intent on puzzling out the weirdness that she barely noticed that many of the bystanders were moving away, giving them privacy.

"I was there. Fuck. This was not the way we planned on telling you." Tucker ground his teeth in frustration. "I was the seal that helped you. The seal that attacked you... was Tobias."

Vivian's world crumbled around her as she stared into Tucker's gray eyes and saw nothing but anger and truth in their depths. Either he was insane, or she'd been lied to. Both options ultimately meant the same thing.

She was about to get her heart broken. Again.

CHAPTER EIGHTEEN

"THIS CONVERSATION HAS to wait until you two are both warm and dry again," Byron was trying to stop the train wreck that was unfolding before him, but he wasn't sure he could. Vivian was suffering from the cold and shock, and there was no way she was going to react well to the truth being thrown at her while she was still wet and shivering after being attacked by Tobias. Twice. He was going to kill the drunken bastard for that, if Tucker didn't beat him to it.

Before she could argue he gathered her into his arms and stood up, making a beeline for the house.

"We need to regroup before we tell her." He sent the thought to Tucker and included a sense of deep concern with the message. All of their plans and hopes for a future with her were hanging in the balance thanks to Tobias's special talent for destroying lives.

They had come back downstairs after meeting with Darius only to discover that Vivian had vanished. They'd been riding on a high, knowing that they could finally share the truth with her. That high had fast faded when they realized that she was not with Jess or Dana. The sound of shouting had drawn the attention of some late arrivals who commented on it as they passed Byron near the front door. That had been all they needed to send them both running outside.

Vivian's screams had sent them hurtling down the slick staircase, Tucker's longer legs giving him the lead. It had been a hell of a shock to Byron to see his blood-brother change forms as he dove into the sea. He knew Tucker had forsaken that part of his life the day the only family he loved had fled and left him behind. For him to use it now to save the woman they loved said more about his feelings for her than words ever could.

"Is Tucker crazy?" Viv whispered as he carried her up the stairs.

"No. He's not. I promise we'll explain it all soon. Just let us get you checked out first." He hugged her hard. "We nearly lost you tonight."

"Yeah, nearly." There was something in her voice that set Byron's teeth on edge. She was already pulling away from them. He could feel it.

"We need to make sure you're not hurt and then get you into some dry clothes. Then we can talk about all this."

"I need to talk to Jessica."

Fuck. That wasn't a good sign. Then again, Jess had a big stake in this too. She might as well be there for this.

"Okay. She's probably organizing up blankets and cocoa. I'll send someone to find her and—"

"No. I want to talk to Jess *alone*," she interjected.

Double fuck.

232

They were only twenty or so feet from the house when he stopped and lifted her higher into his arms. "Viv. Don't shut us out. Please? We love you, and there are things we need to talk about."

She stiffened in his arms. "Things like selkies, maybe?" she snapped, and he groaned.

"Where did you hear that word?"

"From the raving, drunken lunatic who attacked me. He was ranting about human whores and royal blood and selkies, and I thought he was crazy, but he's not, is he? If Tucker isn't crazy, then Tobias isn't crazy, and maybe that means I'm the one who has lost their fucking mind! There is no way you're a bunch of shapeshifting, oversexed seals!"

Byron sighed. "We have a lot to talk about."

"No we don't, because I am not having any conversation that includes the word seal unless you two joined the special forces and never bothered to tell me!" She started to struggle to get free and Byron tightened his grip, using more of his supernatural strength than he'd ever let her see before.

"Stop it, Viv. You're going to hurt yourself. If you want to be mad, that's fine. But not until *after* we know you're okay."

"Jessica!" she yelled. "Jess! Get your ass out here!"

Byron grunted as she managed to slam her heel into his thigh. He didn't want to put her down. He had the sick feeling that if he did, he'd never get to hold her again.

"Sugar, please." Tucker caught up to them and placed himself between Viv and the door. "I'm sorry for what that bastard did. I need to know he didn't hurt you."

"And I need to know what the fuck is really going on! Right now! Jessica, I know you can hear me!"

She squirmed again and Byron accepted that he was going to have to put her down before she hurt herself.

"She's not going to forgive us, is she?" Tucker's thought was laced with pain.

"I hope so. But it's not going to happen tonight."

The moment her feet touched the ground, she wrenched herself out of Byron's arms and bolted for the door. Jess was there before she made it up the steps, and Vivian fell into her arms with a ragged sob.

"We're going to get her warmed up. Tucker, you need to do the same," Jess told them over Vivian's shoulder. "Darius wants to see you too. Tobias has a lot to answer for."

"He does." Tucker growled and Byron rumbled a wordless agreement.

They'd deal with Tobias when the time came, but right now they needed to talk to Vivian. She was the center of their world. They had to find a way to make this right.

"WHAT THE FUCK is going on, Jess?" Vivian blurted out the question the moment they were behind closed doors. Jess had led her to what looked like a guest bedroom that held minimal furniture, a double bed, and a few homey touches but no personal items.

"You're having a really bad day," Jess answered. "Get those wet things off and I'll try to explain."

Viv shrugged out of the dry coat someone had wrapped around her and started peeling off her waterlogged clothing, dropping it piece by sodden piece onto the floor. Once she was down to her bra and panties she grabbed one of the towels Jess had brought with them and scrubbed herself dry.

"Before you say a word, I need you to promise me something," she said and met Jess's gaze.

"Anything."

"No more lies. I don't want to lose my best friend, but if I get told any more lies…"

Jess nodded and Viv watched as tears tracked down her dearest friend's face. "I'm so sorry, Viv. This wasn't…I never…"

"So tell me. All of it." Viv wasn't sure she was ready to hear this or not, but she *was* certain she was done being lied to.

"How much have you figured out?"

"Well, let's see. You left a book about selkies lying around the cabin. I've been wondering why you had that. It didn't seem your usual sort of reading material. Then Tobias freaked out and started going on about bloodlines and human whores and royal selkies right before he pushed me off a dock and then nearly drowned me. At least Byron says it was Tobias who attacked me in the water. I thought it was an animal. And to cap my evening off perfectly, my boyfriend jumped into the water to save me, only I didn't see anything but a seal in the water. So unless I'm off the mark here, selkies are real. At least one of my boyfriends is a fucking mythical monster, and there's a good possibility that I'm currently surrounded by shapeshifters." She dragged an oversized sweatshirt over her head. "How much of that is right?"

"Uh…" Jess winced. "All of it."

"Fuck!" She'd been praying Jess wouldn't say that. "So you married into a bunch of monsters? What the fuck, Jess!"

"We're not monsters."

"Shapeshifters are too monsters! And you fucking set me up with two of them! And...wait a second. Did you say we? As in *we're* not monsters?" Vivian glowered at her best friend. "What, exactly, does *we* mean?"

"It means I have a lot I need to tell you."

"I think that might be the understatement of the year," Viv snarked. "Start talking. And this time, try not to skip any key details."

"I'm so sorry. I wanted to tell you so badly but there are rules! And then you got involved with the guys and I figured they'd have a better chance of being allowed to tell you than I would, so I didn't push and I should have and I'm really sorry for lying to you." The words came at her in a babbling flood and Viv realized that Jess was truly upset. Not as upset as she was, but close. That knowledge made her feel a tiny bit better.

"So what exactly weren't you allowed to tell me? Go slowly and use small words."

"Well, you know that when I came out here I found out that my mother was a local, remember?"

"Right. She never told you, but she was from Kismet Cove and you met a bunch of your family that are still... here." Understanding slowly dawned and Viv sat down on the edge of the bed as the world wobbled a bit on its axis. "Everyone?" She gestured vaguely around her. "All of them?"

"Just about." Jess stared at her, her hands clasping and unclasping in front of her. "Including me."

This night keeps getting weirder.

"So you're a selkie? For real. You turn into a fish-eating mammal that is usually only seen at aquariums and the zoo? How the fuck does that even happen? And why didn't you ever tell me!"

"Yes, I'm a selkie. I never told you because until I got here, I had no clue that they even existed."

"Okay." Viv was trying to keep it together so she could get the answers she needed, but it wasn't easy. "So your mom never mentioned the fact you come from a long line of mythical mon—shapeshifter thingies? And you still haven't explained how the hell it works. Hey, you said your mom was a selkie. What about your dad? Aren't you half human?"

"Where to begin…Yes, I'm half human. Apparently the selkie half is usually dominant for several generations. As for how it works, it's sort of hard to explain. Those furs in the box I told you about? The one my mother left me? One of them was mine. My pelt. The guys had to show me how to use it the first time. Once it was out of the iron box the transformation sort of…happened. One minute I'm human and the next I'm a seal. It's pretty cool. Or it was, once I got over the shock."

"Shock. Yeah. That's one word for it." Viv grabbed the pair of sweatpants Jess had handed her and stood up to tug them on. "And quit standing there looking at me like I'm going to burn you at the stake. You're still my friend." She sat back down, hauled a blanket around her shoulders and then patted the bed beside her. "You are in so much shit with me right now I cannot tell you, but you are still my friend. You're the one person I trusted to always have my back. It hurts that you weren't there for me."

Jess nearly flew across the room, hugging her so hard it was difficult to breathe. Viv returned the hug with one of her own, clinging to the one familiar thing in a world that was suddenly much stranger than she'd ever suspected. "I know I keep saying it, but I'm sorry. I'm sorry I didn't tell you. I'm sorry I screwed up so badly. I'm sorry I was so busy with my own life and hopes that I didn't think about how this would affect you. I was so stunned when I found out the truth I nearly killed them. I never should have put you through the exact same thing."

"No, you shouldn't have. But since I love you like a sister, I'm going to forgive you. Right after you promise to dedicate every book you ever write to me for being the best friend in the whole damned world."

"You got it."

"Seal, huh? Couldn't you at least have been something cool, like a werewolf?" Jess giggled, and the stress of the night bubbled over into a fit of laughter that had both of them in tears before it was done.

As she wiped her eyes and let go of her friend, Viv felt some of her tension ease. She was far from done asking questions and farther still from being ready to forgive anyone, but now she felt a glimmer of balance returning to her world.

"So what else do I need to know? Is there a manual I should be reading? What to expect when your best friend reveals she's a shapeshifter?

"I really am sorry I couldn't tell you."

"I'm sorry you couldn't trust me. Rules be damned, Jess! You should have found a way. Was I the only human at your wedding? Was everyone else laughing at me, the clueless bridesmaid?"

"No one was laughing. And no, you weren't the only human at my wedding. Jenny's human and she's mated to two selkies, and there were a few others there too."

She remembered Tobias's vicious words about Tucker and Byron never being allowed to be with her and her heart started to ache anew. "You encouraged me to go out with the guys, Jess. You should have warned me. I deserved to know the truth before I fell in love with them!"

"I know." Jess hung her head and stared at the floor. "I've missed you so much, and I hoped that maybe you'd stay." Jess's blonde head snapped back up and she stared at Viv. "It's your turn to back up. Did you just say you're in love with them?"

"That was yesterday," Viv said as anger and hurt boiled up inside her again. "Before I found out everyone I care about has been lying to me. I don't know how I feel about them right now. Well, apart from furious, livid, pissed, and totally betrayed."

"But you're going to forgive them, aren't you?"

"Why should I?" she demanded and got up to start pacing the small room. "You all *lied* to me! You're trying to fit around here. I get why you didn't tell me, these people are your family now. But Tucker doesn't even live here! He spends most of his time defying the laws of the colony, so why in the seven fucking hells didn't he break the one rule that would have let me know what I was getting myself into?"

"If they really loved me, they would have trusted me to keep your secrets. *Someone* should have trusted me." Tears stung at her eyes and she swiped at them in annoyance. She wasn't going to cry. She wasn't going to let herself feel anything but righteous anger. Anger she could deal with. Anything else would only make this whole nightmare even worse.

"Do you want to talk to them now? Rory says they're waiting downstairs." Jess tapped her temple with a forefinger. "I should probably mention that there's a telepathic thing that goes along with being a selkie, huh?"

"You're fucking telepathic now?" Viv swore her brain was going to collapse under the weight of all the new information she was trying to process.

"Blood-bonded mates can talk to each other mind-to-mind, yeah. The rest of the colony can only speak this way if we're in seal form."

"Blood-bonded mates." She rolled the strange phrase off her tongue with a frown. "You're telling me that the whole hand-cutting ceremony at your wedding was more than a weird bit of symbolism? And now you can talk to your guys in your head. I swear, if it was anyone but you trying to tell me this I'd be calling them a damned liar! So the three of you shared blood and now what? You're forever linked?"

"Exactly." Jess nodded. "They're bound to me for life, and me to them. If one of us dies, the other two go on. If two of the triad die, we all die."

"Jesus. I don't even know what to say to that. That's taking commitment to the extreme, Jess!"

"No cheating. No doubts. No secrets because of the link. I think it's worth the trade-off. I wouldn't want to live without them anyway," Jess gave her a sad smile. "I couldn't face anyone else leaving me, Viv. This way, they can't go anywhere without me. Not even into the next life."

"Oh, Jess." Viv's throat grew thick with emotions as she looked at her best friend and remembered all the loss and pain she'd suffered in the past year. "I get why you did it. I hope you are really happy here. You deserve to be happy, and so much more." She crossed the room and threw her arms around Jess, still fighting her tears.

"You deserve that too. I want that for you so badly." Jess hugged her hard. "I thought maybe you'd be able to be happy here, but I screwed that up, didn't I? I should have told you everything."

"Yeah, you should have. But if I go, you won't be the reason. Those two idiots waiting downstairs did the one thing I told them I wouldn't stand for. They lied to me. Now I can't trust them. What chance do we have of being happy if I can't even trust them to tell me the truth?"

"They love you, Viv. That has to count for something."

"Love is more than just a word." She could almost feel the ice creeping back around her heart as she untangled herself from Jess and stepped back. "It's a promise. And they broke it. I can't talk about this anymore, Jess. I just want to go home."

"Home to the cabin, right?" Jess queried. "Not home to Toronto?"

Viv pursed her lips and didn't say another word. She wasn't going to make any promises. There'd been enough of those broken already. She needed to get away from everyone and try to figure out what the hell she was going to do with the shattered pieces of the life she'd hoped to build here in Tofino.

I should have stayed home for Christmas Eve. At least then I would have had the fantasy for a little while longer.

CHAPTER NINETEEN

WHEN VIVIAN HAD REFUSED to even speak to them before leaving the party, Tucker knew it was all falling apart.

They hadn't moved from the bottom of the stairs since she'd gone up with Jessica. They needed to speak to her, to explain everything, but Jess had made it clear that Viv wasn't ready to talk to them. Hell, she didn't want to see them, period. Despite that information it had taken both of Byron's fathers plus Rory and Evan to move them to another room when word came down that she was leaving.

The minute she was gone they left too, barely saying a word to anyone. Byron's mother had tried to talk to them, but there was nothing she could say that was going to fix this. There was nothing anyone could say or do to help them with Vivian. Tobias though, he was another matter. Darius had started a full manhunt. It had brought an end to the night's festivities as every able-bodied member of the colony headed out to look for their errant citizen.

They should have done something about him years

ago, before his violent outbursts and vicious temper had forced his mother to flee for her life. Before Tucker's world had been torn apart by a man he despised but was expected to take care of anyway. The colony's archaic rules and traditions had ruined his life once, and now Tucker had the sick sense it was happening all over again.

As they followed the taillights of Jess's Jeep down the gravel road that lead off colony land, Tucker held tight to a single, obsessive thought. The last time his world had come crashing down around him he had been too young to stop it. This time things were different. He'd lost his family once already. He'd be damned to hell before he would let that happen again.

They shadowed her all the way to her driveway before pulling over to the side of the road. "Do we follow her? Or do we honor her wishes and leave her alone for tonight?" Tucker asked and Byron shook his head.

"I don't know. Right now I'm second-guessing every decision I've made since she came into our lives."

"Same here. Looking back, I know we should have told her sooner."

"Maybe. Or maybe tomorrow would have been soon enough if Tobias hadn't fucked this up for us. Your father has a talent for destruction."

"He is not my father!" Tucker slammed a hand down on the steering wheel in frustration. "He's a toxic, vicious son of a bitch that should have been exiled years ago. He has never done a single thing in his entire life to earn the title of Father. As much as I would love to blame him for everything, though, I can't. He attacked Vivian, and that's on him. But *we* are the ones who looked her in the eye and vowed not to lie to her." He struck the steering wheel again. "I've spent the last ten years defying the fucking colony's rules and expectations. Why didn't I tell her?"

"I don't know, I don't know!" Byron exclaimed as he scrubbed a hand over his jaw, looking as frustrated as Tucker felt. "It's not like I've fucking done this before. Until last night it wasn't our news to tell."

"No? So whose news was it?"

"Jessica's, I think. I mean she was the person closest to Vivian, right? She's the one who brought her into our world. The moment we told her about us, Viv would have figured out that Rory and Evan were the same. She knows you two are cousins, and she's not stupid."

Tucker groaned. "I don't think she's going to see it that way. What she's going to see is that we told her we loved her and skipped over the bit where we lied about who and what we were."

"You're right. Fuck!" Byron swore. "Do you think she'll be more understanding once she realizes one of us has been in denial about who and what he is for a decade? If it had been anyone else in the water tonight, you'd still be in denial about who you really are. You never would have done it."

"Done what? Changed forms? To be honest, I didn't plan on transforming at all. I dove in and it took over."

Byron went still and then gave him an odd look. "What do you mean, it took over?"

"I mean I never summoned my pelt. It never even crossed my mind. All I was thinking about was getting to Vivian before she went under. And what is with that look you're giving me? Haven't you ever had your other half take over?"

"Not once," Byron said quietly. "Do you realize what that means?"

"I wasn't aware that it meant anything. Now can we get back to talking about Vivian?"

"We're still talking about Vivian. We have to get her back, bro."

"I thought we established that already."

"You don't understand. We *have* to get her back. Your other half has already chosen her. That's the only reason it would have forced a transformation on you tonight. She's your mate, Tucker. And that means she's my mate too."

"Fuck." Tucker stared out into the darkness as the truth sank in, to be met with a powerful surge of confirmation from the part of him he rarely acknowledged. "We have to get her back."

"That's what I'm saying. She's it for us, bro. There isn't going to be another woman. Not now, not ever. So we better figure out a way to make this up to her, or we're going to be a very lonely, sad pair of bachelors from now until we die."

"But she's human! She's human and we haven't bonded with her. This doesn't make any sense."

Byron's laughter held a bitter edge as he asked, "When did life start making sense? And didn't she tell you her grandmother claimed their family had faerie blood? What if there's something to that? Maybe she's not completely human either."

"I suggest we refrain from telling her she may be part Tinkerbell until *after* we've somehow managed to get her to forgive us."

"You mean introduce the weirdness slowly? That ship has sailed, bro."

"You're not exactly being constructive here," Tucker pointed out, frustration dripping from every word.

"You want constructive? We need to consider the possibility that Tobias isn't done with her yet. He's in the wind and out of his mind. That's a bad combination on a good night. This has been far from a good night for any of us."

"He wouldn't dare." The idea of Vivian having to face Tobias alone made Tucker's blood boil.

"He's insane, and I don't say that lightly. I think the booze and bitterness have finally broken his mind. We'd be smart to assume he would dare just about anything right now."

"She doesn't want us anywhere near her. How are we going to watch over her?"

"You're not going to like what I'm going to suggest."

"This is going to involve spending the night with flippers and fur, isn't it?" The thought didn't bother him nearly as much as the idea of leaving Vivian alone and unprotected. His priorities had changed in the past few hours. Nothing was more important than Vivian. Not the past, not Tobias, not the colony with its archaic rules and backward thinking.

"Can you think of a better way to watch over her?"

"No. We better tell Darius what we're doing though. He'll need to let us know if they find Tobias before morning."

"We can tell Jess." Byron inclined his head toward the cabin, where a pair of headlights could be seen flickering between the trees. "She's going to be here in thirty seconds or so."

"Now let's hope she has good news for us, or barring that, at least some good advice."

VIVIAN STOOD in the middle of the cabin and fought hard not to cry. The entire place was full of reminders of Tucker and Byron and all the joy she'd felt only yesterday. The moment she stepped foot inside she was surrounded by a myriad of scents and sights that conjured up memories she didn't want to face. Her heart hurt, she felt bone-weary and soul-sick. Not to mention she had a bag full of soaking wet clothes she needed to wash before they were ruined.

At least fixing her clothes gave her something mundane to focus on. She took her time, carefully rinsing and then hand washing each piece. By the time they were set out to dry Viv was feeling a little more in control of her world. Not much, but right now she'd take what she could get.

Despite what she'd told Jess about being done discussing things, it hadn't taken long for more questions to arise. Now Viv's head was swimming with all the information she'd been given on the ride back. Blood-bonds and telepathic links were only the beginning. Selkies healed faster than humans, and were immune to most human diseases, though they shared similar lifespans.

Then there was the fact that Darius was more than the de facto leader of the community, he was their king. When Jess married Rory, she became modern-day royalty. Granted, on a very small scale, but it was still hard for Vivian to believe. No wonder Jess had asked her yesterday to keep an open mind and an open heart. At the time Viv thought they were talking about her relationship with Tucker and Byron. It turned out there was a great deal more going on and she didn't know where to begin trying to come to terms with it all.

I think I'm going to start with a stiff drink and go from there.

The first bottle she laid eyes on was the scotch Tucker had sent her. Her hand hovered above it for several long seconds as another host of memories hit her. Laughter and scotch-flavored kisses, the thrum of Tucker's bike as he took her exploring, the scent of leather and cedar that clung to his skin.

She grabbed the bottle and poured herself two fingers' worth of the amber liquid, tossing it back quickly. The liquor left a trail of heat in its wake, but it didn't banish the images dancing around her head. Byron's devilish grin, the way his green eyes danced that first night as he flirted with her. His playful banter and the way he always knew what to say to make her laugh. The vision of him, bare-chested and laughing as he encouraged her attempts to learn to swim. Those lessons had saved her life.

That realization had her pouring another shot of scotch into her glass. She could have easily drowned tonight. If they hadn't come looking for her, she would have gone under eventually. That inky, icy blackness would have closed over her head and that would have been the end. She'd been so busy being angry and hurt that she had somehow managed to avoid thinking about how close she came to dying. As reality crashed in she started to tremble, then shake so hard her drink sloshed in her glass. She put it back down on the counter without drinking it, and made her unsteady way down the hall.

Clothes off. Hot water on. Get into the shower. She was only half aware of what she was doing as she went through the motions and stepped under the steaming cascade of water. She stayed there until every trace of salt was washed away and she finally felt truly warm again.

It might have been only ten minutes or an hour, but finally the dark thoughts and fear receded and she felt like herself again. She was a bit battered, both inside and out, but she was finally past the anger and the shock. Now, she could sleep. In the morning she'd have to decide what the hell she was going to do, but for now, she was too tired to think clearly.

She crawled into bed and tried to ignore the lingering scent of her two men that clung to the pillows on either side of her. She wouldn't think about them. She could not admit to herself that she already missed them despite their thoughtless betrayal and the lies. Not yet. For now it was easier not to feel anything at all.

She had no idea what time it was when she was dragged out of the peaceful oblivion of sleep by a cacophony of howls, barks and snarls. The unfamiliar noises of wild animals in some kind of frenzy had her out of bed and racing for the window before her mind could catch up to her body.

It was too dark to see much, but she could make out several large shapes tumbling over each other where the ocean met the small curve of beach below the cottage.

Bears? Wolves? She squinted, trying hard to pick out some detail that would tell her what was going on. She caught a flash of teeth, followed by the distinct squeal of an animal in pain. Fuck it. Whatever it was, she needed to get a closer look.

She tore through the cabin, wearing nothing but the shirt she'd gone to bed in. As she neared the back door she spotted the bear spray Tucker had given her as a joke and grabbed it. Feeling better for being armed, she yanked open the back door before flipping on the switches for the outdoor lights. The whole backyard lit up, allowing her to finally see what was happening.

There were three seals fighting near the water's edge, two of them working in tandem against another, smaller seal with a golden-brown coat. The two working together were silver and black, and all three of them appeared to be bleeding. As she watched, the smaller seal snarled and lunged, sinking its teeth into the larger one's side. The large one brayed and rolled back into the water, taking the golden-brown one with it.

Why would seals be fighting? Her mind was still trying to shake off the fog of sleep and it took her several more seconds of staring before the truth dawned. Seals wouldn't be fighting like this. Selkies might, though.

"Byron! Tucker!" She screamed their names and the silver seal's head snapped around to stare at her. Dark eyes stared into hers and for a split-second she could have sworn his eyes shifted to a brilliant green.

Byron?

She was still trying to understand what she'd seen when the smaller seal erupted out of the water and charged straight at Byron. At least she thought it was Byron. It didn't matter though, because she was already running down the rain-slick walkway. In her heart she knew those were her men, and seals or not, she wasn't going to leave them to fight this strange battle alone.

As Vivian jumped from the walkway down onto rocky

beach the extent of her mistake hit her. In her hurry to find out what was going on, she hadn't stopped to put on any shoes.

She landed hard, the stones cutting into her bare feet. The footing was too uneven for her to keep her balance and she came down on her hands and knees. Pain lanced through her but she ignored it, fumbling around blindly until she found the canister of bear spray she'd dropped when she hit the rocks. She had it primed and ready by the time she managed to scramble back onto her feet.

In the few short seconds that had passed the small, brown seal had managed to get around Byron and Tucker. It was charging up the beach at her at an impressive speed despite its awkward, rolling method of locomotion. Without hesitating, Jess pulled the trigger and a stream of white vapor shot out of the can and straight into the seal's face.

Ear-piercing barks and howls nearly shattered her eardrums, and then the animal floundered back into the water with one final roar of pain. Silence overtook the beach and Vivian went down to the water, forgetting the residual fog still in the air around her. A gust of wind blew up from the sea and she found herself choking on the noxious stuff. Her vision doubled and then blurred as tears filled her eyes.

"Fuck, that stuff is nasty!" Byron's voice sounded from somewhere to her left, but when she looked that way all she saw was a fuzzy blur.

"Byron?" She wheezed out the syllables of his name and lowered the pepper spray she was still holding out.

"I thought I told you not to use that stuff on me." Tucker grumbled from nearby.

"After the shit you two pulled? If I could see right now I'd probably give you both a snootful just on principle!"

"If it makes you feel better, there's enough of it lingering in the air I think we're all suffering," Byron muttered, and after blinking away more tears she was able to see him standing in front of her, blood streaming down his shoulder from a nasty-looking bite. Tucker moved in beside him and both of them stood, naked, soaked, and streaked with blood.

"Would one of you like to explain why you're bleeding all over my beach?" she asked and reached for Tucker, who was standing closest. She carefully swept away the worst of the blood to check the extent of the bite on his side, trying not to think about how good it felt to touch him again. As her hand inadvertently crossed over the top of a cut, a pulse of heat thrummed through her hand and everything went oddly out of focus.

She was filled with a sense of comfort and warmth that wrapped itself around her heart and eased the pain and sadness that had haunted her since the fight with Tobias. Her knees gave way and she felt Tucker's arms wrap around her, holding her tight.

"Mine." A voice whispered and for a moment she could have sworn it was only in her head.

"Not yours. Not anymore." She tried to push herself out of his arms but her arms wouldn't work right and her mouth felt like it was stuffed with cotton.

"Mine. Always." Tucker's voice came again and then she heard him speak aloud. "Shit! Viv, show me your hands!"

"Why?" she muttered groggily, and lifted her head to look at him. She noticed that her eyes weren't blurred by tears any longer, and her nose and throat had almost stopped burning.

"Show me your hands. Right now," he ordered her again, and she raised her arms to show him her palm and the can of bear spray. That's when she noticed the blood on her hand from the cuts she'd gotten falling on the rocks.

"Holy shit," Byron swore. "Did she—with you?"

"Cabin. Now. You'll have to carry her. I'm still feeling the effects," Tucker muttered, and pointed her toward Byron.

"Effects of what?" Viv tried to ask but her tongue got tangled on the words.

"Effects of a blood-bonding," Byron told her softly as he lifted her into his arms. She would have protested, but she was feeling too woozy to do more than offer up a minor argument.

"Can't be. Not a selkie."

"Shh, we'll figure this out when we get you inside."

"Can't be bonded to him...Tobias said so. You two 'sposed to have a selkie mate. Special bloodline."

Byron's arms tightened around her. "Is that what he told you?"

"Mhmm," Viv hummed in assent.

"Well he was wrong about that," Tucker rumbled from behind them.

"You're ours, slim. We've got a lot to talk about, but make no mistake, we belong together. There's no way in hell we're letting you go."

CHAPTER TWENTY

THE NEXT THING she knew they were back inside the cabin and she was being handed down to someone. Another pair of strong arms wrapped around her, holding her close. *Tucker.* She could smell his familiar scent over the brine of the ocean and the traces of capsicum. Well, at least her nose was working again.

"I've got you, sugar."

"Stop doing that!" she thought back at the invading voice, and Tucker stiffened in surprise.

"You can really hear me?" This time a sense of surprise accompanied the words sounding in her head.

"Of course I can hear you. You're shouting inside my head! How are you even doing that?" she asked out loud, only to be met with silence.

"She can hear you, dude?" Byron asked as he took the pepper spray from her hand.

"And I can hear her, too," Tucker confirmed, and Byron dropped onto the couch down by her feet with a whoosh of breath leaving his lungs.

"Well, that's a surprise."

Viv sat up as the wooziness slowly wore off, and that's when she remembered that neither of them had a stitch on, and she was only wearing a shirt. Her bare ass was across Tucker's thighs and Byron's blood-streaked body was on full display beside her.

"Uh, guys? Clothes would be good."

"In a second. There's something we need to tell you first." Tucker cleared his throat before continuing. "I know you're angry at us. I can feel it. So before we get to the apologies, you might as well hear the rest of it."

Viv groaned. "You still need to explain why you two are here. Who that was who was out there fighting with you, why your voice is in my damned head, and, oh yes, let's not forget you both owe me an apology for lying through your pointy, shapeshifting teeth!"

As her anger returned she tried to launch herself out of Tucker's lap, but he and Byron both latched onto her, preventing her from going anywhere.

"We'll get to that. And believe me, we have a lot to make up for, but you have to understand something first. When you touched me, our blood mingled. Did Jess tell you what blood-bonding was?"

Viv nodded, her stomach turning a slow somersault as her brain caught up with everything that had been said. It wasn't possible. She was human, so it couldn't be. Could it?

"It would seem that it could be, and it is." Tucker's voice sounded inside her mind again and Viv gasped as everything became clear.

"So we're bonded? What the hell does that even mean?"

"It means that I am going to devote the rest of my life to making up for lying to you and seeing to it you are the happiest woman on the planet. You are the only woman I'll ever want from now until the day I die. You hold my life in those pretty little hands of yours, Viv." He cupped his fingers around hers. "Literally."

"Because if I leave you, you'll die." Her heart felt like it was being squeezed by a giant fist and it got tighter with every word she uttered. "And if you die, Byron dies. Like what happened to Jessica's mother when her husband left her. So that's it. I have to stay. If I don't, I'll end up with both of your blood on my hands."

Byron laid a hand on her bare leg and leaned in close. "This wasn't planned. You know that, right? We love you, but we never intended to force you."

"How could you have planned this? No, I know this was fate, not the two of you." Viv closed her eyes and tried to breathe past the terrible weight in her chest. "It doesn't change anything though. You two still betrayed my trust and lied to me. Everyone lied to me, and I don't have a clue where to begin dealing with that."

"I do," Byron spoke again. "But you're probably going to think I'm insane."

"Insane seems to be the theme of the day," she groused. "So let's hear this idea."

"Bond with me, Vivian. We can talk for the rest of the night, but if you bond with me, Tucker and I can let you see what's in our heads, and our hearts. If you can't forgive us after that? Then so be it."

"Bond with you? You're right, that sounds insane. Tucker happened by accident, and now you want me to do it again on purpose?"

"Yes." Byron's voice was raw and his green eyes were full of deep sorrow as he caught her gaze and held it. "I'm sorry I lied to you. I'm sorry I screwed up what we had. I want that back, Viv. I want it back and then I want to make it better than ever."

"How do you think that's going to happen? You two keep talking about making this up to me, but I'm not hearing anything other than airy promises."

"Then let us show you," Tucker whispered, his voice thick with emotion. "Let us claim you properly so there can never be secrets between us again. I don't know how you can share our link, but I'm grateful for it. That link is the only way I can think of to show you how much we love you."

"So show me," she challenged Tucker. "Just you, for now. Show me what it would be like."

"Close your eyes, this might get a little disorienting," he murmured and then it was as if someone opened the top of her head and poured a stream of thoughts, feelings and images directly into her brain.

At first it was too much to make sense of, but then Byron stroked her thigh and gave her some simple advice. "Try to focus on one thing and let the rest fade into the background."

It took her a while longer, but eventually she caught a familiar image. Their first kisses, straddling the back of Tucker's bike as the sun set in a glorious explosion of color. It felt different, and then she understood why. These weren't her memories, they were Tucker's. She was experiencing his needs, his realization that he was falling for her after just one kiss.

Overwhelmed by the power of what he was sharing,

Viv tried to mentally distance herself but Tucker wouldn't allow it. *"I love you,"* he whispered, mind-to-mind, and the echo of those words stirred up other memories. He let her see it all. His doubts, his desires, and all of his love for her.

Then he showed her the rest. The joy he'd experienced last night as they planned a future that would include her. Regret at having to lie to her and the relief of finally having Darius's permission to tell her the truth. He showed her the heart-tearing fear he felt when he saw her in the water, followed by the heartache of seeing the pain and fear in her eyes and knowing he'd caused it.

When she pulled away this time, he let her, shutting down the link between them and letting her head empty of everything he'd put there. "Holy shit. That was…vivid." She had to struggle to find a word that came close to describing what she'd experienced.

"Now do you see?" Byron asked, and she opened her eyes to find him watching her intently.

"I saw. I heard. Hell, I *felt* it," she replied, still a little dazed.

"I want that," Byron murmured, and she could hear the longing in his voice. "I want to have that with you, Viv."

"This would be forever? Linked and locked in until death do us part, literally?"

Both men were silent for a second, and then Tucker answered her. "We don't know. The link is different with humans. You and I already share a very strong bond, so it might tie you to us too. That wouldn't be typical, but nothing about you is." His lips brushed the shell of her ear. "If that happens, would it be so bad?"

"It would be like I had no control. What if you and Byron decided to hurt me, could I leave you then?"

Tucker stiffened beneath her, and she belatedly remembered the fact his mother had done just that. "Wait a second. If your parents left Tobias, how is he still alive? That doesn't make any sense!"

"That's a good question. To be honest, not even the elders know for sure. They think it's because there was never any love between Geoffrey, Tina and Tobias," Byron explained.

"Never?"

"My mother was forced into her triad. In time, she and my father grew to love each other, but Tobias was too cruel and petty to ever win her affections." She could feel Tucker's heartbeat slam against his ribs as he finally talked about his family.

"Their bond was screwed up from the beginning. Selkie men are supposed to protect their mates with their lives, but Tobias was violent and vicious, even to my mother. As he got older, he got nastier. Darius's father was obsessed with bloodlines. He didn't care who was hurt, so long as certain bloodlines were bred the way he thought they should be. Love or even empathy never entered into it. After he died my parents went to the elders and then to Darius looking for a way out. No one wanted to believe that Tobias was that dangerous. No one wanted to believe the blood-bond had been corrupted and that he could hurt his mate...and her son. They fled the colony the night after my twenty-first birthday. My mother left me all her family's money and vanished."

"Shit. And I thought I had a fucked up family. I'm sorry you had to live through that." Viv leaned back into Tucker's arms and automatically turned her head to brush a kiss to his cheek. By the time she realized what she'd done it was too late, but then she caught a riff of satisfaction and yearning along the link she shared with him.

What they were offering her was a lifetime of shared moments and emotional intimacy. It would be absolute, but it would mean the end of doubts and uncertainties. She couldn't deny that the idea appealed to her. Her parents had been indifferent to her, and no matter how hard she'd tried she hadn't been able to change that.

From the day they met, there had been nothing indifferent about the chemistry the three of them shared. Maybe the tarot cards had been right after all. Maybe this was where she was supposed to be. As Tucker stirred behind her she remembered the sense of comfort and security that had wrapped around her soul the moment they had bonded. She had longed for that feeling her whole life, and she'd be a fool to walk away from it now. There was one more thing she needed to know before she gave them her answer, though she already suspected the truth.

"You two were out there watching over me tonight, weren't you?"

Both men nodded and rumbled in assent.

"And that was Tobias out there, fighting with you."

Again they confirmed what she was saying and she sighed. "So he came after me again. And he's going to keep coming after me because he doesn't want us together."

"We'll never let him come near you, love," Byron vowed. "And now we have Darius's blessing, it doesn't matter what Tobias wants. We were going to tell you all of this tomorrow morning and then let you decide. Tobias stole that moment from us. Don't let him steal anything else from us. Please?"

She covered Byron's hand with hers and smiled. "Just remember, you both promised to make it up to me for the rest of my life. I plan on living a very long time."

"Is that a yes? I'm taking that as a yes." Byron bounced off the couch and did a little victory dance in the middle of her living room, completely comfortable in his nudity. As her eyes skimmed over his physique in appreciation, she noticed that the bite she'd seen earlier was almost healed.

"How fast do you guys heal?"

"Very," Tucker told her with an amused rumble. "We'll be as good as new in a few more hours. Which is more than can be said for you." He touched her bruised and battered hands and then frowned as he spotted her bare feet for the first time. "Why didn't you tell us you were hurt?"

Byron broke off his dance and headed for the kitchen without even glancing at her. "I'm bringing something to clean up your feet. We're not doing this bonding until you're all fixed up."

"So that's how you two do it!" Vivian finally understood how her two lovers always seemed to be in sync. "You've been cheating!"

"*Guilty as charged.*" Tucker's thoughts were rife with good humor and affection.

"*Don't get smug yet, buster. I'm not done being mad at you. Not by a long shot.*"

Tucker muttered something under his breath and tucked her head under his chin. "Not smug. Just grateful to have you back in my arms. After everything that happened tonight, I wasn't sure I'd ever get to hold you again."

"After everything that happened, I wasn't sure I'd ever let you," she confessed and then looked up at Byron as he crossed the room toward them, a cloth and a clean towel in his hand. "Either of you."

Byron dropped to his knees beside her legs and began gently washing the soles of her bruised and torn up feet. "You're a mess. How did this happen?"

"I saw Tobias attack you and I started running. I didn't think about the fact I wasn't wearing shoes until I had already jumped off the walkway." She gestured to her feet, knees and hands. "As you can see, I didn't land very well."

"And yet you still managed to get him in the face with a full shot of that bear spray." Byron was grinning as he continued his careful ministrations.

"If he didn't like me before, he's really going to have a hate on for me now," Viv muttered, but she couldn't find it in her to feel regret for what she'd done.

"When the colony finds him, you're going to be the least of his problems. Attacking you and revealing colony secrets are both serious offenses. There was a time that his actions would have led to banishment, or death. At the very least he'll lose his pelt for this, and in many ways that's worse than a death sentence."

"Lose his pelt? Jess tried to explain the whole pelt thing to me, but my brain was on overload by then." Viv leaned her head back against Tucker's shoulder and tried not to wince as Byron cleaned away the last of the sand, stone and blood from her skin.

"If our pelts are placed in something made of iron, we can't summon them. Iron blocks the magic."

"Which is what Jess's mom did to her, right?"

"Right," both of them said together.

"You're all cleaned up. I'd like to get some ointment on those cuts though."

"I don't think there's much in the way of first-aid supplies here." She had meant to buy some basics like ointment and Band-Aids in case of emergencies, but she hadn't gotten around to it yet.

"Will you let us take you back to Breakers?" Tucker asked. "We've got full first-aid kits there. I don't like the idea of cutting your hand if we don't have so much as a bandage to put on it afterward."

"You two shower, then we'll go." She made her counteroffer and both men protested, but she cut them off.

"Have you seen yourselves? You're covered in blood and seawater. If I'm going to forgive you for everything, the least you could do is get cleaned up."

"She's got a point, dude. You're a mess."

Tucker chuckled. "And yet I still look better than you." They managed to get her settled on the couch and tucked under a quilt with admonishments not to move until they got back. Then they both went off to shower, leaving Vivian a few minutes alone to come to terms with what had happened, and what she was about to do.

Despite everything they'd done, she loved them. The connection she had inadvertently made with Tucker allowed her to see that he truly regretted how they'd handled things. It had also shown her how much he loved her. How much *they* loved her.

"And we always will."

"Quit eavesdropping!" she hollered, only to be answered by a chorus of laughter from down the hall. The minute they were done with this bonding thing, she was going to demand they teach her how to block them or she was never going to have a moment's peace.

TUCKER HAD SHOWERED FIRST and then headed back outside to grab their clothes, leaving Byron alone with Vivian for a few precious moments. For the first time in his adult life, Byron was experiencing jealousy, and it was eating him alive.

He wanted what Tucker and Viv had between them. His animal half was near-feral with the need to bond with Viv and form the triad they were always meant for, but he would not give in to it. He would not rush this. He craved her, but he also wanted to give her at least some of the trappings of a proper bonding ritual.

With a towel wrapped around his hips he headed back out to the living room and reclaimed his spot on the couch, gathering Viv into his arms. She came to him willingly, but her hazel eyes hadn't yet regained their sparkle. That was their fault.

"I'm so sorry," he apologized again.

"I know." She wrapped an arm around his chest and let her head rest over his heart. "But that doesn't mean everything is magically fixed." She paused and then snorted with laughter. "Even if magic is actually involved. Which is damned strange to think about despite my beliefs."

"Think how much weirder this would all be if you didn't already believe in magic."

"I don't even want to think about it. This is hard enough as it is."

"For what it's worth, we've known this stuff our entire lives and we still had no idea how the hell we were going to explain it to you."

"You've never told anyone else?" She tipped her head up and he caught a glimmer of amazement in her beautiful eyes as she stared at him. "No one?"

"Never. You're the first we've ever wanted to share this with. The first one who mattered enough to take the risk."

"That makes me feel a little better," she confessed, and her lips curved up into the briefest of smiles. He dropped his head and kissed her before he even considered what he was doing. His lips tingled as they touched hers, and then the tingle turned to a shimmer of heat. His tongue swept over her mouth and he could still taste the fiery remnants of the pepper spray that had blown back onto them all.

"Spicy," she whispered as her lips parted and she invited him to take the kiss deeper.

"Yes, you are."

Her laughter buzzed against his tongue, and in that moment he knew that it was going to be okay. The universe had taken pity on the two of them and given them back the only woman in the world that could make them whole.

"Thank you," he murmured to his lover and whatever deities had chosen to help them this day. Then her kisses stole his mind and he drifted, blissfully content until Tucker reappeared and it was time to go.

CHAPTER TWENTY-ONE

THEY WAVED off her attempts to get dressed and wrapped her in another layer of blankets before carrying her off to the truck. Byron held her in his arms the entire time. Touching her was the only thing keeping his selkie half satisfied, and it was barely enough. When they got to Breakers she tried to get them to put her down and let her walk, but neither of them had any intention of letting her feet so much as touch the ground.

"Indulge us," Byron requested as he carried her through the back entrance and into the dark interior.

"Like I have a choice," she grumbled, a rebellious look on her pretty face.

"Not really." He deposited her on the edge of one of the bar's pool tables and gave her a lopsided grin as he unwrapped her from the blankets. "Tucker, you want to get some of these lights turned on?"

Tucker flicked on a handful of lights and joined them. He was carrying a duffle bag and Viv was gawking at it as he hefted it up beside her.

"That's your idea of a first-aid kit?" she asked, clearly amazed. "What's in that thing, a heart and lung machine? Everything a Do-It-Yourself surgeon needs?"

"This? It's an industrial first-aid bag. We invested in the courses after our first few bar fights." Tucker was busy rummaging for bandages and the other items they'd need.

"It saves us having to sit around the emergency room too often," Byron chimed.

"Very practical of you," she snickered, and then held out her hand toward him, palm up. "So how is this going to work?"

His heart slammed hard against his ribs as he took her hand in his and traced a finger over her palm, following the line that started beneath her index finger. "I'll cut you there, just a shallow slice, and then I'll do the same for me." He showed her the faint scar that marked his palm. Tucker held his hand up too, displaying the scar line that was normally unnoticeable.

"You cut along the life line." She stared at their scars and smiled. "Of course you do. I'd say it's a pretty bit of symbolism, but given that you're both actual, magical beings, I suppose it might be more than that, huh?"

"Life line?" Tucker frowned and looked down at his hand. "You're a palm reader too?"

"Of course she is," Byron couldn't help but grin as he lifted her fingers to his mouth and brushed a kiss across her open palm. "She's our fae princess."

"Oh, I like the sound of that!" her missing smile reappeared as she beamed at them both. "Jess can deal with being royalty. I only want to be *your* princess."

"You'll be that, and more," Byron vowed. Tucker handed him a pocket knife and came to stand beside him.

"I love you. And I promise I will spend the rest of my life showing you how much you mean to me, in every way I can think of." He cut himself and then ran the blade along her palm. He hated the idea that he had to cut her to claim her, but if he had his way this would be the last pain he'd ever cause her.

As they clasped hands, palm-to-palm, a surge of heat passed through him and he felt the same sensory shift he experienced the day he'd been bound to Tucker. She was his. He was hers. It was done. Now not even death could part them for long.

The legends of his people claimed that souls bound to each other this way would find their mates in every incarnation, recognizing each other and falling in love all over again. Byron believed in the legend, and as her blood mingled with his he knew that they'd shared this moment before. Just as he knew that they would share this moment again and again, in lifetime after lifetime, until the stars faded and the universe ceased to be.

THIS TIME she was prepared for the strange sensations that accompanied the bonding, but it didn't stop the dizziness or the way her mind went muddy and fuzzy around the edges. Tucker's arm went around her shoulders and she leaned into it, grateful for the added support.

"I've got you," Tucker murmured.

"We'll always be there for you, love." Byron's voice sounded inside her head and Vivian knew that it was done. For better or worse, she had tied herself to both men for the rest of her days. Emotions began to appear along

with his thoughts, and Viv's heart swelled, then overflowed.

She wouldn't have guessed that Byron was the one with the soul of a poet, but his thoughts and feelings were just that, poetry. There were no shadows on his soul, and every element she explored gave her more insight into the man she loved. She took in his heart and gave hers back in return while both of them held her hands.

"Lie back and let me fix you up," Tucker finally spoke, breaking the trance she'd fallen into. "While Byron takes a minute to get his bearings. I hope I didn't have that goofy grin on *my* face when we bonded."

"You looked goofier," Byron shot back.

"No fighting, you two," Viv interjected, as she allowed Tucker to ease her back until she was lying on the pool table with her feet dangling over the edge. "This is surprisingly comfy."

"Don't tell us that or we'll be joining you instead of cleaning up this impressive array of boo-boos you managed to gather charging straight for the one man we were trying to keep away from you," Tucker placed a piece of gauze against the cut Byron had given her. "Make a fist and keep some pressure on that."

"In my defense, I wasn't charging toward anyone. I was defending my beach from a bunch of unruly seals that woke me up after the worst night of my life."

"I'd apologize, but since waking you up is what led us all to this point, I'm not going to. If Tobias hadn't come after you again, we'd still be trying to figure out a way to get you to forgive us for being idiots." Byron's voice had the same far-off and fuzzy tone to it that hers did, and Viv knew he was also feeling the effects of their recent bonding.

Tucker's hands were incredibly gentle as he smoothed ointment over her injuries, finishing with her hand. She let herself drift as he worked, and somewhere in the fullness of time two hands became four, and their touch went from therapeutic to sensual.

Callused hands caressed and stroked. Eventually one of them slid her shirt up, exposing her breasts.

"Hands over your head, please." Tucker whispered. The moment she moved her arms he whisked her shirt off, only to tangle it around her wrists, snuggly enough she couldn't wriggle free without serious effort.

"Hey!" she yelped in protest. "No fair!" He gave her an unapologetic grin from where he stood at the top of the table, her bound wrists captured between his hands.

"We just want to be sure you don't strain yourself." Byron's thoughts were tinged with amusement and thrumming with the beginnings of lust.

"Let us love you, Viv." Tucker's voice joined Byron's and she felt his desires flow through her.

She didn't give them a direct answer. Instead she mentally pushed some of her own nearly kindling passion back at them and was rewarded with a pair of low groans.

"She's learning fast," Byron commented as he tore off his clothes in a few quick tugs. He surprised her by climbing onto the table beside her and slanting a heated kiss across her lips. Tucker still held her hands captive, so she couldn't do much more than open her mouth to Byron's kisses. She nibbled on his lower lip and he responded by thrusting his tongue into her mouth, the plunge and press a subtle promise of what she hoped was to come. Before too long though, he broke their kiss and moved away despite her soft mewls of disappointment.

"Eyes closed," Tucker's words had a note of command that sent a thrill right down to her toes.

"Who made you the boss of me?" she sassed as she closed her eyes. Seconds later something soft, warm and imbued with Tucker's woodsy scent was tucked under her head as a pillow, and she cracked an eye open to peek.

"No peeking! Right now, we are in charge," Byron informed her as Tucker laughed from his position above her.

"Says who?" she guffawed, and deliberately tugged at her wrists. "Come on guys, let me—" her words choked off as something cool and wet was trickled between her breasts. "What the hell is that?"

"I think you're about to find out, trouble."

Byron's hot mouth closed over one peaked nipple, his tongue swirling around the taut nub, leaving a strange, tingling sensation in its wake. He released her with a soft pop of suction and then dropped his head to the valley between her breasts, licking up every trace of the unknown liquid he'd drizzled on her skin. Again there was a faint tingle and then she gasped as he lifted his head and blew a puff of air across her wet flesh. Instantly her nipple puckered as her skin chilled and another, far more powerful tingle hit her.

She arched upward as his mouth claimed her other breast and repeated the process, leaving her panting and squirming on the table as she tried to put as much of herself into contact with him as she could.

"Incoming," Tucker warned her silently as more of the cool liquid hit her skin, tracking down her stomach and

filling her navel. Byron's mouth followed the trail of liquid, and each time he blew on her chills zinged across her stomach and chased each other down to her drenched pussy.

As his mouth grazed her piercing he paused to play, lapping every drop from the tiny pool of her navel and toying with the jeweled ring nestled there. His touch was arousing and teasing at the same time, and her swollen clit throbbed with every caress. She drew up the leg furthest from him in a blatant appeal. "Please?" she asked softly, and he rewarded her with a caress up her inner thigh.

"Please, what?" Byron coaxed. "Come on, gorgeous. Use your words."

"Smug, arrogant, jumped-up jackanapes! How's that for using my words?" she sniped, and Tucker burst out laughing.

"Bro, if she can still sound like a thesaurus, you aren't doing it right. Do I need to take over?"

"No." Byron growled before nipping at her navel ring and giving it a last lash of his tongue. "I know what she wants. I want to hear you ask for it, Viv."

Viv lifted her hips off the table and writhed, hoping she looked sensuous and not silly. *"I want this."* She sent the mental message to both of them, accompanied by a vivid image of Byron's face between her legs as she came.

"Fuck! I liked it better when she was cursing at you. If you don't move it, I'm tagging in."

Vivian laughed at the frustration and longing she could hear in Tucker's voice. "If you let go of my hands, you could join us."

"Don't think I'm not tempted, but watching you get all turned on and squirming while I restrain your hands is a serious turn-on, so you're going to have to wait a little while longer."

Hands slid up the delicate skin of her inner thighs, coaxing her legs further apart. "Legs up," Byron instructed as he lifted each foot so her knees were on his shoulders and she was laid open beneath him. "Now that is a beautiful sight. You have such a pretty pussy." Strong fingers stroked over her swollen folds, making her moan with need.

Hot breath fanned overheated skin, making her inner walls tighten in anticipation. Then his mouth was feasting, touching, tasting and devouring her with barely restrained intensity. Everywhere his mouth touched the strange tingling sensation followed, making her nerves sing and sizzle. When he lifted his head to blow across the hood of her clit she cried out in shock as icy heat flowed over her pussy.

"Peppermint schnapps body shots was a damned good call," Tucker murmured, giving Vivian the answer to what had been poured on her skin. "And right now, sugar, you're projecting every single sensation you're feeling. Fuck that is hot."

She glanced up at Tucker, catching his rapt expression as he watched Byron push her ever closer to orgasm. "Reminds me of the first time the three of us were together." She winked up at him and he nodded, his eyes gleaming with lust.

"Oh yeah. That memory is forever burned into my brain." He kept her wrists pinned lightly with one hand and unzipped his jeans with the other, pushing them down far enough to free his cock from the denim.

"Skipped underwear, did we?" She tipped her head so she could watch as he stroked himself from root to tip.

"I was in a hurry to get dressed and get back to you."

Byron's teeth closed on her clit, nipping her sharply enough to snap her full attention back to him and what he was doing.

"Much better," he whispered inside her mind. *"You can play with Tucker after I get you off."*

"Yes, sir," she muttered out loud.

"I like that. Sir. You can call me that anytime you like."

"Why do I get the feeling I'm missing a fascinating conversation?" Tucker asked. He pumped his fist faster over the slick head of his cock, spreading the moisture along the length with each pass of his hand. "Come for us, Viv. Let us feel what we do to you."

Byron went to work with an intensity that left her breathless, lapping and sucking until she was arched off the table and her toes were curled in anticipation of the release that was blossoming deep in her womb. Just as she crested he slid a finger into her aching cunt, pushing her into a soul-shattering orgasm that sent her into orbit.

She was still coming back to Earth when Tucker's lips locked onto hers and she realized her hands were finally free. She buried her hands into his dark hair, kissing him back with so much passion she felt like she was dancing on the edge of madness.

When Tucker finally broke their kiss he winked at her before switching his focus to shedding the rest of his clothes. Byron moved in, spooning his body behind hers so she could feel his rock-hard cock pressed tight against the soft flesh of her ass. The feel of him had her aching, needing to have him inside her.

Tucker quickly joined them on the table, stretching out beside her. He was on his side, his hips near her shoulder and his head propped up on his hand so he could watch the two of them.

"Very soon, I'll be where we both want me to be." Byron's words whispered through her mind like a delicate caress as he lifted her upper leg and draped it over his thigh.

"Now that's a hell of a view," Tucker said with approval.

"Now you know about us, we can tell you that we are immune to human disease." Byron shifted his body so his dick now rested along the seam of her pussy. "Since you're on the pill that means we could do this without condoms. With your permission, of course."

"No diseases either, huh? There are some serious perks to this selkie thing. Too bad it's not possible for me to become one of you. Now that I'm getting used to the idea, I might even consider it." She paused before adding, "And no condoms is fine by me."

"There's one advantage to you being human," Byron murmured, nuzzling her neck. "Selkie women can only have two children at the most. One from each father."

"So Jess gets one each? That's it?"

"That's it. Some sort of magically enforced population control." Tucker shrugged. "None of us really understand it."

"But I'm not selkie, so that means…"

"It means that if we decide that we want kids, we can have as many as we wish." Viv could hear the longing in Byron's voice and despite his attempts to hide it, some of that yearning bled into the connection that linked them together.

At that moment, she let go of the last shreds of her doubt and accepted that she had found herself a home, and a fairytale ending with two men who loved her so completely it made her heart hurt. A family of her own was never something she let herself believe she could have, but deep in her soul she'd never stopped hoping. "Then I guess when the time comes, we'll need to have at least three, just to rub everyone else's face in it, huh?"

Both men were totally still and silent for a moment, and then she was hugged around shoulders and hips by two big men with tears in their eyes. Joy and love filled her mind and her heart, all of their thoughts tangling together until she couldn't tell them apart. Not that she wanted to. She had never felt so loved, or so complete, in all her life.

"You're ours, Viv." Byron eased himself into her tight opening, his teeth nibbling along her shoulder as he teased her with several short, shallow thrusts. She reached out and caught Tucker's tattooed hip, drawing him in close enough she could capture the tip of his cock with her mouth.

Both men groaned and she closed her eyes as they began to fill her head with very different thoughts. Lust, raw and hot, coursed through her. She played her tongue over the thick crown of Tucker's dick, swirling and suckling as Byron rocked his hips and fucked her slowly.

When Tucker's thumb brushed along her slick folds she quivered. When he pushed that thick digit deeper to stroke her clit Viv moaned so loudly she felt his balls tighten in response to the vibration.

"Thank you for forgiving us," Tucker whispered. "If you hadn't I—"

She stopped his words with a carefully judged nip to

his shaft.

"Just love me and never stop." She sent her request to both of them and they answered without words, letting their actions speak for them.

Byron's hand came round to toy with her breasts, his mouth and tongue tracing the lines of her dragon tattoo as he drove into her again and again. He curved his hips to change the angle enough to hit her elusive G-spot with the head of his cock, stroking over it with each back-and-forth motion until she was trembling with the need to come.

"You have gone the prettiest shade of pink, sugar," Tucker crooned as his thumb continued to circle and rub her clit, not quite hard enough to send her over the edge. "Do you want to come now?"

She moaned an affirmative and sucked every inch of his hard length into her mouth, sending as clear a message as she could.

"Come on my dick, gorgeous. I want to feel your pussy squeeze me tight and milk me dry. Goddamn do I like fucking you without a condom. You feel like you were made for me."

"She was made for us, thank the gods." Tucker flicked the callused tip of his thumb over her clitoris hard enough to make the entire nerve bundle pulse and swell. "Come for us. Show us how good it feels."

He and Byron must have coordinated their attacks, because both of them moved together and she lost the last vestiges of her control. Her orgasm tore through her and with her last shreds of awareness she pushed every sensation she was feeling into her lovers' minds, taking them with her into a world of pure pleasure.

She swallowed Tucker's seed down as he groaned and

thrust lightly into her mouth. Behind her Byron shuddered and bucked, driving himself deep into her body as he came. The three of them lay back, panting and replete after what she knew had been the most intense sexual experience of her life. How could it be anything else when she had gotten a sense of everything her lovers had felt, physically and emotionally?

"So, sex is going to be like this from now on?" she asked, unable to keep herself from smiling in contentment.

"Fuck, I hope so. This shouldn't be possible though. Not considering you're human," Tucker said as he swapped ends again so he could kiss her.

"So what does it mean that I can hear and feel you the way I do?"

"Well for starters, it means that there's a very good chance you're fully bound to us, selkie-style." Byron didn't look at all concerned about that idea. In fact, he looked downright smug.

"Details please. Jess's book of selkie stories didn't mention half this stuff. Just lots of talk about you guys being the gigolos of the sea."

"Gigolos?" Tucker snorted. "Not hardly. We're oceanic love gods, thank you very much."

"You're cute when you're delusional," she shot back, and then returned to her questions. "So that bit's true? If some heartbroken chick cries into the sea one of you might show up and give her a reason to smile?" Shock and a trace of jealousy coursed through her at the idea of *her* men being summoned that way.

"Not once we're bonded. Now there's only one woman we will ever want." Byron nuzzled her cheek and then kissed her softly. "You."

"And we'll want to protect you too. Actually, we'll need to. It's programmed into us to defend our mate. That means we won't want to be parted with you for long. At least one of us will be nearby, because otherwise we get...twitchy."

"For the record, I don't need protecting."

Both men burst out laughing.

"Says the woman we fished out of the frigid waters of the Pacific Ocean a few hours ago. Sugar, Jess warned us about you the first day we met her. She said you were a trouble magnet, and she was right. Keeping you safe is going to be a full-time job."

"For both of us," Byron chimed in. "And to answer your earlier question, if you are bonded to us, you won't be tempted by any other man, and you'll feel it when we're not with you. You'll miss us, a lot." He grinned. "I really hope we're all bonded and you're locked into this too. We'll figure out the why and how later."

"So I guess this means I'm moving in?" she asked, barely able to believe she'd said the words.

Both men looked pleased to hear her question, but Tucker answered first. "We've got a lot to talk about, but we'd be very happy to have you living with us. We're a family now, we should be together."

"Okay." Jess yawned as the events of the day started to catch up with her again. "Just one thing. Wherever we end up living, we have to invest in a first-class espresso maker."

"Whatever our fae princess wishes," Byron murmured as Tucker scooped her off the table and carried her upstairs to bed. Maybe now she could finally get some sleep.

CHAPTER TWENTY-TWO

WHEN THE STRIDENT scream of the alarm first tore him out of his dreams, Tucker was too sleep befuddled to do anything more than blindly flail with one hand until he smacked the snooze button. When the noise didn't stop, he finally cracked open an eye and then launched out of bed as the acrid scent of smoke hit his nose. "Fire! Move it you two!"

His bedmates were already moving by the time he bellowed his warning. He hit the lights and dragged on the first pants he found, then turned to find Byron doing the same. Viv was limping toward the dresser where she had stashed a few of her clothes, but Tucker knew they didn't have time for her to hobble over there by herself.

Byron must have had the same thought, because he was still tugging a pair of sweatpants over his hips when he darted past her and tossed the first things he found at her. "No time. We need to get outside, now!"

They helped her dress and then Tucker gathered her into his arms as every instinct screamed for him to get her away from danger. They headed down the backstairs, Byron following behind with their phones and shoes. Tucker could already hear him on the phone as they damned near flew down the last few steps and out into the wintery night.

"...I'm outside now and, fuck yeah, there's smoke and I can see flames on the south side of the building." The wail of the volunteer fire siren started before Byron could say anything more, and he shouted a thank you into the phone and hung up. "They'll be here shortly."

The three of them stood and watched the smoke rise up into the night sky. There weren't many flames yet, but what few there were cast a strange, orange light over the far side of the parking lot.

"So what's with the siren?" Viv asked after it had faded away to silence again.

"We've got a volunteer fire department. They're all getting automated calls right now too, but for the ones in town, that's the call to arms. They'll head to the station, grab the trucks and be here as soon as they can. Until then, we just have to wait." Not that he wanted to. He wanted to go in with an extinguisher or a garden hose and try to control the fire, but he knew that would be foolhardy. It was unbearable to have to stand and watch as the fire spread, threatening his home and his beloved bar.

At least our insurance is paid up.

"Fuck!" Byron swore and ran for the back door before either of them could stop him. "I have to go back in!"

"Byron! Don't you dare!" Viv was screaming, her fear and anger broadcasting to both of them so loudly it made Tucker wince.

"It's important!" Byron called back as he vanished into the dark doorway.

Viv squirmed in his arms as if she was considering going after Byron, and he locked her into his embrace with a grunt of denial. "Not a chance, trouble. Bad enough Byron's lost his mind, but I sure as hell am not letting you go in after him."

"I had to go back for our pelts. We forgot we brought them here for when we talked to Vivian." Byron sent him an explanation that Tucker somehow knew Vivian had not been able to hear.

"Fuck! I forgot they were here!"

"Good save, but move your ass, the fire is spreading!" Tucker sent to Byron and then explained to Vivian. "He's fine, sugar. He's still nattering away like an old woman in my head. He'll be back out in a minute."

"Why isn't he talking to me too?"

"Because you're still yelling at me in your head and it's giving me a headache!" Byron shot back. *"I'm already seeing a downside to this bonding thing!"*

"Get back down here and I'll show you a downside, buster!"

"Meet me around front," Byron's words were tinged with laughter and Tucker knew that he was going to be fine. At least until their mate got a hold of him.

"You heard him, around front! Move it!" Vivian managed to kick him in the side as she pointed to the driveway. "I swear, if he stopped to save a keg of his favorite beer on his way through I will kill him myself! Shit! I should have told him to hide that painting you're working on. The one of me naked. If the firemen see that, I'll die!"

Tucker couldn't help it. As he jogged around to the

front of the building with an irate Vivian still in his arms, he burst out laughing. If this was what life was going to be like from now on, he was never going to be bored.

"And what are you laughing about? Odds are good your home is at the very least going to have smoke damage, so it looks like *you* are moving in with me or Byron. No more man cave for you!"

He grinned down at her as she hissed and spat, knowing every second of anger was only because she was terrified for Byron. As she rounded the driveway and arrived out front, sirens could be heard in the distance and he felt relief rush through him. It looked to him like they'd get there in time to save the bar.

Byron came staggering out the front doors in a cloud of smoke, a hand-crafted wooden box cradled in his arms and a triumphant look on his soot-smudged face. "Safe and sound, as promised."

"Only until she gets a hold of you, bro. Our mate is pissed!"

"Did you tell her what I went back for?" Byron asked, his eyes narrowing as he realized Tucker hadn't bothered to explain.

"Nope."

"Why the fuck not?" Byron demanded of him, and Vivian turned her head to scowl up at him.

"Yeah! Why not?"

"Because, trouble, you're really hot when you're ticked off." Tucker knew he was going to pay for that comment, but the truth was he didn't care. Even now, with Breakers burning, he was happy.

"That's it. I'm in love with two of the craziest men I've

ever met. It's a good thing you're both drop-dead gorgeous."

"For the record, I'm not crazy." Byron hefted the box in his arms. "These are our pelts. We took them out of their fireproof box and brought them down here to show them to you when we told you the truth."

"Oh." She stared at the box for a moment and then sighed. "Then I suppose I understand why you went back for them. Jessica explained to me about your pelts. That it's more than just fur and flesh, it was the source of your magic. Tell me if I have this right. If it's taken from you, then you're basically enslaved to whoever possesses it. You said earlier that if it's locked in iron, then you guys can't transform. And Jess said that if a selkie's pelt is actually destroyed, you basically become human, no magic at all. It's like part of you dies."

Byron felt a chill pass over him at her last words. No selkie wanted to imagine that kind of life. "You've got it right. There's something else important in here too, but now doesn't seem quite the right time." Byron inclined his head toward the lights and sirens speeding in their direction. "Ask me once we've got this mess sorted."

"Oh believe me, I will." Viv was still obviously rankled about Byron's stunt. "How could this have happened? We were downstairs a little while ago and there wasn't anything wrong."

"Tucker, take a deep breath and tell me what you smell. Besides smoke."

He inhaled, and then did it again as something familiar tickled the back of his nose. It was out of place and pungent and he finally realized what it was. "Gasoline? What the fuck is going on?"

"I caught a whiff of it when I came out the front door," Byron confirmed. This whole area reeks of it."

"It wasn't at the back though."

"Nope. Almost like whoever poured it out knew that would be the way you'd get out and left you an escape route."

"That makes no goddamned sense at all! Who would set a fire like this?"

Vivian went rigid in his arms, her eyes wide and wild. "Oh shit. I think I know who would do this!"

The firefighters arrived at that moment, their sirens drowning out her next words.

"Tobias!" She used their link to convey the name and showed them her memories of Tobias's earlier ramblings. Tucker's vision went red as he saw what Tobias and done and said to the woman he loved. Byron snarled under his breath and Tucker knew his blood-brother was as enraged as he was. They should have killed him on the beach instead of trying to subdue him to face the judgment of the colony.

The man was completely, dangerously insane.

Firefighters ran past them shouting to each other and a hand clapped down on Tucker's shoulder, snapping him back to the present. "You three need to get back."

It took a second for him to make out the features behind the new arrival's faceplate. "Luke?"

"You were expecting the Easter Bunny maybe? Of course it's me. Now get your asses moving so we can save my favorite watering hole from burning to the ground."

Luke ushered them over to a quiet spot at the side of one of the trucks where there was enough light to see by. He brought blankets for each of them and got them semi-comfortable leaning up against the side of a red and silver pump truck. "Now we're alone, tell me that wooden box doesn't contain what I think it does. How many times have I told everyone to secure those in *fireproof* fucking containers!"

"You can lecture us later. First, save our bar. Oh, and we smelled gasoline. Lots of it." Byron pointed to the doors. "I don't think this was an accident. We're pretty sure it was Tobias."

"Perfect. Merry fucking Christmas to all." Luke growled into his radio and had a short, terse conversation with several other firefighters before turning his attention back to the three of them.

"Since these two are a bit distracted, I'll forgive them for not introducing me. My name's Lucas MacPherson, and you must be the very beautiful Vivian Waverly I've heard so much about."

"Back off, Luke. She's ours." Tucker didn't bother reining in his beast when it added a rolling growl to the end of his warning.

"Easy, big guy." Luke laughed and backed off a step. "I'm just letting her know she's got options."

Viv decided to end the pissing contest that was about to start and held up her newly cut hand so Luke could see it. "Actually I don't have options. I'm off the market for good."

Luke's dark eyes widened behind his faceplate and then he grinned. "Well then, welcome to the colony. You are one brave woman taking these two on."

"Actually, they're the brave ones," she said and smiled at her two lovers before turning back to the firefighter. "Is the bar going to be okay?"

"Looks like it, but there's going to be a hell of a mess to clean up." Luke's radio squawked again and he stopped talking to listen in. "All indications are that the fire started on the south side, maybe even inside the tattoo shop. More signs of gasoline use around too. We're going to have to call for an arson investigation."

"Do what you have to do," Tucker said, relief thickening his voice. "We got out with everything that matters. The rest we can rebuild." He bowed his head to brush a kiss over Viv's hair and she knew he meant her. They hadn't even taken their pelts with them the first time. The three of them, and what they had together, that was all that mattered.

"I need to get back there. I'll come back and update you later." Lucas nodded to them and headed toward the fire.

"Now we know the bar is okay, I think it's time we told Viv what else I've got in this box," Byron suggested.

"Now?" Tucker shot his best friend a look that was somewhere between incredulity and panic.

"Yeah, now," Byron responded, his eyes gleaming with too many emotions for her to be able to read him. "We should have done this last night, dude. We were too busy doing, uh, other things though. Or would you like every other single pup in the colony to try and put the moves on our mate?"

"No!" Tucker snarled and Byron snickered.

"So, it's time."

"Would one of you like to explain to me what the hell

you're talking about? I can't read either of you and I'm totally confused." Vivian kicked to punctuate her sense of frustration. "And I'd really like to be put down now."

"As the lady wishes." Tucker set her down and she yelped as her feet hit the cold, wet pavement. When she went to tell him off she found him smirking, his brow arched and his dimple flashing as she danced from foot to foot despite the tenderness of her bruised soles.

"Shit, no shoes!" she swore before looking up at her two grinning mates with irritation. "Very cute."

"Yes, you are," both of them told her unison, and Tucker leaned in and picked her up again, adjusting her blanket around her shoulders as he did so.

Byron set down the rather artistically carved box on the chrome step of the truck and opened it enough he could slip a hand inside. He retrieved whatever it was he needed, placing it in his pocket without letting her see it. "There's a tradition among our people that when a woman agrees to be mated, the men give her a gift to celebrate. We had this ready for you, in hopes that when we told you everything you'd agree to wear it." He held up something that glowed golden in the streetlights, offering it to her. "Will you wear it for us?"

Viv took it and gasped as she got her first look at their present. It was a gold necklace with a three-sided Celtic knot at its center. The mazelike pattern filled the downward pointing triangle, and as she stared at it she knew where she'd seen the design before. It was the same pattern as the tattoo that covered Tucker's body from neck to thigh. Hanging from the bottom point was a teardrop-shaped piece of amber, while the upper points were attached to the golden links of the necklace. "It's stunning.

Of course I'll wear it." She tried to open the clasp but her fingers were shaking and she finally gave it to Byron. "Will you put it on me?"

"It would be my greatest pleasure." He fastened it around her neck and settled it so that the amber lay flush against her skin. "Each generation's necklace is different from the last, because it is usually a combination of both of *their* parent's patterns. Yours is different though. Tucker's family crest isn't part of this design. This is something new, belonging just to us."

"A fresh start for all of us?" she asked, understanding why Tucker wouldn't want to have his family represented. Not after everything he'd been through. "That explains the amber then." She reached up to stroke the golden stone with a smile. "It's imbued with the power to cleanse and heal."

"Actually, I didn't know that. But I bet my mother did. Mom gave that to me and told me it would be a good piece to put in our bonding pendant."

"Smart lady."

"You're only saying that because she likes you and told us not to screw this up." Tucker's finger tucked under her chin to lift her head so he could see the pendant. "It looks good on you, sugar."

"She told you not to screw this up? Well next time we see her I can tell her that our boys did good. Eventually."

"I'm feeling damned by faint praise over here," Byron grumbled.

"You and me both, bro."

They sat in the darkness and watched as the last of the flames were doused. Smoke still rose from the area where the fire had started, but the danger was over. Luke came by from time to time to keep them updated on what they'd found. When he appeared yet again, none of them were prepared for what he told them.

He had his helmet in his hands and a lingering sadness in his dark eyes. "Tucker. Fuck. I don't know how to tell you this, but we found a body in the tattoo shop."

Tucker's shoulders sagged and Viv hung onto to him as tight as she could, offering him her silent support. "It's okay, Luke. Just say it."

The firefighter ran a hand through his sweat-soaked curls. "Tobias didn't make it out after he set the fire. I'm sorry."

"He attacked Vivian twice tonight and tried to burn our business to the ground. He doesn't deserve anyone's remorse. Now at least everyone will know exactly what kind of man he was." Tucker's skin was gray and he looked drained as he met the other man's gaze. "You're sure it's him?"

Luke nodded slowly. "The way he fell, his face was protected from the worst of the fire. I know you aren't going to like this, but the coroner is going to need you to make an identification later."

"Whatever needs to be done," Tucker said, sounding tired now.

"We're going to need statements from the three of you, but then you're free to go." Luke scrubbed his hand over his face, leaving more soot and ash behind than he managed to wipe away. "I called Darius and they're on their way. They don't know about Tobias yet, but I thought they'd want to know what happened here tonight."

Byron nodded, but Tucker tensed and Viv felt resentment surge through their link. She sent back soothing notes of love before lifting her head. "Don't, Tucker. They should be here. This concerns all of us." She reached for Byron and he moved closer, catching her fingers in his. "We said this was a fresh start for us. So let's do one better and make it a fresh start for everyone. Tobias is gone, and carrying this anger and pain around with you isn't going to change anything that happened before this moment. It's time to let it go, lover."

"I've been angry at them so long. I don't know how to feel any other way."

"We'll help. But if I can forgive you two and Jess for everything, then you can do this." Viv moved in and kissed Tucker, then tugged Byron in for a kiss of his own. "Besides, as I recall Byron's place is the only one of our residences that has a king-sized bed. That means we're moving to Kismet Cove. All three of us."

Tucker opened his mouth to protest but she stopped it with another kiss.

"I like that idea," Byron said. "The three of us making a home for ourselves out there. Come on, Tucker. Say yes. It's time."

Tucker sighed and then nodded. "Okay. But I am really going to miss not having to commute to work."

Everyone laughed and Vivian nipped at his lower lip before whispering. "I promise to find a way to make that up to you." Then she beamed at both of them. "Merry Christmas. I love you."

EPILOGUE

It HAD TAKEN six weeks to get Breakers ready for re-opening, but they were nearly there. The rebuilding had been the center of their waking lives for every day since the fire, and the entire Kismet Cove community had pitched in to get it done on time.

Vivian had thrown herself into the work with joy, helping her men decide on new furnishings and improvements that would transform Breakers from an aging dive bar to a comfortable hangout for locals and tourists alike. The kitchen and storage areas were cleaned out and updated, while the rest of the building underwent a complete facelift. Breakers was getting a fresh start too.

She was behind the bar, setting up the glassware when her men found her, both of them grinning like lunatics as they approached. "You know, you look pretty good back there, trouble."

"Yeah, you do. So it's a shame we're firing you," Byron said and crooked his finger at her. "You don't work here, slim. We're ejecting you from the premises."

They were looking far too pleased with themselves to be serious, so Viv decided to play along. "So if I don't work here, does that mean you want me to go home and bake you cookies? Maybe put on some pearls and high heels to greet you guys when you come home at night?" She glowered at them both and wagged a playful finger in their direction as she came around the bar to where Byron was standing. "That is *so* not gonna happen."

"Damn straight it's not. If you're home one of us is going to need to check in on you, not to mention the cove is too far away to run home for a quickie on our breaks."

"So if I'm not working here, and you don't have delusions of trying to make me into a fifties housewife, what am I going to do with myself all day? Is this your way of telling me to go find a job?" She laughed because they knew she'd already been looking, but the hair salons in town weren't hiring right now.

"Nope, this is our way of telling you we found you one."

"You found me a job? Don't they want to at least meet me before they hire me?"

"You're asking too many questions. Just come with us and let us surprise you." Tucker joined them and took one hand while Byron took the other. Together they led her out into the parking lot, where she noticed there seemed to be a great many people standing and grinning at her.

What the hell are they up to?

"Why's everyone standing around staring at me?" she asked, feeling decidedly uncomfortable at all the attention.

"They're not staring at you, they're looking at the owner of Tofino's newest hair salon," Byron told her, and they both turned, pivoting her around to look back at the front of Breakers. Beside it, where the T-Spot's sign used to sit, was a shiny new one. *Vivacious* was written in bold red letters across a black background, and her jaw dropped. That was the name she'd always wanted to use for her own shop. The one she'd been scrimping and saving to be able to open one day. Jess must have told them about her plans, it was the only way they could have known.

"But that's…" She trailed off as words fled, leaving her flapping her hands in shock.

"That's the former business establishment of a slimeball ex-tenant who is currently facing charges of arson and insurance fraud. And now it's all yours. Two businesses are better than one, right?" Tucker arched his brow at her and she nodded and launched herself into his arms, still too overwhelmed to speak.

In the beginning Trask had denied any wrongdoing, but when a key to his front door was found in Tobias's pocket he had stopped saying anything at all to investigators. Once it was discovered that only a week before the fire Trask had taken out a new, very large insurance policy on his business without revealing he'd been evicted, the pieces fell into place and it looked like he would be going away for a very long time.

"Hey, if you're done mauling the big guy, I deserve a hug too!" Byron interrupted them as the crowd around them laughed and cheered. Vivian kissed Tucker's cheek and then threw herself at Byron.

"It's incredible! You both deserve hugs and more." She was filled with elation as she looked up at the sign again to be sure she hadn't been hallucinating. "I've put away nearly every penny of my inheritance from my grandmother and all my tips for years trying to get enough together to make this happen. We'll have to figure out rent, and oh goddess I'm going to need to make up a list of equipment and inventory."

"Back up the train a bit!" Tucker was laughing so hard he could barely talk. "No rent. That wouldn't make any sense. We'll figure out what your share of the utilities and stuff is going to be, and you use your money to buy the equipment and scissors and stuff. This is going to be a family-run business. Only we're going to have two very different businesses housed in the same building."

Tears stung her eyes as she looked at her two lovers. They had made one of her lifelong ambitions come true. She was going to be her own boss. "That sounds really good to me. Incredibly good, in fact. So I am going to agree to it, with one addition."

"What's that, slim?"

"I want first pick of Tucker's artwork so I can decorate my salon in style. Maybe even sell a few pieces for you if I can."

Tucker made a strangled noise and shook his head, but all around them people were nodding and she knew she was going to get her way. He was too good to hide his talent anymore. She was going to see to it that when he finished the new murals inside Breakers, he'd be putting his name to those too. The last few weeks had been joyful and challenging as the three of them had planned for their future while coming to terms with their past.

Tucker, Vivian and Byron were now living in Kismet Cove full time, and the place was slowly beginning to feel like home. Tucker's childhood home had been cleared of Tobias's things by a few of the colony members, who had gone on to clean it from top to bottom in preparation for new owners.

Well, not so much new owners, as old owners that were finally coming home. That had been the hardest thing of all to deal with, and the one thing none of them had considered that cold, wet Christmas Day that Breakers had nearly burned down. Tucker's parents had sensed Tobias's death, and had called Darius not long afterward.

So far there had only been one strained phone call between Tucker and his long-estranged parents, but Viv hoped that once they came home, the three of them could start rebuilding the relationship they'd once had. They had a lot to make up for, but they seemed to know things wouldn't be easy.

Her own parents had responded with mild surprise to her news that she was moving out west, but they hadn't asked for details and Viv hadn't offered them any. She got the feeling that it would be a long time before they came to visit her.

Maybe when I start giving them grandchildren.

Or maybe not. It didn't matter anymore if they approved of her choices or not. She had Byron and Tucker now, as well as Jess and a host of people who cared about her happiness. The winds of fate really had been blowing that day she'd flown out west. They had carried her out of her old life and into a new one full of love, laughter, and more magic than she'd ever dared to believe could exist.

She was home.

ABOUT THE AUTHOR

Susan lives out on the Canadian west coast surrounded by open water, dear family, and good friends. She's jumped out of perfectly good airplanes on purpose and accidentally swum with sharks on the Great Barrier Reef.

If the world ends, she plans to survive as the spunky, comedic sidekick to the heroes of the new world, because she's too damned short and out of shape to make it on her own for long.

You can find out more about Susan and her books here:
www.susanhayes.ca